The Last Billable Hour

The Last Billable Hour

A Novel by

Susan Wolfe

St. Martin's Press
New York

Editor: Jared Kieling
Production Editor: Sabrina Soares
Copyedited by Deborah Manette
Design by Judith Stagnitto

Library of Congress Cataloging-in-Publication Data

Wolfe, Susan, 1950–
    The last billable hour.
    I. Title.
PS3573.05256L38   1989   813'.54   88–29865
ISBN 0–312–02566–1

First Edition

10 9 8 7 6 5 4 3 2 1

To Ralph,
with love and gratitude.

Acknowledgments

I thank Carol Kersten, Teresa Kersten, and Susan Termohlen for their help and encouragement; Susan Maunders for her generous and valuable editing of my first draft; Detective Jim Simpson and Detective Ron Williams of the Menlo Park Police Department; Mike Ladra, who put me in touch with a fine editor; Jared Kieling, for being a fine editor and fun to work with; and Fred Hartwick, for all his help and counsel, and just for being himself.

Most of all I thank my husband, Ralph DeVoe, who made this book possible in so many ways.

The
Last
Billable
Hour

1

Chips of Gold

Howard sat in the waiting room. His shirt was stuck to his back. He rotated his left shoulder furtively, trying to calm an itch between his shoulder blades. This happened with every interview. The minute you found the lobby your suit didn't fit. The worst part—well, almost the worst part—was waiting to get started.

This was definitely the most lavish firm so far. Beams from the soft track lighting burrowed into the salmon-colored carpet, highlighted the white tulips in the centerpiece, and reflected faintly from the rosewood tables. In front of him, muffled by a brass-railed glass wall, six men and a woman worked at a long rosewood conference table.

Even the receptionists were plush: black curls against red silk, blond hair cascading over a gold necklace, obscuring a dimple. This would make law firm number, let's see, eleven. His uncle was being pretty damn loyal to keep setting these up.

He wasn't alone in the reception area. There was a continuous influx, first of dark-suited men, then of younger men in short-sleeved polyester shirts, who kept their eyes fixed on the carpet. Occasionally uneasy groups combining both types hovered momentarily, conferring softly among themselves, before being greeted and whisked away by a secretary. An old couple sat next to each other on one of the big sofas, the gentleman consulting his watch with increasing irritation. And seated near Howard, their knees separated only by the corner of the coffee table, was the Neat-hair who was going to get the job.

Howard spotted him immediately. The guy was in his mid-twenties like Howard, right out of law school like Howard. Unlike Howard, he was a *New Yorker* ad for Stanley Blacker. Navy pinstripes, vest, the suit had obviously been pressed on the way up in the elevator. His nervousness expressed itself as eager intensity instead of damp dread.

Howard knew how he looked by comparison, even if the gold-flecked glass panels hadn't been there to remind him. His tie was wrinkled, and the cuffs of his gray pants made his legs look short and wide. The lines of his body sloped down and out, from his horn-rimmed aviator glasses to his mustache to his soft shoulders. The tails of his navy blazer splayed out at the back to accommodate a body that did not exercise. Gravity had been hard on Howard Rickover. Surrounded by sun-baked joggers (the Neat-hair was certainly a jogger), Howard looked slightly melted.

"Jesus," the Neat-hair muttered suddenly. "Dan Block. They say he's the next Charlie Sporck." Howard followed his gaze to a barrel-chested man who was stepping off the elevator. Howard opened his mouth and then closed it again. You had to watch Neat-hairs. They might buddy up to the partners by joking about the guy who didn't know who Charlie Sporck was. Client, maybe. Probably not a lawyer. Howard had looked up the lawyer list in *Martindale Hubble*; Sporck didn't sound familiar.

He wondered idly what the people in the glass conference room were working on. Whoever those people were and whatever they were doing, they'd been at it a long time. The men had their shirtsleeves rolled up. Dark circles stained their armpits. You could almost smell the nervous sweat, the stale smoke. The woman talked on the phone, a fat man in short sleeves paced in front of the plate-glass windows. Beyond him, chunky clouds drifted easily through the blue sky, and the sun ricocheted through the parking lot, where Howard's Civic was sandwiched between a 380SL and a DeLorean.

"Tweedmore and Slyde, Tweedmore and Slyde," the receptionists chanted pleasantly, their frantic fingers racing over the telephone consoles.

His view of the conference room was momentarily obscured as a skinny woman with stringy red hair raced into the lobby and almost collided with a blonde in a low-cut dress who was carrying a tray of soft drinks.

"Candy, *please* stay out from under other people's feet."

"Well, you shouldn't be running in the lobby, Mary Belle."

"Those of us who work have to run sometimes," the skinny woman said over her shoulder as she disappeared around the corner. The blond woman shrugged so that her cleavage heaved and walked on.

"Incredible," the Neat-hair muttered again. "Isn't that Jimmy Treybig?" He shook his head and smiled with disbelief. "Twenty-two lawyers, and they represent the whole damn Valley."

"Yeah," said Howard. "Pretty amazing." This was going to be worse than he'd expected. Nemesis Neat-hair knew the clients by sight.

Okay, might as well get it over with. But the prospects of speedy execution were small. Nemesis had been there when Howard arrived; his rolled-up interview list was starting to look positively creased. The old couple on the sofa had probably been newlyweds when they sat down.

The attorneys who had come into the lobby to greet clients were surprisingly casual. One wore a camel blazer that set off his blown-dry hair. Here was a guy in a sports coat, tie loosened, his curly hair rumpled. Both were fit and very tan. Their casualness said "New money here." Uh-oh, Neat-hair was furrowing his brow. Was his perfect New York interviewing suit somehow . . . somber?

"Mr. Wheeler?"

A young woman approached Neat-hair, smiling pleasantly. He stood up a little too eagerly.

"I'm afraid there's been a mistake. Mr. Slyde tried to call you himself, but you'd already left for the airport. We've had an embarrassment of riches, everybody has accepted, there's just no opening for another person of your experience. We don't want to waste any more of your time by keeping you for interviews."

"But I—"

"And anyway, Mr. Slyde is in Japan. I'm so embarrassed." She was holding his elbow lightly and steering him toward the elevators. "Send us an itemized bill, won't you? The least we can do is pay expenses. Have a pleasant trip back."

She deposited him into the elevator and pushed the down button. Howard glanced at his interview list as she turned back to the reception area. Slyde was the very first guy on the list. Fuck. He'd sweated a quart into this stupid coat for nothing. He rose to meet her, hoping to avoid the bum's rush with his elbow.

"Mr. Rickover?" she said pleasantly. "Mr. Slyde will see you now."

2

The Billable Hour

Gerard Tweedmore of Tweedmore & Slyde called Howard three days after he interviewed and offered him the job. Displaying the charm that had undoubtedly helped to skyrocket the firm to dominance in the Valley, Mr. Tweedmore informed Howard that the pleasure of receiving and reviewing such a solid résumé was surpassed only by the pleasure of learning that such credentials were possessed by a person of warmth and good judgment. They were offering him the position, and every member of the firm stood ready to exert influence to gain Howard's acceptance.

Really, they needn't have tried so hard. It was only Howard's astonishment that prevented him from accepting the offer on the spot. When he did accept the following week, he returned the lavish flattery that had been showered on him by stating that the firm was absolutely his first choice. With uncharacteristic reticence he omitted to tell them it was his only choice.

Howard's uncle, who had wangled the interview for him by calling upon threadbare college ties to Gerard Tweedmore, shared Howard's astonishment. Using the metaphor "manna from heaven," he offered Howard the sound if blunt suggestion that for once in his life he not blow it. Howard felt lucky that his uncle took an interest in his affairs, and he accepted the advice with good-humored gratitude. When he began work the following week he intended to follow it. That left four days to celebrate.

*   *   *

He drove down the coast to see the sea lions at Point Lobos. Sitting on a granite boulder at the water's edge, he squinted at the tiny brown lozenges dotting the rocky island offshore. Amazingly, their loud croaking could be heard even above the booming waves. As the ocean spray tickled his pale Bostonian feet he considered.

No more interviews. He had a job. Hey, and not just any job. His uncle thought Tweedmore & Slyde was the hottest up-and-coming firm in Silicon Valley.

Well, not *in* the Valley. The T&S lawyers boasted proudly that they had attained their dominant position without ever leaving San Mateo. "Gerry knew. He knew that if we were good enough, if we had the right people, we wouldn't have to go to Silicon Valley. The Valley would come to us."

And so, apparently, it had. By the end of his day of interviews, Howard knew that the BMWs and Porsches and Alfa Romeos that streamed into the Tweedmore parking lot brought the Valley's finest talent, eager to benefit from the renowned T&S courtroom presence, and from its talent for doing deals, innovative deals on the cutting edge of securities law. Helping high-tech engineers get money to produce computer stuff.

Judging by the interviews, the classic T&S client was a guy in blue jeans and cowboy boots who made millions by working out of his garage between midnight and four in the morning. What was it the T&S lawyers called them? "SVMs." For Silicon Valley Millionaire. Apparently there were too many to keep saying it in longhand. To hear those guys talk, there was so much money around that the lawyers just inevitably ended up being SVMs, too. Fine, only he'd settle for SVS: Silicon Valley Solvent.

He just hoped Leo Slyde, the new boss, hadn't made

a mistake. Not that Howard had misled the guy. He hadn't gotten the chance. Slyde hadn't really asked him that much. He mostly kept winking at Howard and saying "There's a lot of money to be made around here." Howard guessed he looked like he needed some. He wiggled his toes to dislodge the sand between them and headed up the path to his car.

Hopefully they didn't expect him to know much about computers. He kept wanting to say "silicone," as in breast implants. But why should he have to know about computers? he reassured himself as he pulled onto the highway. He'd be doing estate planning. And some litigation at first. T&S was known for its antitrust litigation, too. He wouldn't be doing trials, just helping to get ready for trials, until the new probate department got off the ground.

It looked like his uncle's strategy to bring him out to California was going to pay off. He rounded a curve and was startled by the beauty of the rocky coast stretching for miles below him.

Howard had only the vaguest idea of what it meant to get a probate department off the ground. After a few days on the job he could see that for the partners, it meant lavish entertainment of SVMs while touting T&S as a full-service law firm. For Howard it meant drafting general purpose will forms. The consequences of this division of labor became apparent over time as Howard became conversant with the one all-encompassing legal precept upon which the great T&S legal machine was founded, the Billable Hour.

He had an appointment with Bill Madras at nine-thirty. He knew he was in the right office. Although

Madras, rising star of corporate acquisitions, wasn't there in person, his dark eyes beamed at Howard from the photos on the credenza. In one photo Madras had his arm around a woman whose face was hidden in shadows. The other showed Madras in a baseball uniform, bat over his shoulder, tilting his cap back and grinning at the camera. Even under the baseball cap his black hair looked blown dry. Another Neat-hair. Howard hoped he and Neat-hairs had more in common than he had always supposed.

The wall opposite Madras's desk contained two diplomas and several certificates of admission to practice, all in antique gold frames that contrasted curiously with the clean lines of the modern wood furniture. The wall by the door sported an antique oval mirror, which reflected the bright empty sky in the windows opposite. Howard was standing by those windows, looking straight down six stories at two oddly foreshortened figures who were walking in the courtyard, when Madras arrived, his tie flying out beside him like a yellow flag.

"Big How, sorry I'm late. I guess I'm your den mother for the next few weeks. I got a client coming in about five minutes, we need to get you up to speed on billing. Have a seat. You know about time sheets?"

"Sort of. I brought one."

"Great. Let's look at it. They give you your attorney number yet? That goes here. All right, billable hours, we do them by tenths. Every six minutes." He was talking faster than he walked. "Every tenth gets billed to somebody, that's how the firm gets its money. Every matter has a separate billing number, you get it from here." He opened his drawer, lifted a fat book, and dropped it back in. "It's alphabetical. The only trick is some of our guys have a lotta different deals going, be sure you get the right deal.

"Then you write a description. Here's a set of codes.

TC for telephone conference. RS is research. Then you just put whatever detail on this line here. Who you talked to, that stuff. Couple things you want to avoid. Don't put much time under RVF, review file. Looks lazy. Same with ACF, attorney conference, clients don't like it. Make that time look like something else.

"That's the mechanics. Want some philosophy? This stuff matters. Every month your hours get added up. They go in a report to all the partners. It's how clients get billed, how partners divide up the bucks, how they decide who's a team player and who's just doing a yeoman's job. You follow?"

"I guess so. It's better to have lots."

"You got it. Especially during this probationary stuff. Anything else?"

"Wait. During what?"

Madras frowned. "This hundred-and-twenty-day thing. Leo talked to you about it, right?"

Howard shook his head. "I'm pretty sure he didn't."

Madras shrugged. "I must have misunderstood."

"Misunderstood what? What did you hear?"

"Evidently I heard nothing. What I thought I heard . . . who cares?" He grinned. "Hey, auditory hallucinations aren't the worst that can happen on a job like this. Let's finish with billing."

"Okay. Maybe I should talk to Leo, just in case."

"Don't do that." Madras jabbed the air with his forefinger for emphasis, then relaxed. "Look, it's gotta be bullshit, right? Because nobody talked to you. Leo's got a lot on his mind right now. He hired you to help him. I don't think he'd want to be spending his time on personnel problems right out of the chute. You know what I mean?"

"Yeah. I guess so."

"Anyway, it's no big deal. Just do what you'd do

anyway. Work your butt off. Impress the hell out of them. You'll be fine. Anything else about billing?"

"Well, yeah. What about the time I spend that isn't for a particular client, like these general will forms I'm doing, or reading about new law? What do I do with that?"

Madras grinned. "What you do with your spare time is your business."

"I don't even write it down?"

Bill held his palms up. "Billables, How, billables. Forget the rest. My client is here." He stood up and walked around the desk. "Listen, you have any questions the next few weeks, let me know." He straightened his tie in the antique mirror. "Linda? Let's get him in here. See you, How."

Bill was right, Howard told himself several times in the next few days. Leo would have told him. And a new guy was always on probation. Formal or informal, what could he do differently? He certainly couldn't try harder.

A hundred and twenty days. That would be, let's see, four months. Sixteen weeks, maybe seventeen. Not that it mattered. He didn't know why he was even bothering to count.

In addition to the nonbillable hours he was putting in to develop the probate department, Howard received work from the litigation department. First one partner and then another would drop by his office to invite him to join the team on the KashPro litigation or the TechSkill securities fraud case.

". . . So this is a substantial case for a very significant client," Stan Pierce or Cal Forman or John Maddis would say. "We've got a tough opponent, I imagine he'll keep us busy." Wry smile. "What we need now is a talented young associate to round out the team. I see this case as a real learning opportunity, with substantial client contact and significant responsibility. How does your schedule look for the next few weeks?"

Howard always said yes. Billable work in probate was temporarily scarce, and Howard felt flattered that these various fine lawyers were eager to get his help. By the end of the second week he noticed with satisfaction that his file cabinet was already taking on the bulging, slightly unkempt look of a real lawyer's.

T&S had no formal training program for its new recruits, and encouraged its young lawyers to learn primarily by doing and secondarily by observing. Accordingly, one morning Howard found himself seated in the front conference room with the sun streaming in on a small crowd of well- and conservatively dressed people who were about to take part in a deposition. Howard had been given the twin duties of educating himself and taking notes.

The court reporter sat at the head of the table with a small machine like a typewriter to record what was said. Seated on one side of the table were three dark-suited men who alternated between whispering to each other and frowning at pieces of paper. On Howard's side of the table sat the witness (a pleasant-looking man in his forties who was being sued for securities fraud), and his attorney, Constance Valentine of Tweedmore & Slyde.

Valentine had briefed him. "This case against Trillobyte Memories started out looking serious six months ago and then evaporated when we investigated the facts. Our purpose since then has been to educate the plaintiff and his lawyer about how very weak his case is. While our efforts have been impeded by the lawyer's faulty intellect, I think we've finally succeeded." She smiled. "Now they're stalling. Today they're deposing Lyman Mink, a former director and investor in the company. This is the last of their so-called big depositions, at the end of which we should have softened them up for settlement. It's a five-million-dollar suit, I expect to get rid of it for twenty thousand.''

Watching her make last-minute notes before the deposition began, Howard felt he would prefer not to be softened up by Connie Valentine. There was nothing even slightly coquettish about her indisputable good looks. In contrast to the other women attorneys at the firm, who wore drab tailored suits with little bright ties, Constance dressed to be noticed. Today she wore a dark, wide-belted dress with diagonal slashes of orange that highlighted her reddish brown hair. Her bold lipstick was a warning: ''This is my mouth. I use it to win.''

Howard recorded the proceedings accurately and carefully. The witness testified under oath that his name was Lyman Mink, he was a real estate developer, and yes, from time to time he invested in other Silicon Valley ventures. He was describing in some detail the courses he had taken in junior college before becoming self-employed when a skirmish occurred.

Ms. Atty: May I remind you that I have made Mr. Mink available for one day only. You may wish to move quickly over the routine matter of Mr. Mink's credentials to the heart of your questioning.

Mr. Atty: (*Expanding his already formidable chest*) Of course you realize Mr. Mink is here for as long as we need him. In a case of this magnitude, it would be perfectly appropriate to depose this witness for several days or even weeks.

Howard summarized the foregoing as ''Discussion of appropriate number of credentials.''

The deponent went on to discuss his investment in Trillobyte Memories Corp. He was describing the reasons he had found the investment appealing when a second argument broke out.

Mr. Atty: Now when you say that the Trillobyte computer was portable, what precisely do you mean?

Witness: Why, that it could be carried from place to place.

Mr. Atty: *(Smiling indulgently)* Well, but a building could be carried from place to place if one had the proper tools and implements.

Ms. Atty: *(Doodling geometric patterns)* Objection. Harassing the witness.

Witness: Well, then, something that could be carried from place to place without the benefit of tools and implements.

Mr. Atty: *(After pausing, slyly)* Including wheels?

Ms. Atty: Objection. Irrelevant and not reasonably calculated to lead to the discovery of admissible evidence. The Trillobyte computer did not have wheels. No computer has wheels.

Mr. Atty: *(Sarcastically)* Are you testifying for this witness, counsel? There has been no testimony that the Trillobyte computer was without wheels.

Ms. Atty: If that troubles you, Mr. Neece, I suggest you elicit that testimony now.

Mr. Atty: Thank you, Ms. Valentine, I would prefer to conduct my own inquiry if you don't mind. *(Sighing luxuriously, settling into his seat)* Now, Mr. Mink, would a computer or would it not, in your opinion, be portable, as you understand that word, if one were able to move it about only with the benefit of wheels?

Witness: I don't know, I never thought about it.

Mr. Atty: Perhaps you could trouble yourself to think about it now.

Ms. Atty: *(Rubbing her eye)* Objection, harassing the witness. Why don't we simply stipulate to Webster's definition of "portable" and move along?

Mr. Atty: *(Patiently)* Such a stipulation would seem to serve no purpose whatsoever, Ms. Valentine, since we would then know Mr. Webster's definition of "portable," when what I want to know is Mr. Mink's definition. I am posing a set of hypotheticals designed to elicit that information. Such methods are perfectly appropriate in cases of this magnitude. Now, Mr. Mink, what about a carrying case? Would a carrying case be considered a tool or implement, in your view, such that the need of one to carry a computer from place to place would obviate the possibility that such computer was portable, as you understand that word?

Ms. Atty: *(Sighing)* Objection, instruct the witness not to answer. Wheels are not an issue in this case. Portable is not an issue in this case. If you persist in this fruitless line of inquiry, Mr. Neece, I will terminate the deposition and ask Judge Scarvelli for sanctions.

Howard was uncertain what to record about this interchange. He was sure he shouldn't record what was interesting to him, including, for example, the apparent boredom with which Connie Valentine issued her objections. Or Howard's assessment of the other lawyer. Reluctantly he crossed out "Fatuous asshole" and wrote "Discussion about need for definition of portable."

The deposition continued for several minutes in peace. The witness turned from his reasons for purchasing stock in the company to reasons for selling it. Then another fight broke out.

This time Howard must have been daydreaming, because the first thing he heard was the tense, indignant voice of Connie Valentine.

Ms. Atty: . . . client is exhausted, and expect you to have the common courtesy to grant his request for a break.

Mr. Atty: He has asked for nothing of the sort, counsel, you are coaching him to request a break. I insist that we continue uninterrupted.

Ms. Atty: We will recess for ten minutes while I confer with my client. Mr. Mink?

The conference door slammed. The three dark-suited men glanced at Howard, perfected their posture, and exchanged hooded glances of bewilderment. After a moment they got up and went into the lobby.

Ten minutes passed, then fifteen, then thirty. Howard finally got up, leaving the court reporter staring vacantly out the window, and went in search of Connie Valentine.

He was raising his fist to knock when her door swung open and Ms. Valentine, her hair in disarray, pushed a decidedly pale Mr. Mink into the hallway. "No more depo," she called curtly over her shoulder as she hurried the weakly smiling Mink down the hall. "Drop your notes off with my secretary."

His notes were embarrassing. Only three pages after two hours, that couldn't be right. He obliterated "Fatuous asshole" completely, then looked at the last notation: "Needed his $2.5 million out of Trillobyte to protect real estate investment." What crisis could possibly be revealed by that perfectly ordinary remark? He assumed it was a crisis. You didn't just routinely stop a deposition in midsentence. Did you? He opened his mouth to verify this bit of civil procedure with Connie Valentine's secretary, but something in her gaze stopped him. Was it amusement? Contempt for a jerk on probation? Perhaps he only imagined it. He scribbled "Declined to furnish specifics" and dropped the notes into her waiting hand.

3

Saint Gullible

With all the lawyers working so hard, Howard was pleasantly surprised that they found time to socialize away from the office. He seemed to run into them wherever he went. First it was Peter Bonifacio, the T&S trademark lawyer, with Leo Slyde's secretary at the *Mikado* performance on the Stanford campus. Seated by himself in the balcony, Howard was attracted by the play of light from the chandeliers on Candy Gilley's thick gold curls in the crowd below. She and Peter were seated with their heads bent together a few rows from the stage. Feeling slightly guilty, Howard watched Candy swing her long hair as if daring Peter to become entangled. As the lights dimmed, Peter leaned toward her and froze, breathless at the edge of a precipice.

Then a week later it was Leo himself. When his uncle invited him to dinner in the city, Howard chose a little place with fifties' decor called Max's Diner. As he and his uncle followed their waiter down a narrow corridor, Howard saw somebody with Leo's sculptured blond hair and full cheeks bend to slide into a booth a few yards away. Of course it couldn't be Leo, because Howard knew from Candy that Leo was on the East Coast on emergency business. He was therefore startled when the Leo look-alike caught his eye, made a "sssh" sign, and winked as he slid into the booth. As the waiter led Howard past the booth, Howard glimpsed the profile of Connie Valentine.

By the third week he could see that being in the office from eight A.M. to six P.M., as he had originally planned, wasn't enough. He began grabbing a quick dinner at Burger King and working through until eight. Riding up in the posh elevator with the acrid smell of fries coming from his cheerful red-and-yellow paper bag, he felt camaraderie with the other associates carrying the same bags. Although they griped effusively, he could see that they shared his sense of importance.

He worked through the cocktail hour of the annual attorney dinner. By the time he arrived at the Atherton Country Club, gritty and exhausted, the others were already seated at four round, linen-draped tables in a private room with an open bar. Cal Forman and Leo were carrying on a loud joke on the far side of the room. After hastily surveying the possibilities from the doorway, Howard took the nearest seat, which was between Martha Lewis, T&S's second newest associate, and Bill Madras. Although Martha professed to be delighted, Howard soon realized that she didn't care who sat to her left, since she was devoting her full attention to Peter Bonifacio who was seated on her right.

"I assure you I share your alarm," Peter was saying. "I personally am going to say the rosary in the shower every morning until they hire somebody. Maybe that new guy who came through today."

"I don't know how much help he could be," said Martha. "He seems greener than I am. How old do you think he is?"

"He must be older than he looks," said Peter. "He looks like a fetus. Could I trouble you for the butter?"

Peter was said to have spent several years in a Catholic seminary. If so, his Jesuit training had not diminished his social skills. Seated between Martha and Paula Levi, two of T&S's four women lawyers, Peter was having no difficulty keeping them both entertained.

His face was dominated by round, jet black wire-rims. His thick black hair parted reluctantly above his right eyebrow, and his mouth curved slightly up and then down again, as if he were repressing an irreverence. A faintly pulsing vein by his upper lip lent intensity to his continuous pantomime of longing for the women around him. He apparently expressed this longing without actually indulging it. He had a longtime girlfriend who was making her way through a psychiatric residency in Los Angeles.

Bill Madras was bent over a thick stack of papers that he was revising enthusiastically with a red pen.

"Can't they get any light in here?" he muttered, pulling one of the candles closer. "I feel like fucking Abe Lincoln, wax all over my goddamn prospectus."

"May we assume 'fucking' is here used as an adjective?" Peter said. "Or are you abandoning the closet this evening?"

"Adjective, Big Pete," he said to his document as Paula laughed into her wineglass.

"Wait!" Peter cried in a stage whisper as Howard lifted his soup spoon to his mouth. "Let Leo test it. We're young and have too much to lose." Martha and Paula nodded in mock solemnity. They craned their necks and watched across the room as Leo sipped, hesitated, and swallowed.

"Looks like virulent but not lethal," Peter interpreted, whereupon the others began to eat.

"Why single Leo out? If the food's so bad," Howard asked Martha, "why do we eat here?"

"Owned by a client. We'll sacrifice anything for a client, even our health."

"And how come Leo's the food tester?"

Madras didn't look up. "Hey, Big How, we're optimists. We keep hoping every cloud really does have a silver lining."

Peter barked one spare burst of laughter as Gerry Tweedmore approached the table and put a hand on Peter's shoulder.

Gerry Tweedmore was aging gracefully and with dignity, as only a highly successful male can do. He was still fit inside his shapeless Brooks Brothers coat. His gray mustache and the short gray hair that fell across his forehead accentuated his blue eyes. The creases in his tan face bespoke wisdom instead of decay. His shockingly ugly red-and-white tie was probably a Stanford club tie, although Howard couldn't be certain from across the table. Gerry gave the impression that once he had developed a loyalty he would not easily abandon it. Hence the firm's stubborn insistence on remaining in San Mateo while the electronics revolution fermented and then exploded to the south. After three weeks, Howard found Gerry more intimidating than all the other lawyers put together. His respect was too big a prize; Howard never felt equal to trying to earn it.

"How is it that you always have the best-looking company in the crowd?" Gerry asked Peter. There it was, the combination of power and friendly charm that Howard found disconcerting.

"Hard work," said Peter. "You may recall that you once extolled the virtues of hard work to me in another context. Don't you wish I had been as receptive?"

"But I know you have been working hard. I've been looking over your cross-complaint, and I just don't see how it could be any better. One of the most innovative pieces of lawyering I've seen in a long time. Why did we let you bury your talents in trademark law? Let's serve it on them next week. We're going to have some fun with this one." He patted Peter on the shoulder and returned to his table.

"Well," said Martha.

"What was that about?" Paula asked.

"DeLuth case," Peter replied. "We had some exceptionally worrisome facts, and I had the felicity to discover that those same facts could be even more worrisome to the opposition. This cross-complaint is a u-shaped tube that we're about to install between the guy's out box and his in box. We're going to stand back and watch the water show when he flushes the toilet." They were giggling when Gerry Tweedmore got to his table and tapped on his wineglass.

"Well, folks, the bad news is you're going to hear two speeches tonight, and the good news is they'll both be short. The thing I want to share with you this evening is some thinking I've been doing about the word 'quality.'

"I know you all share my belief that the quality of our practice is second to none. We wouldn't have it any other way, and I guess maybe we sort of take it for granted. I don't think we should. We are every one of us so busy these days that the temptation to take short cuts is a serious one.

"You all know what I'm talking about. It's two-thirty in the morning, and opposing counsel is so weak that those last two cases he cited couldn't possibly say anything you should know about. Or one of our paralegals is so good with incorporation papers that there's no need to go over this set. Or the basic arguments are right there in the brief, if it seems a little disorganized you can always make that up in oral argument.

"I think our sense of pride and integrity as top-quality professionals is one of our greatest assets. The only way we can love the practice of law is to insist on producing the very finest quality, always.

"Maybe more important than the quality of our practice is the quality of our lives. Too many of us get so focused on what we're doing here in the office that we forget about what we ought to be doing outside. Family,

for those of us lucky enough to have them. The time to
pursue other interests. The time to just sit back and think
about where our lives are going. The pressure on us to
sacrifice these things is enormous, and I think we have to
resist that pressure as if our very lives depended on it.

"That's about it from me tonight. I'm very proud to
be part of this outfit, and I want to thank all of you for
helping me feel that way. Leo?" As the applause faded,
Leo Slyde rose tippily to his feet.

Leo was short. Although he probably wasn't over-
weight, his round cheeks and full, soft mouth created the
impression that he was pudgy. He was in his thirties, but
his pink skin and devilish smile made him seem younger.
Perhaps to counteract this, his face was heavily weighted
by dark-frame glasses.

Just now his tie was loosened, and the candlelight
played across his gold watch and cuff links as he opened
his palms and spread his stubby fingers in benediction to
quiet the crowd.

"Okay, guys, listen up. Bottom line is, money's
rollin' in. [Laughter, applause.] The other partners and I
just wanna say thanks, and keep up the good work.

"You know, sometimes we get so busy talkin' and
thinkin' and tryin' to make things happen for our clients
that we forget to say how much we appreciate the great
work you all do. We know you're all makin' some sacrifices, 'cause we make 'em, too." Suddenly Martha giggled, and several heads turned in her direction. She was
watching Peter, who was doing something with his dinner plate. "Some of us don't get a whole lot of vacation,
or even a whole lot of sleep, and several of you have
mentioned how my golf game's goin' to hell. [Laughter.]
And in all seriousness, some of us don't see as much of
our families as we'd like." Martha giggled again, and
Howard turned in time to see Peter slide his plate to one

side, revealing something on the paper place mat underneath, then slide it back again.

"But we like to think these sacrifices are more than
compensated for by the pleasures of a job well done and
the pleasures of being in a service business where we are
constantly putting the client first, even when it costs us
something personally." Here Martha giggled again, and
this time she turned her back on Peter and buried her
face in her dinner napkin.

"Anyhow, we think it's important to take time out
like this once in a while and let you know how much we
appreciate the way you all give a hundred and twenty-
five percent. Course we wish it could be a hundred and
thirty. [Laughter.] You'll be getting a memo about that
shortly. [More laughter.]

"When all is said and done, guys, there's a lot of
money to be made out there. So rest up tonight, enjoy
yourselves, then get the hell in there tomorrow and make
us all rich." A shout of enthusiasm rose from the crowd
as he dropped heavily into his seat.

"Wait a minute, wait a minute!" Cal Forman shouted
above the applause. "I have a few words to add." The
crowd murmured in anticipation and turned its attention
to T&S's antitrust litigation partner.

"Gentlemen, and ladies, I feel compelled to share a
bit of news with you this evening, a bit of bad news and
a bit of good news about our own Leo M. Slyde. The bad
news is that, after some hard drinking and some hard
working and some hard other things [shouts of laughter],
Leo up and died. And the good news is that, quality control being in a very sorry state, he actually got into
heaven. [More laughter.] So when Leo got up to the
pearly gates and gave his name, the angels rushed off
and brought back St. Peter himself.

"And St. Peter said, 'Good to have you here, son,
we've been waiting. I left instructions for them to come

and get me, because I want to personally welcome the oldest man who ever got into heaven.'

"And Leo said, 'There must be some mistake, St. Peter, I'm only thirty-three years old.'

"But St. Peter just wagged his finger at Leo like this and said, 'Don't try to kid us, boy. We've seen your billable hours, we know you're a hundred and ninety-five.''

The laughter that erupted was so loud that couples strolling by the windows stopped and looked in on the candlelit festivities. Shortly thereafter people got up to go, and Howard took advantage of the milling to see what Peter had been doing during Leo's speech. He reached over and pulled aside Peter's plate. Printed in tidy block letters on the paper place mat was the word BULLSHIT.

4

The Village Expert

The work kept coming. In the fourth week Howard's phone began to ring. Whenever he was making headway with one client's problem, he would answer his telephone to find another client demanding immediate information on an unrelated matter. Or a secretary would say she had Mr. Thus-and-so on the line, and Mr. Forman would like Howard to handle the call. (Never once would Howard have heard of Mr. Thus-and-so.) Or a partner was asking him to step into his office right away.

"Candy said you wanted to see me?" Howard said, standing in the door of Leo's office.

"Howard," said Leo heartily. "How are ya? Listen,

close the door, have a seat. You just got your most important client."

"I did?" Howard perched stiffly on the edge of a maroon leather chair.

"Yeah, me. I need a little will change and can't seem to get to it. I figure what the hell, you'd probably like the experience." He touched the cleft in his chin with his index finger as he spoke.

"I'll certainly do my best. What needs to be changed?"

"Just the beneficiaries. Right now the money goes to my wife, Nancy. I want to change that. I want half to my kids, you can get their names from the will. The rest goes to Connie."

Howard kept his eyes on his yellow pad. "Connie?"

"Yeah, Connie Valentine. The one who works here." Howard looked up and Leo winked. "Cheap at the price."

"That, uh, shouldn't be so hard. Where do I get a copy of the will you have now?"

"It's in the vault. Easier still, get a word processor to run one off for you. Any questions?"

"Well, does Mrs. Slyde have a will?"

"Yeah, she did it separately. Forget about it."

"And, uh, if your kids are minors, I guess we need a trust."

"You worry about that." He grinned and waved his hand. "Be creative. Show me what's new since I was in school. Creative and discreet. Hey, I'll bet you're good at being discreet. Do we understand each other?"

"Yes, I think so."

"I think so, too. How you liking your job so far?"

"I like it a lot."

"Good. I know you'll be creative and discreet. Catcha later, okay? I got a few calls to make before the East Coast shuts down." He swung around to his credenza and was dialing as Howard left.

*   *   *

He was frantically trying to decipher the index to a looseleaf on revocable trusts when the phone rang.

"Howard Rickover."

"Hi, Tom?"

He recognized her voice. "Hi, Candy, no, this Howard. You want Tom?"

"Oh, no, I'm sorry, I meant Howard. Leo wants you in his office right away."

He put on his coat and tried to smooth the crease out of his tie, irritated that his heart was beating faster for no reason. The pour-over trust? The adoption papers? Wouldn't hurt to take the adoption papers, just in case.

He reached behind him on the credenza for the adoption papers. They weren't there. Except of course they were there. He'd put them there himself, less than an hour ago. He flipped rapidly through the other documents on the credenza and glanced over his desk. The hell with it. Leo probably wanted something else anyway.

"Leo mention what it was about, Candy?" he asked as he passed her desk. "Is he with anybody?" She was wearing a blouse as sheer as a spider web, and he watched her mouth intently while she answered him.

"No, he didn't say, Howard, but he's in with Mr. and Mrs. Donahue."

"That's not Mr. and Mrs. Donahue, Candy." Mary Belle Strick issued this criticism over her shoulder, without breaking the rhythm of her typing. "That's Mr. and Mrs. Smith. That was very poor client relations when you called him Mr. Donahue just now." Mary Belle and Candy shared the secretary's cubicle outside Leo's office.

"Well, how can I help it? Look right here, Howard, in his appointment book: 'eleven A.M. Donahue.'"

"Don't worry, Candy, it's not important. Donahue is probably settling down in the waiting room with his very

first cup of coffee." He didn't know a Smith or a Donahue, and he relaxed. Leo was bringing him in on a new
client. As he knocked on Leo's door, he heard Candy say
into the telephone, "Good morning, Mr. Dona— I mean,
Mr. Slyde's office."

But Leo wasn't in the office at all. The only occupants were two gray-haired people whom Howard took
to be Mr. and Mrs. Smith.

"Look here," said Mr. Smith. "Are you this expert
on the generation-skipping trust?"

"Hi. I'm Howard Rickover. Has Leo stepped out?"

"That's one way of putting it," said Mrs. Smith.
"After we waited an hour for him, he brought us in here
and then the phone rang. He jumped up and ran out and
said he'd send in the office expert to help us take care of
our problem. Is that you or isn't it? I'm starting to think
we're getting the runaround."

"No problem," Howard said without conviction.
This was Leo's perfect little joke. Although Howard had
heard of generation-skipping trusts, he knew virtually
nothing about them. "Leo was certainly exaggerating
when he called me the expert, but that is my area. Let's
get all the facts and questions today, and if there are
some I can't answer then I'll look them up and be sure I
have it right before we meet again."

Mrs. Smith inhaled sharply and exchanged glances
with her husband. But they had been waiting over an
hour, and nobody else was available. Grudgingly, they
started telling Howard their problem. Howard didn't
know any of the answers, but he tried to ask lots of questions to show he was thorough, and also because he was
hoping he would somehow end up with the relevant
facts after he looked up the law. He took a long time, and
after forty-five minutes he noticed that the Smiths were
getting restless.

"Well," he said cheerfully, "I guess we don't have

the answers yet, but we certainly have all the questions." The Smiths stared at him in silence. "Let me be sure I have your phone number, and then . . ." The door opened and Leo entered. He seemed startled for an instant. Then he grinned.

"Mr. and Mrs. Smith," he said heartily. "How's it goin'? Just about got that trust worked out?"

"Well, not completely," said Howard. "We hit a few minor snags, but I think—"

"What snags?" Leo asked. "Maybe we can work it out now."

Howard started reading some of the questions from his yellow pad. Leo knew the answers to every question, and asked some others that Howard hadn't thought of.

"This doesn't sound so tough. I think we need an irrevocable trust, one that has a contingency clause allowing the funds to revert back according to certain contingencies beyond your control. That way you won't have to worry about probate, and at the same time you won't have to worry about somebody contesting the will. Then later if you decide that you really can entrust the management to one of your children, come on back in and we'll make that person the trustee. After all, some kids turn out all right in the end, and there's no reason to hurt feelings unnecessarily. Right?"

Leo had been in the office for five minutes. Mrs. Smith was sitting forward in her chair, Mr. Smith had sunk back into the cushions. To Howard's irritation they were both smiling. Didn't they feel just a little bit curious about where Leo had been?

"Now, did Howard go over any of the tax consequences with you?" A ridiculous question, since even Howard knew that the tax consequences of this kind of arrangement were both complex and unusual.

"No," the Smiths said in unison, glancing uncomfortably into Howard's corner as if they were embarrassed that he was still there.

"Well, no problem. Let's not take up your time this morning. We'll just have Howard write them up in a letter and send it along to you. He'll get it in the mail tomorrow, will that be all right?" Leo stood up. "Fine, then, thank you very much for coming in. We'll draft this trust and put together the tax memo and send it along. Look it over, and don't hesitate to give Howard a call if you have any questions. After all, he did my will, he *is* the office expert." He gave Howard a conspiratorial wink. "Howard, why don't you show the Smiths out? I've got a little nuisance settlement that's going to hell on me."

As Howard left the office, Leo had swung around to his credenza and was holding his red phone receiver between his cheek and shoulder.

"George! What's happening?" he said, at the same time dialing the black phone.

Back in his own office, Howard sank into his chair and closed his eyes. The water under his armpits felt like ice. And now he was committed to all that tax research by tomorrow.

He opened his eyes and saw the adoption papers. They were on the credenza, by the telephone. He leaned forward and stared at them. Exactly where he had remembered putting them. How could he possibly have overlooked them? He flipped slowly through them. Page five of the petition was missing. Somebody had been in his office.

Why would somebody be in his office? The probation. Madras had been right. They were monitoring his work. They saw how few hours he was billing. They were afraid he wasn't doing anything at all. He got up and opened his door.

"Excuse me," he said to Mary Belle Strick, the secretary closest to his door. Apparently she didn't hear him. He said it louder.

"Mm?" Mary Belle said, continuing her typing.

"Have you been here for the last hour?"

"Mm," Mary Belle said, still not looking up.

"Did anybody . . ." Suddenly he felt ridiculous. People were so busy they were barely in control. Who would have energy to creep around and inspect his meager output? Mary Belle had paused, her fingers still resting on the keys, her raised eyebrows inviting him to finish his interruption.

". . . uh, leave any messages?"

She resumed typing. "Four," she said, motioning with her head to his message spindle. "You're getting popular for a new guy."

He took the messages back into his office. There under the roller of his chair was the missing page from his adoption petition. He picked the paper up, dusted it against his shirt, and reinserted it into the stack of papers. Bill had talked about auditory hallucinations; why not visual ones? He went to get coffee before he started the tax research.

He stared glumly into the fire in his fireplace, tracing patterns in the cold condensation on his glass. After a month on the job it was clear that NYU had left out some things. Like how to do any of this stuff. Like how to read the indexes of books that purported to explain how to do this stuff. He pressed the cold glass against his forehead. Like how to be sure he was looking at the right index.

And what about this hours problem? He was doing nothing but work and he was billing only six hours a day. Some people had been talking at lunch about a deal where Leo was billing forty hours a day. What did that mean? How was that physically possible?

And then this probation rumor . . . But something else was bothering him even more. Had he really gone to law school to help Leo Slyde cheat his wife?

Leo was treating Howard to a joke about three Chinamen and a Jew as he flipped through the motion papers he was supposed to be reading. Mercifully, Candy stuck her head in. "The police are here to see you."

Leo looked up sharply. "The police? What about?"

"Your car."

He exhaled and grinned. "Couldn't be that bad. They're paid for. Which car? What about it?"

"She didn't say."

"She?" His grin broadened as he put down his pen. "Let's see what this is about."

The woman who entered was an unlikely police officer. She looked more like an otherworldly intellectual and dreamer, with short curly hair that did what it wanted and a navy polyester suit that had been lived and possibly slept in. She looked like her hands were always cold.

"Hey," Leo said to Howard, winking. "The cops are getting better looking." He turned to her. "Don't they let lady officers wear uniforms?"

Her gaze was steady, unreadable. "I'm plainclothes," she said, holding out her badge. "I was in the neighborhood when the call came through."

"Okay. So what'd I do?"

"Do you own a sixty-seven Aston Martin DB6?"

"Yeah, but it's been in the parking lot all day. What've I got, a lapsed meter?"

"It appears you've been the victim of malicious destruction of property."

His smirk evaporated. "My Aston Martin? Something's wrong with my Aston Martin?"

"I wonder if you'd step down to the garage with me to inspect the property."

He pushed away from his desk and headed for the door. "You're telling me somebody wrecked my Aston Martin? This had better be a mistake."

Howard said quickly, "Leo, this is due in court by five."

"Shit. Bring it. Let's go."

As they entered the underground section of the lot it was obvious there was no mistake. Leo stood silently in the doorway, then walked slowly down the cement steps, holding onto the rail, to where the car stood. Suddenly he screamed, "Fuck!" and slammed his hand down on the hood. "Fuck!" The sound echoed off the cement pillars. "What've they done to my car?"

A Day-Glo pink ASSHOLE was sprayed in foot-high letters across the windshield and along the dark-green paint of the driver's door.

Leo stamped his feet and shook his fists in the air. "Who did this? I want to know who did this to my car." He grabbed his blond hair with both hands.

"I'm sorry about your loss, Mr. Slyde."

Leo was growling through clenched teeth.

"We'd like to help you find the person who did it."

"You fucking better find the person who did it."

"Any suspicions about who it might have been?"

"How the hell should I know? That's your goddamn job. It was obviously some lunatic."

She watched him levelly. "Have you had any major disagreements recently that might have provoked this sort of retaliation?"

Howard thought he saw fear flicker in Leo's eyes and then vanish. The police officer's gaze registered nothing.

"Yeah," said Leo. "Lots of major disagreements. My job is major disagreements. But that's business. Nothing for anybody to get . . . personal about."

"It may have been random. What time did you park here this morning?"

"Seven-fifteen, as usual. No, seven. First car in the lot."

"And you haven't moved it since?"

Leo shook his head.

"We got the call about an hour ago from somebody who parked down here. She said it looked like the paint was still wet. We'll post somebody here tonight from five to six-thirty and ask for witnesses." She glanced around. "You might post a sign in your law firm, see if anybody saw anything. Here's my card. Call me if anything occurs to you that might help."

He stuck the unexamined card in his pocket, staring beyond her face. His sudden smile was boyish. "Listen, Officer, so you'll help me out with this, won't you? You're going to give it your best, right? I'd really appreciate it." For the first time her watchful dark eyes changed a shade.

"I'll call you immediately if anything turns up," she said. She nodded to both of them. Howard watched her climb the cement stairs and disappear. What was that look at the end? It reflected some opinion of Leo. Howard felt confident the opinion was an intelligent one.

"What's her name?" he asked Leo. "I mean, in case you need to get in touch with her."

Leo pulled the card out of his pocket silently and handed it over. His shoulders were drooping and he sighed. "I don't know," he said doubtfully. "Maybe this means somebody doesn't like me." Howard was so startled that he almost missed his cue.

"Uh, no. I'm sure it doesn't. Probably just some crazy who wanted to wreck the best-looking car in the lot." Nelson. Inspector Sarah Nelson. He handed the card back. "Won't your insurance cover it?"

"Doesn't matter," said Leo, his eyes growing moist.

"I'd always know this had happened to it, you know?"
He contemplated the car for another moment, then
pulled out his wallet. "Have Triple-A tow it to B and F
Motors. Here, you'll need the key. And have Candy call
Nancy to pick me up."

"Listen," said Howard, reaching into his coat
pocket, "I know this seems irrelevant right now, but
shouldn't we sign the summary judgment motion?" Leo
accepted the outstretched pen and signed vacantly.
Howard left him standing in the underground parking
lot, apparently paying his last respects.

"This is Sarah Nelson," she said into her car microphone, "following up on that malicious destruction at
sixteen hundred Cabrillo, intersection of San Ysidro. We
need a uniformed officer in the underground parking lot
behind the building at seventeen hundred hours to seek
witnesses to the incident. Continuing to nineteen hundred hours. Over."

"Nelson, affirmative on uniformed officer. Over."

"Nelson here. Also requesting central computer
check on the owner of the vehicle. Over."

"Nelson, affirmative on central computer check.
What are we looking for? Insurance fraud? Over."

"Negative on insurance fraud. Any type of criminal
record. Over and out.

"In other words," she said cheerfully as she replaced
the microphone, "I'll know just as soon as I find it."

5

The Taste of Manna

Howard went in on Saturday to spend time in the library without the phone ringing. He spent Sunday in his cottage working on will forms. He began to have trouble sleeping, lying in the dark going over and over his various deadlines and trying to satisfy himself that he could meet them all. He called his doctor and got a prescription for sleeping pills.

Still the work kept coming. Cal wanted to bring him in on the Gobbit team, which was rapidly preparing for trial. They needed a summary judgment motion in two weeks. They needed motions *in limine*. They needed jury instructions as soon as possible. Hiding in his office and looking up "motion *in limine*" in his law dictionary, Howard felt astonished by how little law school had prepared him for this job.

He was surprised to hear that he was going to court with Peter Bonifacio.

"I thought he did patents or something," he confided to Bill Madras, who had decided to use his time at the urinals to ask how Howard was adjusting to life as a lawyer.

Madras grinned. "Hey, Big Pete's done plenty of court work. Not that he likes it much. You better do the talking," he said with a decisive zip, "but he can definitely tell you what to say."

Howard didn't take Bill's time to explain that it was

going to be the other way around. Howard didn't feel that his very first time inside a courtroom should be an actual court appearance. He had explained this to Leo by means of a note, and Candy reported back a couple of days later that Peter would do the appearance for him.

Howard explained the issues from a prepared outline as Peter negotiated the morning traffic on 101. He wondered whether Peter always honked at other drivers so much. When they climbed out of the BMW in the parking lot, Peter's impeccably tailored, perfectly pressed, lint-free navy suit was suddenly too big for him, and he slunk into the courtroom behind Howard like a defendant in an armed robbery case. When the judge called their case half an hour later, Howard braced himself for the humiliation of Peter being unable to speak at all.

"Well, Mr. Bonifacio," said the judge, raising his eyebrows and peering down through his bifocals. "Haven't seen you in a long time. Are we expecting any fireworks today?"

"—cretin!" Peter muttered violently under his breath. Howard stood up taller, willing himself not to turn and stare. No. That couldn't be what he had said.

Peter then proceeded to croak out concise, well-organized if barely audible paragraphs through his constricted throat. Although the judge asked him to speak up twice, with increasing irritation, Peter won the motion. On the trip home he became hilarious, and Howard was laughing, too, when they pulled into the Tweedmore parking lot. Suddenly Peter said through clenched teeth, "Look at these bastards who park where they're not supposed to. I feel like slashing all their tires."

Was this the man Madras had credited with lots of court work? It wasn't possible. The guy wouldn't have survived.

One of the bigger surprises of those first weeks at T&S occurred a few days later. When Howard asked Connie

Valentine whether Peter had really done much trial work, he was astonished by her emphatic confirmation.

By the seventh week files were spilling out of his file cabinet and onto his expensive brown carpet. He decided to become more organized. He made a large chart with squares for each day of the month. First, he wrote in the court- or client-imposed deadlines in red, then penciled in what had to be accomplished each day to meet those deadlines. He saw that in the ninth week he had six court briefs due in five days. He stopped taking lunch and worked with his door closed.

He was crossing the lobby to the mailroom when he heard glass shatter. He turned to see a big man sprawled facedown on the coffee table. Tulips and yellow roses were strewn on the sofa, and water was soaking into the cushions. The man was struggling. Heart attack. Call the ambulance. Then the man said, "Bastard," and Howard realized he had Leo Slyde pinned beneath him. Leo's head hit the glass tabletop. "Jerk." Slam. "You think you control everything, don't you? Well, control this." Cal Forman ran into the lobby.

"Whoa! What's going on here? Take it easy. Let's take it easy." He rushed to the table and started pulling the two men apart.

"Come on now," said Cal. "I know Leo's an ugly son of a bitch, but that's no reason to kill him." Howard grabbed the big man by the arm and started pulling.

"There," Cal said. "That's it. Let go." He pulled Leo from under the big guy and pushed him at Bill Madras. "Get him out of here." There was blood on Leo's shirt, and he had a hand over his nose. Bill led him as far as the sofa, where Leo sat down heavily. The big man called over to him.

"Hey, asshole!"

"Al, that's it," said the man holding his elbow. "Get control of yourself." The big man shook him loose.

"I said 'asshole.'" He was pointing his finger, and Howard could see that his hand was shaking. "People have limits. The law may not, but people do. Let's get out of here." The big man and the guy on his elbow disappeared into an elevator.

"Leo," said Cal. "You all right? We oughta get a doctor."

Leo shook his head. "No." Behind his open hand his sniff sounded bubbly. "Anybody got a handkerchief?" he asked. Howard handed him one.

"Broken?"

Leo touched the bridge gingerly with his thumb and forefinger. "Don't think so. Probably just a nosebleed. Hey, I think he likes me." He winked painfully to the sound of nervous laughter.

"Who in the hell was he?" asked Cal.

"Guy opposing us in the Sullivan case."

"That guy was a lawyer?" asked Cal, incredulous.

Leo shook his head slightly. "Plaintiff. I was deposing him. I don't think he liked my interrogating style."

"Jesus, we better call the cops."

"Nah, hold off. I've gotta figure out how to play this." The elevator door opened and Leo tensed, then relaxed when a well-dressed woman stepped off. "Maybe I'll threaten him with a civil suit. That'll soften him up on this other case." The corners of a grin appeared from behind the bloody handkerchief. "Hey, how do I bill this one? Settlement negotiation, physical." He tried to get up, Bill helped him. "Shit, my suit's ripped. Cost me forty dollars for another one." There was thin laughter as he disappeared around the corner on Bill's arm.

That night at eleven-thirty Howard happened on Leo, nose taped, turning the knob of Connie's door. When Leo winked conspiratorially and slicked back his hair with both hands, Howard wondered how either of them found the energy.

Howard had been standing idly by Candy's desk for at least ten minutes while she tried to set up a conference call. It was peculiarly bad luck that Gerry Tweedmore was himself standing in the hall less than twenty feet away, from which vantage point he could and did observe Howard doing absolutely nothing.

Gerry was standing outside Bill Madras's closed door with a three-piece companion that Howard didn't recognize. "Gosh, Barry," he said. "I hate to keep you standing out here in the corridor like some kind of a brush salesman. Bill must be on a pretty important call." Irritation showed plainly through his transparent smile.

Barry shrugged. "Emergencies happen. Especially in a place like this. I haven't worked with your office before, but my wife told me what to expect. She did some work for you guys a couple of years ago. Wendy Hite."

"She sounds familiar," said Gerry. "Linda, does Bill know we're out here?"

Howard could feel Gerry's eyes on him again. He grabbed the weekly calendar from Candy's desk and started flipping through it.

Gerry turned back to his companion. "What did Wendy help us out with?"

"Come to think of it," said Barry, "I guess she worked for your partner. Slyde."

"Darn," said Candy. "Darn, darn. I lost them again." This had to be the third time. If Gerry had been elsewhere Howard would have taken over and done it himself.

He heard Linda say, "Mr. Madras is off the phone." Good. Get Gerry into Bill's office. Then he heard Linda call, "Mr. Tweedmore?"

Howard looked up to see Gerry with his hand on

Barry's shoulder, shepherding him down the hall. Madras opened his door and stuck his head out as Linda called, "Mr. Tweedmore!"

Gerry looked back without stopping. "Oh, Bill. Stick around awhile, will you? We'll be back."

"Where's he going?" Linda asked Bill. "I thought he was going to knock your door down."

"Okay," said Candy. "Finally. They're on."

It did seem strange for Gerry to wander off like that. Linda and Bill Madras were still staring at each other when Howard entered Leo's office.

"Mr. and Mrs. Smith," Leo was saying heartily. "What's happening? Listen, Howard and I've been doin' the research we told you about, and it turns out we've got something even better than that irrevocable trust we considered. Yeah, it's called a Dingle Plan. The thing about it is, you don't have to worry about contingencies at all. We do one clean set of documents and it's settled. You can forget about it. Yeah. Yeah, I know I did, and it would do a fairly good job for you. The point is, this new way is even better.

"Now, I know you'll want details, and I've asked Howard to give you a call to set up a time. Yeah. I know you are, and we're going to wrap it up right away. After you talk to Howard you're gonna agree this little delay was well worth the time and trouble.

"Okay, great. I just wanted to call you with the good news. Let me know if I can do anything else. Talk to you later."

He hung up the receiver and grinned. "What'd I tell you, it's all in the packaging. No reason for them ever to know we had a little screw-up the first time. That take care of it?" Two phones rang. "Hey, catcha later."

In the eighth week he was assigned Mary Belle, the skinny little redneck secretary who shared a cubicle with

Candy. Mary Belle was in her mid-twenties, with stringy red hair and a crescent-shaped scar on her forehead. She blew a cloud of cigarette smoke around him every time they talked.

"Okay, Howie, let's do some ground rules. I go home at five, I got a boyfriend who gets mean if I'm late. I don't care about lunch hour. I won't do your personal insurance forms, and I'm not a maid. It'll be awhile before you know whether I'm doing anything wrong, but if you last that long, let me know. That way I can fix it and we both look good. Don't do your own filing, you'll screw it up. You'll try to oversupervise me, I'll straighten that out as we go. Questions?"

"Uh, actually, my name is Howard."

"Yeah? Well, mine's Maria Bellina, but we go informal around here. You got a call on forty-one."

She seemed to have a delicate ego, so he was careful to be respectful. "Please keep a copy of this for the file," he wrote on a draft of his first brief. An hour later it was back in his box: "NO."

He ran into Bill Madras at the urinals again.

"Hey, Big How, keepin' up with the dead guys?"

"Probate? It's going okay, I guess. I feel like I'm churning it out so fast I don't know how it's going."

"Yeah? Not what your time sheets say."

"I know. I must be incredibly inefficient. These will forms are taking forever and they're not even billable."

"Tough break." Madras shook himself. "Gotta make it up in the billable stuff."

"But how? I'm putting in as many hours as I physically have in my life, and I'm still coming in at the bottom."

Madras stopped in midflush and looked at Howard with concern. "Shouldn't be happening, How, you're screwing up." He frowned at the speckled wall for a moment. "Look at it this way. Don't bill the time you actually spend on a project, bill what it's worth. See what I mean?"

"Not really. I mean, how would I judge that? And don't we tell the clients we bill by the hour?"

But Madras was already halfway into the lobby, Howard could barely hear him above the thundering water. ". . . the hell, it's your probate."

Mary Belle called after him in the hallway.

"Whoa, Howie, hold on a minute, your writ's all screwed up." Was she hooked to an amplifier? Through the haze of her cigarette smoke he could see that many eyes were upon him. "You gotta have a petition, and then your set of points and authorities is a whole separate document. And where's your draft order? Good thing this isn't due today." She tossed the writ over the top of the partition. "There's a CEB book on this stuff, check the library."

"I'm worried," said Emily, Gerry's secretary. She and Liz, one of the word processors, were standing over Howard in his office, analyzing a Xeroxed recipe for cheese torta striped with pesto. "This looks complicated. It looks like you need a food processor."

"Absolutely not," Howard said. "You need a blender, but you can use mine if you want."

"I have a blender," said Liz. "Look, we asked Howard for something sort of special. I bet this'll work fine. Wait. What's a Charlotte mold?"

"You don't need one," Howard explained. "Just use a small mixing bowl. The only thing the least bit tricky about any of this is the ingredients. Be sure the basil is fresh. I'd go to Bernini's. And use unsalted butter. For some reason the salted butter makes this weird—"

Leo burst in, slamming the door against the wall.

"What in hell have you done to Jim Macaffee?" he shouted from the open doorway. All typing in the secretaries' cubicles stopped abruptly, then a single typewriter resumed anemically as Emily and Liz escaped through the closing door. "For five years I cultivate that guy. We've taken three of his companies through start-up and venture deals, and then I've got him screaming on the goddamn phone for fifteen minutes today. We're not responsive anymore, we're too big for our own good. And why? His goddamn estate plan, can you believe that? What have you done to him?"

"I was late getting the trust papers over to him. I couldn't let them go without a thorough review, and I couldn't do that by Friday without blowing the Huffman deal."

"I don't want to hear about the fucking Huffman deal. Where's the Macaffee file?" He started tossing the files on Howard's desk.

"It's out by Mary Belle. The agreement is done, she's typing a cover letter."

"I want it hand-delivered. Today. And for God's sake, send it over my signature." He slammed the door against the wall again on his way out. Mary Belle stared at Howard smugly through the closing door. A moment later she buzzed him on the intercom.

"A Mr. Bangsund on the line."

"Get a number, okay? And hold my calls for an hour or two."

"Not good, Howie. Clients don't like it. Better get used to the interruptions now before it gets busy. He's on forty-one." She hung up.

Leo saw Howard in the parking lot that night and motioned him to come over.

"Howard," he said halfheartedly. "What's doin'?

Listen, I got a little excited today. Don't worry about Macaffee, I'll get him calmed down. He's sort of an antsy bastard, anyway." He held up his hand to block Howard's response. "Look, I want to give you some advice. Late is bad. Don't be late. But that's not the reason Macaffee called me. He called because he didn't feel confident that you were in control of his problem. This is a service business, you aren't some ivory-tower professor. Macaffee doesn't know a trust from Shinola, if he did he wouldn't pay you to do it for him. How would he know whether the job you're doing is good or lousy?

"You tell him. You remind him every day that he's lucky to have you. I don't give a damn if you don't listen to him, he's a boring bastard. But you gotta make him think you're listening all the time. Make him think he's got the most interesting legal problem you can think of."

He held his chubby hands out in front of him, palms flat toward Howard, and began swaying his chunky shoulders rhythmically, a look of rapture on his face. "You've got to dance with the client, you've got to show him that you're right there with him all the time."

"I guess I'm still trying to dance with the probate code."

Leo stopped dancing and opened his eyes. "That's your mistake, you underestimate yourself. Any bimbo can master the probate code. You did a great job on my will. And you do seem to know the meaning of 'discreet' so far. . . .

"My point is this job is ten percent lawyering, ninety percent showmanship. The sooner you figure that out the richer you'll be." He winked and patted his new silver Aston Martin affectionately. Howard noticed that it didn't yet have plates. "My methods may not be the best"—he grinned—"but they work. See you tomorrow."

In the tenth week Howard received yet another invitation to join a litigation team, which he tactfully and regretfully declined. It sounded like one of the most exciting cases in the office, he told Stan Pierce, and he was looking forward to working with Stan particularly. However, with his present caseload, he felt it would be an injustice to everybody concerned to take on another client.

It seemed Howard had made a mistake. Apparently it had already been determined that he was the person for the job. It seemed, in fact, from a review of billable hours that Howard could pick up the pace just a little bit. Indeed, he was lucky to be chosen for this particular plum, because it could shield him from other less tasteful matters that would surely come his way. Because Stan liked Howard he was willing to give him a valuable bit of advice. One of the qualities most valued in associates was their Enthusiasm. If a lawyer got the reputation of being a complainer or a resister of work, it would sour the whole relationship. Howard thanked Stan for his help and agreed to prepare the motion to dismiss by Friday. He began wearing his coat in the office to conceal the wet stains under his armpits.

He glared through the windshield at the pavement racing into the arc of his headlights. One in the morning. He was wired. He'd be lucky to sleep five hours. And it wasn't just the amount of work that was getting to him, or the elusive probation, or the daily, devouring fear that he was sowing the seeds of future disaster. It was Leo.

Leo was getting to him. Not (primarily) because Leo had hoodwinked the Smiths into paying all those extra hours for Leo's fuck-up. Not (really) because Leo had an obscene way of stroking his car. It wasn't even (exactly) that Leo treated Howard with complete contempt by throwing him at Leo's clients with no warning. It was that he winked while he was doing it.

That wink really made you feel greasy. Like Leo was generously including you in some highly prestigious conspiracy. The greaseball conspiracy. As Howard turned into his driveway he whispered, "Fuck."

By the twelfth week the sleeping pills had stopped working. On Monday, trying desperately to finish a motion to dismiss for lack of federal jurisdiction, he was distracted by Peter Bonifacio's voice in the next office: "Settle? Why would we settle? I worked my butt off on this thing, Gerry, we agreed the arguments were sound. Why would we settle? Aren't I entitled to know that?" Howard hoped it wasn't that DeLuth case they'd been talking about at the attorney dinner. In any case, Peter's voice had a pleading quality that kept Howard staring at the wall long after the voice fell silent.

On Tuesday he failed to file the brief by five P.M. This meant a desperate petition to the court to allow the papers to be filed late. Stan Pierce, who liked Howard personally, offered him the valuable piece of advice that there was no quality that could destroy a young lawyer's career like Carelessness. After that, it seemed to Howard that faces were averted as he passed down the hallway.

In the thirteenth week Cal Forman, John Maddis, and Leo all whipped into Howard's office with SVM estate plans to be drafted immediately. It seemed the probate department was finally getting off the ground.

"Do my guy first," said Leo. "He's got a brain tumor."

"God, how awful."

"Yeah. Doesn't give us much time."

That week Howard realized the elevator had begun opening and closing in slow motion, its rubber-lipped doors lingering wistfully at every floor, hoping to entice a reluctant passenger. At Burger King the cashiers taunted him by fumbling over the cheerful red-and-yellow bags and mocked him with their uncanny need to open a new roll of quarters every time he needed change.

6

The Near Miss

Howard was an unlikely hunter. He thought animals belonged in woods and fairy tales, or else roasted and accompanied by a good wine. He was unprepared for the suggestion that they served another purpose.

"Candy said this was a good time to talk to you about the generation-skipping trust?" he said, standing in Leo's doorway.

"Marty! How's it goin'?" Leo said into his phone, gesturing to Howard to close the door. Howard had been waiting more than a week for this audience, and he shut Leo's door with determination. Leo never even pretended to concentrate on anything Howard said for more than five minutes. Also, Howard lacked the status to get Leo to hold his calls. The five minutes could be spread over an hour, while Leo talked into first one phone and then another and then two at once, winking conspiratorially in Howard's direction as the only acknowledgment that Howard was there. To contend with this, Howard had so perfected his own concentration that he could be interrupted in midsentence and continue smoothly fifteen minutes later as the receiver left Leo's ear.

Today the calls were surprisingly sparse. After only

ten minutes Howard had asked nearly all his questions. Then Leo looked up wistfully from the draft document and said, "How can I concentrate on this when yesterday I was with the President?"

"It must be difficult," Howard agreed, glancing at his outline and wondering vaguely which president of what. "What were you and the president working on?" Leo's dark-framed glasses were on the desk. Without them, his pale blue eyes seemed to recede into puffy skin.

"He was dedicating the new space shuttle! Don't you read the *Chronicle?*"

"Oh, you mean *the* President. As in United States." He did dimly recall a picture in the morning paper of the President standing in front of an airplane.

"That's the man. A few of us got together with him for a little barbecue afterward at the base commander's. The Reagans were there. Sally Ride. I sat with Senator Glenn. I guess John's quite a fisherman, I told him to use the island for a few days this summer."

His eyes focused on the invisible distance for a moment, then refocused benevolently on Howard. "You've never been to the island, have you, Howard? I'd like to have you join me up there this summer."

Not very likely, Howard thought sourly. Leo owned an island called Montgomery Island off the coast of British Columbia, and periodically took the boys there to go deep sea fishing. "The boys" were generally partners and presidents of companies, not first-year associates.

"Hey, in the meantime, let's go hunting this weekend! Harry Vinelle's got a buncha guys flying down to his ranch, and I think it would do you good. Just regular guys: Harry, Jack Lincoln, me, anybody else I want to bring." He grinned. "You know, Harry and Jack have some money to put into generation-skipping trusts."

Howard was unable to form a single thought, much

less an excuse. Leo was beaming as he handed back the forgotten trust agreement, deeply touched by his own generosity. "Besides, we can get to know each other better."

Just what he needed, for Leo to know him better, he thought as he sat in his kitchen at 3 A.M. eating Hostess cupcakes. After all, Leo might still harbor the illusion that they had something in common.

And where was he supposed to get time to chase . . . what did they chase? Ducks? Seemed like the wrong season. Probably not rabbits, not macho enough. Deer? Something vicious that would hunt you back. Wolverines, maybe, with those droolly, pointed teeth. Wild pigs. For Leo's sake he hoped it wasn't pigs. Somebody might get phonetic and shoot the wrong boor.

Maybe he wouldn't have to go. Maybe Leo had forgotten all about asking him by now. You couldn't count on that. Maybe Howard could get sick. He licked the cream from the center of his last cupcake and relaxed into the fantasy of being sick and not going.

He should go. He couldn't afford to hide out in his cottage listening to Puccini when he could be trading anecdotes over a campfire with Jack Lincoln. But Jack Lincoln was scary, nearly as scary as some bristly hog who just wanted to root and slobber in peace. And how would he finish the motions *in limine*, the Casselman estate plan, answer the KashPro interrogatories? Lying in the dark, imagining himself in jodhpurs clutching an elephant gun, Howard actually whimpered.

He got sick. To make it look authentic, he complained of a headache on Thursday and called in sick on Friday, summoning a messenger to his house with files.

That weekend he stayed inside for fear of being seen. He worked. He ate. He worried.

He worried that he had squandered an opportunity to dance with the clients. His job was slipping away from him, he was a technocrat, a detail man. He belonged in some bureaucrat's job, buried deep in the bowels of some giant organization where he couldn't do any harm, and all he had to do was dance with the Xerox machine. He was starting to envy Mary Belle. Her job might be boring, but she was always equal to it.

The phone rang. As if summoned by his thoughts, Mary Belle said, "I hope you're faking, 'cause we got problems. Bonifacio shot Leo."

"What is this, a bed check?"

"No joke, Howie. Peter fell into a ravine at the Vinelle ranch and his gun went off accidentally."

"Holy shit. Is he. . . ?"

"Not dead. We don't know how bad he is yet. But you're the only guy left who can get the Roy Albrecht papers together by tomorrow at eight-thirty. I'll meet you at the office in half an hour."

When he got to the office, Mary Belle reported that the bullet had just grazed Leo's ear. "Peter cracked his head pretty good, they're both laid up with the shit scared out of them. You know, if people keep taking little bitty pieces out of Leo, pretty soon there won't be enough left to make it to court. I hope you've got five gears on that pen of yours."

It was almost, Howard reflected as he settled in with the Albrecht papers, as if Peter had thought up the boor joke and found it too good to resist.

7

Double Farewell

Even with the extra work that had rained down on him in the wake of Leo's accident, Howard felt he should drop in on John Maddis's honeymoon send-off. Judging by gossip in the corridor, every lawyer in the firm faced the same dilemma. With both Leo and Peter temporarily at less than capacity, every able-bodied lawyer had been pressed into emergency service.

The party started at five o'clock in the Tweedmore lobby, with the receptionist area turned into the bar. The elevators were locked off to the general public, and John the messenger poured Henry Weinhardt's into giant red cups and champagne into plastic stem glasses. In the adjoining conference room little meatballs bubbled slowly in a silver chafing dish and giant shrimp lay in pale pink heaps among the triangle sandwiches.

By five-thirty it was clear that, despite the increased workload, the accident had probably helped rather than hurt attendance. And war stories about office crises were only the second most popular topic; the group was buzzing with speculation about the accident.

It was reported (without citation to authority) that Leo and Peter had spent Sunday night in the same hospital. It was speculated they insisted upon separate floors. Neither of them had come into the office on Monday. Somebody said Leo had been forbidden by his doctor to fly the rented plane home, so that when he had finally arrived in the office just before lunch today his principal

complaint had been the stranded Cessna. Peter's continued absence was attributed to the long number of days it
might take to walk from Santa Barbara.

Although Leo had reportedly been in the office since
about eleven-thirty, it seemed he had been too tied up
with emergencies to talk with anyone. His appearance at
the party was eagerly anticipated but shrouded with
doubt. Fears about this deal and that court appearance
were voiced. John's clever ploy in getting married to
avoid the extra work was remarked until the bride's
lovely smile began to wear thin. It was, Howard reflected, almost certainly a more lively gathering than if
Leo and Peter had been intact and among them.

Howard knew he couldn't drink without falling
asleep, and he had at least six hours of work ahead of
him. As he stood near the meatballs with a glass of flat
beer, he was momentarily distracted by the large number
of Tweedmore secretaries who were bursting with radi-
ant sexuality. Some sensualist with an eye finely cali-
brated for long legs and dimples lay camouflaged within
the protective Tweedmore professional veneer. Laser-
bright silk dresses dotted the pinstripe landscape, and
fresh laughter seemed to blow the nervous exhaustion
away from the male lawyers' faces, revealing momentarily eyes more vulnerable than confident.

The women lawyers, of which Tweedmore sported
four, seemed to Howard to be generally uncomfortable
and out of place at these parties. Howard found Martha
and Rebecca strikingly pretty, but when they stood
around this sex-charged setting in scratchy suitcoats,
low-heeled shoes, and no makeup, they seemed stiff—
neither fish nor fowl. The women lawyers were a lot
better off than their secretarial sisters, but Howard wondered whether they minded the way their sensible shoes
kept their legs from looking long and the way their tailored suits hid their bodies.

Only Constance Valentine seemed completely in her element. If Leo's brush with death had frightened her, she was disguising it as only a top-notch trial lawyer could. She wore bold colors, a blue velvet blazer with blue cashmere turtleneck and a heavy pendant. Obviously expensive, as always. As always she was confident, eager to be seen.

Just now she was standing in a circle with three of Tweedmore's partners, flashing her characteristic smile. Although the smile was apparently intended to put people at their ease, there was too much tension around her eyes, and her eyeteeth gleemed too brightly. Howard found her smile hungry, more of a warning than a social grace. Her success within the firm seemed natural, but he continued to puzzle over the idea that she and Leo found enough heat between them to make illicit sex worthwhile. He flashed on Leo, grinning and slicking back his thick blond hair as he turned the doorknob of Connie's office. What business was it of his? He felt vaguely nasty as Gerry Tweedmore touched his arm.

"Howard, how goes the paper chase in estate planning?"

"It hasn't buried me yet, which I count as a success." Careful. Too sarcastic. "Actually, it's very interesting. I'd say it's going fine." He resisted the urge to call him "sir."

"I'm glad to hear that," Tweedmore said lightly. "You know, the first year of practice can be pretty tough. I remember my first year I just seemed to get dumber and less confident every day. Every single thing I did was for the first time, and there was nobody telling me how. Oh, the older guys know how to do it, all right, but they just don't seem to get around to showing you."

"Thank God Mary Belle catches my dumb mistakes about three times a day."

"Yes," he said. "Of course, she makes you pay for it, doesn't she?" His eyes were amused as they watched

Howard's face for a hint of recognition that Howard couldn't produce. "Well, these secretaries act tough, but don't let them get to you. And don't let Leo get you down, either. Leo is a damn good lawyer, but it's pretty hard to catch him sitting still. I guess maybe you sort of have to learn by osmosis. Watch him. Watch what he does and figure out why it's so darned effective. Beyond that, just keep working at it. One of these days you'll realize you're doing fine." One of these days. Like he thought Howard was going to be around for a while. That was hopeful. Gerry patted Howard's shoulder just as Bill Madras joined them.

"Hey, big Ger, what's new in the world of start-ups? We closed the Slater deal today. Two and a half mil sailed through my palms into the Slater R and D account." Howard stood watching, hoping the two of them couldn't see that, as far as he was concerned, they might as well have been speaking Navajo. Occasionally he put his lips to his glass to show that he was still alive.

Connie Valentine speared a shrimp and joined them.

"Well, Con," said Madras, "are you braced for all the abuse you're going to get at the partnership meeting on Saturday?"

Constance flashed her teeth in Tweedmore's direction. "Thank God I won't be there to hear it. Presumably in the retelling Gerry will be kind."

"Oh, I shouldn't think you have much to worry about from us, Connie. We hardly ever outright kill a lawyer, we mostly just chew on them a little. I predict you'll come through it fine." So she was feeling the strain, Howard thought, studying her face. Maybe that had eclipsed her worries about Leo. On Monday she would either be Tweedmore's first woman partner or she wouldn't. Howard couldn't imagine her failing at anything, but from the tension in her jaw, her imagination was apparently better than his.

Gerry Tweedmore excused himself and headed toward the drink counter, leaving Howard flushed and defeated. It was hard to banter with someone who could squash you like a bug.

"This is a pretty intense time, eh, Con?" said Madras. "But seriously, you can't be worried. Leo loves you."

If Constance thought the remark referred to anything other than professional esteem she didn't betray it. Slowly she said, "No, I'm not worried about Leo. Assuming he manages to get there. I feel extremely confident that he won't say anything against me. I'm worried about that bastard Pierce, what about . . ."

Madras looked warningly in Howard's direction, and Connie laughed. "Oh, I don't think we need to worry about Howard. Who would he tell?" She reached out and patted Howard's arm lightly. "I'm going to get some more wine," she said to Madras. "Why don't you join me?" The two of them made their way through the crowd toward the drink counter.

As he watched them cross the room, Howard heard laughter and turned to see Peter Bonifacio step off an elevator. With a solemn frown he placed his hands gingerly against the sides of his head and muttered something that was greeted by shouts of beery laughter. Apparently his brush with death hadn't damaged his libido. When Candy reached over to pat his cheek he looked appreciatively down the front of her dress.

Howard knew he should get the Gobbit brief back to word processing, but he went and stacked a couple of sandwiches on his plate. Mary Belle pushed her way into the table next to him and said, "What? No chocolate stuff? What're they pouring, Weinhardt's? I can use a slug a that. Howie, you planning to work today?" She headed toward the drink counter.

Cal Forman caught Howard's eye and beamed. "Howard, you're a patient man," he said, inclining his head toward Mary Belle. Cal was big and solid with thick, dark eyebrows and white hair so thin on top that you could see precisely where each hair was planted. His brown eyes were bright with pent-up humor.

"How's your trial going, Cal?"

"Oh, about usual. I just got back from court, halfway through my guy's testimony. He's in my office, about to crap in his pants, I told him I'd get him something to eat. I hate these damn parties, don't you?" Howard hesitated, and Cal laughed loudly. "Hey, don't answer. Gotta figure out your politics first. Look, there's Peter, back from battle. Peter! Over here."

Peter made his way slowly through the crowd toward them. He paused to stare with mild distaste at the coagulated gravy in the meatballs, then speared a shrimp before turning to Cal.

"Well," said Cal, I hear you missed him." He giggled wildly.

"So glad you're amused. I assure you Leo wasn't."

"You didn't hurt him, did you?"

"Well, I was closer to his head than either of us was comfortable with."

"Oh, his head. I was afraid it was something vital, like the family jewels. Hell, a little hole in his head wouldn't even slow down his billables. What happened?"

"I don't precisely know what happened. I was standing by a ravine. We had located an animal which I am not permitted to identify at this time of year, but which bore an uncanny resemblance to Bambi. I had just been ordered to shoot at this animal, when something loathsome slithered across my foot. As I was falling into the ravine I heard a deafening sound."

"Your gun went off, huh?"

"I presume so. Either that or Leo's lying about

having his ear pierced. We are all still here by the grace of God. I assure you, this will not happen to me again."

"God, that really is something. Glad you're both all right. Did I tell you the latest Leo story? I'm not in bad taste, am I, with him wounded there in the next room? He brought one of his real estate clients in to see Tom about a tax shelter last week, and Tom told him that only farms can use that shelter. So the guy said, 'Hey, I'm a farm!' Now Leo has Tom doing research to see if the lemon trees by the guy's garage can qualify as a farm."

Peter turned to Howard. "You could have had that plum, you know. Leo would have given it to you if—"

A loud scream silenced the party chatter. Suddenly people were running to Leo's corner, and somebody reached for Candy. She was pointing into Leo's office, and she looked like her blood had rushed into her very high-heeled shoes.

8

A Blow to the Billables

Successful lawyers come from varied backgrounds. Tweedmore & Slyde could boast not only a former basketball player and a lapsed theologian but also a veterinarian among its ranks. Exhibiting the confidence and bedside manner that had undoubtedly made him as popular with his former patients as he was with his present business associates, he pronounced in under twenty seconds that Leo had danced with his last client. Thus the ambulance crew that raced in on the heels of the police moments later found itself useless in every regard.

"Dead!" Cal Forman said at Howard's elbow. Howard could barely hear him above the din. "What in hell is he talking about?"

"We could look it up in *Words and Phrases*," said Peter, "but I don't think he's using it as a term of art." Peter's voice was peculiar, and his face was suddenly so pale that his eyes glittered.

"He can't be dead," said Martha. "We've got a closing tomorrow."

"This isn't possible," Connie Valentine said, pushing her way to the front of the crowd. "Excuse me. Excuse me, can I get through?" Howard saw her come to a stop in front of one of the uniformed officers near Leo's door.

"May I have your attention," called the officer who was standing with Connie Valentine. The noise wavered and then dropped to a low hum. "A homicide inspector is on the way." The crowd erupted into a roar.

"Homicide?" Howard said in disbelief to the backs of the heads in front of him.

"Dead? What did he die of?" asked Emily, Gerry's secretary.

"I think it's more a question of who," Howard said. "Guy just said homicide."

"Stabbed," somebody in front of him said. "Craig says he was stabbed with some special technique." The word stabbed ricocheted through the crowd.

"May I have your attention," the officer shouted. "Until Inspector Nelson arrives, I have to ask that you refrain from further conversation. Will you all please move back into the lobby. Back to the lobby. Find yourselves a seat and please remain silent. Your cooperation is appreciated." The noise surged for an instant, then trailed off into silence as the crowd began to move. Howard found a space on one of the glass end tables and sat heavily down as people pushed against his knees to get past him. Several people headed for the drink counter and silently poured themselves drinks as they waited for the inspector to make his appearance.

"He" was Inspector Sarah Nelson, and as she emerged from the elevator with one of the uniformed officers moments later a wave of surprise tinged with contempt rippled through the crowd. These people were accustomed to being in control, and Howard felt their rush of confidence that they would remain in control with Inspector Nelson.

She was wearing the same navy polyester suit that Howard recognized from the day Leo's car was wrecked. As she passed through the lobby she surveyed the crowd politely, making no effort to take control. She would be pretty, Howard thought, if she wore makeup, if she got more sleep. She disappeared into Leo's office behind the man in uniform.

"Now what?" Bill Madras asked. "Are we supposed to sit here all night waiting for Mother Nelson to hear our confession? This is bullshit." He tried to follow her into Leo's office. A uniformed officer blocked his path, letting him bounce off his forearm. "Excuse me, Miss?" he called through the doorway. "Can you tell me who's in charge here?" The uniformed officer was taking him by the elbow when she appeared in the doorway.

"That's all right, Officer Zatopa. Is there a problem?"

"Is there, uh, somebody in charge here?" He stretched his neck to look past her into Leo's office. Her gaze was steady. "I guess it's you. Look, this is absolutely terrible and I want to help in any way I can, believe me. But I have to leave now."

"Your name is—?" she asked. He told her. "Mr. Madras, for a few moments at least, everyone will need to stay."

"You know, I think maybe I'm expressing myself badly." He bent toward her slightly, and spoke slowly and earnestly. "As terrible as this is, and jeez, it's really terrible, but I have to leave. Never mind my billables, of course, but I have responsibilities. I've got a deal that has to close tomorrow or my guys lose their financing. My obligations to them . . . I simply can't let that happen. I'm terribly sorry." He turned to go and was blocked by Officer Zatopa.

"We know you have obligations, Mr. Madras," Inspector Nelson said. "We'll operate efficiently, I promise you. Officer Zatopa, would you see if Mr. Madras would like an escort to his office to pick up something to work on here in the lobby? At least maybe we can help him salvage his billings."

"Billables," he said to her back as she disappeared into Leo's office. Somebody snickered as he pulled away from Officer Zatopa and sank into a seat.

One of the uniformed officers took people's names and returned to Leo's office. A moment later Inspector Nelson set herself up in the glass-walled conference room with what looked like a small Dictaphone machine and a pad of paper. Two uniformed officers appeared and called names from their respective lists. Inspector Nelson called for Candy Gilley.

Candy had disappeared into an empty office long before the police arrived, and all eyes watched as she made her way through the lobby to the conference room. She was obviously shaken. Her face was splotched, and her chest heaved expressively beneath the fan of her long blond hair. Her smile was slightly crooked. Still, she paused at the door of the conference room and glanced quickly around.

"Ooh, so *you're* the detective. Well, I'm sure you'll figure out who killed poor Leo." Then the drama turned to pantomime as she closed the conference room door. From the back, Howard recognized the little roll of the shoulders that made her boobs jiggle slightly as she sat down opposite Nelson. Flirting was apparently such an inherent part of Candy's personality that she automatically flirted even with a female detective, even over a dead body.

Inspector Nelson said something, then started up the recorder. Candy seemed to be doing most of the talking. Twenty minutes went by, then Inspector Nelson escorted Candy to the elevator and asked for Mr. Madras.

Madras emerged ten minutes later, smiling confidently at the now-exhausted group remaining in the lobby. At the elevator he insisted on pumping Inspector Nelson's hand.

"Well, Inspector, we all appreciate the great job you're doing, and we wish you the very best of luck." He smiled into her eyes as if he knew she found him very appealing. Then he dropped her hand and waved at the crowd in the lobby. "Bye, guys. See you tomorrow." He disappeared as Nelson consulted her list and called for Peter Bonifacio.

The crowd was diminishing as the officers made their way through the names. Less than half the original group remained. Howard was beginning to feel as stale as the beer that sat flatly puddled in the cups that dotted the tables. He was relieved when Nelson called his name. He closed the door of the conference room and sank into a chair, nodding his permission for her to use the recorder.

"Mr. Rickover, do you know who may have had a motive to murder Mr. Slyde?"

"No."

He was too exhausted to fill in the silence that followed.

"You worked with him?" she said finally.

"Yes. I've seen you before. The day Leo's car got wrecked."

She studied his face briefly, then nodded. "Of course. You were working on something together."

"Right. I was in his department."

"And I take it you loved him."

"Of course not, I thought he was a flaming asshole like everybody else did. I mean, a successful asshole, I don't mean to be disrespectful. . . ."

Inspector Nelson smiled faintly. "Why was Mr. Slyde an asshole?"

Howard sighed. "Officer, it's been a long day. For about two hours I've been watching a steady stream of people come in here to talk to you. By now you know as much about Leo as I do. Why ask me what made him an asshole? God made him an asshole, nobody else had the talent." He paused. "I'm being really rude. This whole thing has sort of freaked me out."

She was resting her chin on her fist and watching him, not unkindly. "Shall I tell you what I've learned about Leo so far today? He was one of the chief rainmakers around here. He was a shrewd negotiator. He talked into several telephones at one time. He did big favors for some people's careers. And everybody but you loved him."

"Who told you everybody loved Leo?"

"Everybody I've seen today except you."

"Are you shitting me?" He sank back in his chair. "Well, maybe they all did. They sure didn't act like it, though."

"Did you notice anybody acting strangely at the party?"

"No. Well, yes. But strangely like always, you know what I mean?"

The corners of her smile were barely visible behind her fist. "I meant was anybody acting atypically strangely."

"No. Not that I saw. But then I was pretty busy trying to look like I knew what 'R and D' stands for."

"Research and Development, I think. Are you very successful here?"

"What's that got to do with anything? Hell no, I'm not successful here. I've been here a total of about four months and I feel like each day may be my last. They all said they *liked* Leo? What the hell, I hope they did. It's terrible when people die that you don't like much."

"Yes."

"It hasn't happened to you."

"Not yet."

"Yeah. Family's the worst."

To his astonishment she blushed. He was surprised that he didn't mind her eyes assessing him.

An officer knocked and put his head in. "Coroner's investigator is here."

"Crime lab finished with the body?"

The officer nodded.

"You or Pitlack be there for the bagging. Be sure about the clothes."

"I'll handle it. Crime lab is finishing up. Soon as the body's gone they'll be ready to seal the room."

Nelson shook her head. "Ask them to put you in custody until I get there. Twenty minutes or half an hour. Then I'll take over until morning." She turned back to Howard as the door closed. "Where is your office in relation to Mr. Slyde's?"

"Next door."

"Were you in there this afternoon?"

"Some, with my door closed. I was also in the library. And down in word processing."

"Can you hear what goes on in Mr. Slyde's office?"

He shook his head. "Well, I can hear his phones ring, and if somebody really laughs or yells. Not much else."

"Did you hear anything this afternoon?"

"I don't know. I'm pretty used to that stuff by now.

Nothing caught my attention." Through the slats of the Venetian blind he saw a police officer and a man in a white coat shouldering a big black bag on its way to the elevator.

"We'll be contacting witnesses in the next few days to set up more thorough interviews." He nodded and stood up.

"Listen," he said, "we're pretty sure the guy's gone now, right?"

"The murderer? Yes, the murderer is almost certainly gone. Would you like an escort to your car?"

"I wish. I know this is disgusting, but I think I have to work."

"Here? I'll be right next door all night."

"Great. So, uh, if I scream you'll come, right?"

"I will," she said, nodding emphatically. "Either that or I'll call the cops." A smile flickered across her face as she walked him to the door.

9

Hunch

Inspector Sarah Nelson found Officer Zatopa leaning one hand on the door frame of Leo Slyde's office, the other hand hitched in his belt. He stepped back to let her enter. She set her tape recorder on one of the off-white upholstered chairs.

"Doesn't look much like a murder scene, does it, Andy?"

"Nope. No mess, no blood, not even on the chair he was sitting in. No defense wounds that we could see.

Looks like he was completely relaxed right up until they speared him."

"They?"

He tilted his head toward the credenza. "You tell me who was on the other end of that phone."

"Have we checked with P.D.?"

"Not yet."

She picked up the beige phone and dialed. "Carol, Sarah Nelson on the Slyde homicide. We think he was on the phone when it happened. I need to know whether anybody called this afternoon to say they were on the other end. Right. Could be a message from another jurisdiction. There's probably a switchboard that controls the main number, but he's got another phone number here that might work." She read off the number of the beige phone. "Thanks."

She could see that the receiver from the black phone had been picked up from the carpet and placed on the credenza.

"Nobody hung it up?"

Zatopa's eyes flashed. "No, Sam, nobody hung it up."

"I'm not badmouthing the department. If this were the L.A.P.D. somebody would have hung it up. Anyway, we should assume the trace won't work."

Zatopa nodded. "I'll be after his phone records first thing in the morning."

"We'll have to have a release. Were the phones in Slyde's name or the law firm's?"

Zatopa shrugged.

"While we're at it let's get the records for all three phones." She looked around. "I'll do the wastebaskets tonight. And the desktop. There a Rolodex?"

Zatopa held up two fingers and grinned. "He either had a lot of friends or a lot of enemies. There's also an open phone book." He pointed to a directory lying open on the credenza.

She snorted softly. "What about the floor below us? Anybody down there hear anything?"

"The elevator's locked off. Pitlack's down at the building directory trying to get names and phone numbers."

"And Mrs. Slyde?"

"Wizbiski's over there now."

"Other buildings where the occupants could see in here?"

"Doesn't look likely." They walked over to the bank of windows and looked down at the red-and-white lights snaking along Cabrillo Drive. "Most of the stuff around here is pretty low. There are a couple of possibilities across the street there."

"Follow it up, will you, Andy? The credenza's up against the window. If he was killed in his chair somebody down below might have seen it." She paused, watching the traffic. "This isn't my first encounter with the victim."

"Yeah?"

"Somebody took a paint sprayer to his car a couple of months ago. No suspects. I had a feeling about Slyde, though. I ran a computer check that didn't turn up anything."

"Maybe that was round one."

"Maybe." She was silent a moment. "What do you think? Premeditated?"

"The method suggests premeditation. But to murder somebody when the elevators are locked off . . ."

"Exactly. Unless it happened before the party started." She turned away from the window. "Take the number from the beige phone. Tomorrow morning is fine to get back to me unless you have something. Thanks."

The centerpiece of the office was a huge oak desk with pie-shaped panels radiating out from the black leather chair like rays from the sun. After hesitating for a moment with her hand on the chair, she pushed it out of the way and dragged one of the upholstered chairs to take its place. She pulled a small black notebook from her pocket and placed it in front of her.

Several of the desk panels to her right were thickly covered with paper, organized in long rows so that only the title of each document was visible. She read a few of the titles. Indemnification Agreement, with cover letter. Cold Comfort Letter. Narrative Statement of B. Grizzly. Plaintiffs Third Set of Interrogatories. Motion for Temporary Stay, Last Will and Testament of B. Chilton, Red Herring Prospectus . . .

On her left was the beige phone, surrounded by two more or less discreet piles of pink phone messages, each about an inch high. A few of the messages had doodles on them. Also one of the Rolodexes, which was actually a long box of cards with a brown plastic cover. The cover was closed.

She opened the drawers quickly to get an overview, then turned to the credenza behind the desk. Besides the two personal phones the top held another Rolodex, also closed. Another page with doodles and a couple of words that looked like names. Also a brown leather daily appointment book. Inside the credenza doors were rows and rows of files, each suspended from metal rails in green Pendaflex files.

She pulled the wastebasket from under the desk. In among the balled-up pink message slips and the typed pages marked with red ink she found an empty Trojan condom wrapper. Farther down she she could see shreds of lettuce and mayonnaise sticking to some wax paper.

She opened her notebook and began writing.

Several hours later she checked her watch, flipped through her notebook and whispered, "Shit." She reached up and raked her fingers through her short curly hair until it stuck out from her head in a wedge. Then she went and stood by the windows.

After a few moments she closed the office door and set her tape recorder on the desk. She loaded one of the tapes and adjusted the volume. She crossed back to the windows and stood looking down as the voice of Howard Rickover began to speak.

As he left the conference room Howard realized that, for once, he was more exhausted than hungry. He hesitated in the lobby, struggling with a distinct aversion to his file-strewn desk. But the motion on federal jurisdiction was due tomorrow. He headed down the corridor, past the uniformed officer who was standing in Leo's doorway. On his way past Mary Belle's desk he carefully avoided looking at his message spindle, dreading to see the pink messages from angry clients that had certainly accumulated there.

A memo had been taped to the back of his chair. Gerard Tweedmore wanted everybody to meet tomorrow in the back conference room at nine A.M. "I think it is important for us to take a few moments to understand and express our feelings about the terrible tragedy that has struck Leo."

He dropped into his chair and leaned on the palm of his hand with his eyes closed. After a few moments he heard Inspector Nelson's voice in the corridor, then the sound of Leo's door closing. Leo's door, except Leo wouldn't be using it anymore. There was no Leo. Howard's body sagged with fatigue, he put his ear against the desktop . . .

He sat up with a start, his heart pounding. Ten after ten, he'd been asleep for twenty minutes on his notes. He could hear the detective opening drawers in Leo's office. He picked up his Dictaphone and forced himself to start talking.

*　　*　　*

Questions of federal jurisdiction had never impressed Howard as being susceptible to ready analysis or easy communication. In giving him the Gobbit brief, Pierce's only advice had been to "be relentlessly logical, and hit with the sexiest argument first." Three days of intensive research had yielded nothing remotely erotic about *in personam* jurisdiction. Howard had therefore spent the better part of two days pursuing the phantom of relentless logic.

It seemed hopeless that a task which had thus far proved so elusive could be accomplished on a night when there was fierce competition for Howard's attention. But law school yields up disciplined graduates. After several hours Howard looked up from his stack of *Fed. 2d Reporters* to find Sarah Nelson watching him.

"You haven't screamed," she said, as he very nearly did.

"Not yet. I've been swearing a fair amount. Twenty after one. I could use some coffee."

"There's coffee?"

"Well . . . I'll show you."

A moment later they stood stirring powder into Styrofoam cups filled with lukewarm water. "So I guess you haven't found the murderer in a drawer or anything."

"Uh-uh." She threw the plastic stick into the trash. Her hair was sticking out at a peculiar angle.

"Are you sorting through the stuff okay?"

She shook her head. "Half the stuff is totally incomprehensible. I'm surprised you guys understand what you're talking about."

"Who says we do? What's hanging you up? Probably all the pretrial papers."

"I guess. What's a cold comfort letter?"

"Merger file. Maybe. What's that got to do with your murder?"

She shrugged. "Probably nothing. Unless that's what he was working on when he was killed."

"Was it on his desk?"

"Yeah, but so are some other things." She headed back down the corridor, Howard following.

"Maybe you should go through his phone log. Or his time sheets."

"Haven't found a phone log. I think I've got time sheets, but I don't understand the codes."

"You mean billing numbers. They're in the drawer with his Dictaphone." They paused in front of Howard's office. "Listen, if you think I could help . . ."

She looked at him over the rim of her Styrofoam cup.

"I mean, you don't want me in there smudging fingerprints, but I might be able to help you set up a system."

She tilted her head toward his desk. "Don't you have some more swearing to do?"

"Yeah, but what will another twenty minutes matter? Here, at least let me show you the phone log."

In half an hour he had identified most of the contents of Leo's desk. "Well, that's the extent of my expertise. I better get back to forum *non conveniens*."

She was standing by the windows, looking down on Cabrillo Drive. "Mr. Rickover, do you have a few more minutes?"

He hesitated, suddenly wary. "I guess so. If it's really a few. What for?"

"I keep remembering what you said earlier about Slyde's unpopularity. I'd like you to hear something." She walked over to her tape recorder.

"Wait. Are you sure you want to do that?"

She paused, watching him, her hand on the recorder button.

"I mean, isn't that secret police stuff?"

She nodded. "Yes, it's confidential."

"So why me?"

"A hunch. That you might hear something, make a connection. Bear with me for a minute. I'll try to save time by just playing the highlights." She adjusted the recorder and sat back.

10

We Loved His Guts

"Ms. Gilley? Come in. I'm Inspector Sarah Nelson."

After a pause Candy's voice, slightly grainy, came over the recorder.

"Ooh, so *you're* the detective. Well, I'm sure you'll figure out who killed poor Leo." She agreed to have the interview taped, warily.

She had left the party early, she said, because Leo had a document that had to go out Federal Express, and the last pickup was at six-fifteen. The document was ready for his signature at five, but Leo was on the phone, so she went to the party. At five-thirty, the console on her desk showed that Leo was still on the phone, so she went back for another glass of champagne. Which phone? You mean phones, she said, giggling. Leo had a talent for talking into two phones at one time. These were the red-and-black personal ones, she thought.

At five-forty-five she started to worry and decided to risk Leo's anger by interrupting. She opened the door as quietly as possible and saw him hunched over his credenza, leaning on his elbows. She saw the red phone against his ear.

She tiptoed up behind him and tapped him on the shoulder. He didn't move, so she whispered, "Leo?" That was when she noticed that the receiver of the black phone was dangling by its curly cord.

"Well, that just seemed wrong, Inspector, you know what I mean? So I said it louder, 'Leo?' and I grabbed the arm of his chair and pulled on it. When I . . . when I pulled, the whole chair swung around, and Leo's head flopped back hard against the top of the chair and rolled to the side. Then I saw . . ." There was a pause, then Candy continued, quietly. "Then I saw the blood on his shirt. Anybody would have screamed, his face looked so cheerful. He was almost laughing, except he was dead."

Inspector Nelson interrupted the tape and sat with her finger on the button. "I'm sorry if that was grisly," she said, "but I thought you might be curious about how he was killed." She pulled a sealed plastic pouch from under her chair and showed it to him. "This was the murder weapon. I don't know what it is. Have you seen it before?"

The plastic was smeared on the inside with dark blood and something like mucus. Howard leaned over the bag as it lay on the desk between them, careful not to touch it or bring his face any closer than necessary. Inside was what looked like a long nail, thin, but threaded at one end like a screw.

"It was pushed up under his breastbone all the way to the threads."

Howard leaned back in his chair as far from the bag as possible. "God. No, I haven't seen it before. Is it an ice pick?"

She shrugged. "Could be. But why would an ice pick have a screw-on handle? Which we haven't found, by the way." She put the bag under her chair.

"When I got here," she said, "his hand was still locked around the red receiver. Do you know what kind of calls he made on that phone?"

Again, Howard shook his head. "I think it was some kind of personal line," he said, "but the only call I ever heard on it was Leo buying a Ferarri and pretending to be totally blown away by the guy's asking price. I remember, because he winked at me while he was sounding indignant."

She turned the machine back on. Candy had last seen Leo alive at three P.M. She saw by her console that he picked up the red phone at four-thirty. Mr. Tweedmore was with him for a short time in the afternoon, and left just as Leo was dialing. She kept everybody away from him after that, even Howard Rickover, who was sweet but kind of a pest. Of course, she wouldn't know who was with him between five and five-forty-five. "You might ask Mary Belle," she said brightly. "She doesn't like parties and she keeps track of everybody's business."

"Ms. Gilley—" Inspector Nelson's voice came back over the recorder.

"Oh, please, call me Candy."

"You were Leo's secretary, did you know him well?"

"Well . . ." The recorder was silent for a moment. "I guess a secretary always knows her boss pretty well."

"Do you know who his enemies were?"

"Oh, Detective, Leo didn't have any enemies, I'm sure of it. Everybody *loved* Leo. Just the other day one of the associates leaned across the banister toward my desk and said, 'Candy, I love his guts.' Really, he said that. It was Peter Bonifacio. But it doesn't matter which one said it. That's how we all felt."

She fast forwarded the tape, listened, adjusted it, and sat back. Howard recognized Bill Madras's voice.

"Come in, Mr. Madras, I'm Inspector Nelson. We met earlier."

"Hey, Inspector, you know, I'm really sorry about

that. I was wrong to be uptight, you have a lot of things on your mind right now."

"It's all right."

"But really, I'm very sorry. Say, that's a nice suit you're wearing."

"Mr. Madras . . ."

"Really, it goes well with your eyes."

"Does this firm practice any criminal law?"

"Not intentionally." He paused. "No, but really, we do the full range of civil cases for the firms here in Silicon Valley. And start-up stuff, financings, trade secret, antitrust, taking companies public. Me, I do securities, because that's where the sharks swim."

"Was Leo Slyde a shark?"

He laughed. "Sharpest teeth in the ocean. He was one helluva lawyer."

"Did you work with him?"

"Some. As much as possible, just like everybody else. Leo and I tried a case last month, and I was so excited that the Lakers lost and I didn't even care. That's how exciting it was to work with Leo. Damn."

"Mr. Madras, who had any reason to want Leo Slyde dead?"

"Nobody. Well, I guess the guys on the other side of all Leo's cases, maybe." He paused. "No, but really, I just can't help you there. We loved the guy. Except maybe for Rickover. But he's no murderer.

"Who is Rickover?"

"A guy who works here and shouldn't. Leo decided the firm needed a guy to do estate planning scutwork and pissed off the hiring committee by leaving us out of the decision. Leo assured us it was a probationary hire, but apparently he never got around to telling Rickover. Anyway, the consensus is he blew it."

"In what way?"

"You know how I said we're all sharks? Rickover is a

tuna. He mopes, his clothes aren't sharp. He watches Julia Child on TV and *talks* about it, for God's sake. I think Leo wanted somebody he could use and throw away, but even then he screwed up. He and Leo just don't hit it off. Didn't—"

"But apart from Mr. Rickover, you can't think of anybody who disliked him?"

"Miss Detective, Leo Slyde was our chief rainmaker around here. Canceling Leo would be like canceling our own meal ticket. We aren't the kind of people who would do that."

She sat forward and stopped the recorder. "Time for one more?"

"Time, maybe, but I don't know about ego. Does the next guy like me as much as the first two?"

"I hope it wasn't rude to play it for you. That was why I asked you whether you felt successful here. I had a couple of clues that you might not be happy."

"You don't think I—"

"No," she interrupted, "I don't. That's why I wanted to talk to you. Do you really watch Julia Child?"

"Yeah, I tape it on my VCR and watch it when I get home. You think that's weird?"

"No. Do you really talk about it?"

"I guess so."

"To Bill Madras?"

"Apparently I must have."

She grinned. "The last interview?"

"Yeah, go ahead."

She adjusted the recorder, and Howard recognized Peter Bonifacio's voice. Nelson listened, then fast forwarded. "This was about the hunting accident," she said. She pushed another button and sat back as her own voice spoke from the recorder.

"One of your coworkers characterized this as a place where sharks swim. Does that seem right to you?"

Peter's laugh was explosive and mirthless. "Let me see, which of our poets laureate summoned that metaphor from his innermost soul? I couldn't begin to guess. Yes, there are a couple of assholes here, but then they abound generally, don't you think?"

"Was Leo Slyde an asshole?"

"Oh, I don't know. On the whole, he amused me. But those can't have been his observations."

"Do you remember telling Candy Gilley you loved Leo's guts?"

The recorder fell silent except for a tapping sound.

"What's that?" said Howard.

"Clicking his pen," she said quickly, demonstrating.

Peter's voice resumed. "I may have said that, I don't remember."

"Did anybody have reason to dislike Leo?"

"I don't really know. Leo cut a lot of deals, and my impression is that the other side sometimes felt it had been, shall we say, fleeced? Maybe somebody really got angry. Beyond that, I wouldn't know."

"I'm sorry, if you told me this I've forgotten. Why did you love Leo's guts?"

Another pause, except for the staccato clicking sound.

"I said that, *if* I said it, because I owe a lot to Leo. He did me a very big favor once, he saved my career when it was in trouble." His pen fell silent, and for a moment no sound at all came over the recorder. Then Inspector Nelson thanked him for his time. Howard heard the door of the conference room open, and Peter's voice from across the room. "This turn of events is remarkable. This place has always been amusing in its way, but this, Leo, you . . . I shall be very curious to learn what you find."

"Well, Mr. Rickover, there you have it, everybody loved Leo."

"What the hell, maybe they all did. I wonder why they picked on him so much when he wasn't around."

"You know, you've already been helpful. I'd like to talk to you again."

"Inspector Nelson, you seem like a nice person, you really do. In a way I'd like to help. But I can't. I'm already on the outs around here, if they got the slightest idea that I was spying on them I'd be a total pariah. And that's only the beginning. I already have trouble sleeping at night trying to take care of my own business. I spent a lot of time and money getting through law school, and you heard the impression I'm making around here. And now with Leo gone, Jesus, estate planning is going to be hell." He sat forward in his chair and sighed. "Anyhow, I don't think you'd better count on me. People who do tend to get disappointed."

"Well, I'm sorry, but of course it's your decision." She stood up, allowing Howard to do the same. "Here's my card. If you change your mind, if anything occurs to you at all, I'd like to hear about it. I give you more credit than these guys do. Maybe more than you give yourself."

Howard had been right. Her hand was cold.

11

Eulogy for a Shark

The firm had outgrown even the large back conference room in recent months, so people picked up their pastries and assembled in the front lobby. The lobby showed no traces of last night's ordeal, and even sported a new arrangement of fiery red tulips on the glass-topped table. The operators at the telephone console expertly deflected all calls, and Emily, Gerry Tweedmore's secretary, sat by the elevators with a pad, noting the name of each visitor, whispering an explanation, and sending him on his way.

Howard found a spot on the floor near Connie and settled in with his three butterhorns just as Gerry arrived. Howard noticed the uncharacteristic bags beneath the blue eyes of his thin face.

"If I could have your attention for a few moments," he said softly, almost modestly, and immediately the room fell silent.

"I haven't had much sleep since yesterday afternoon, and I guess maybe a lot of you had trouble sleeping, too. I sat up thinking and wondering what I could say to you this morning that might help us to help each other in the tough days ahead.

"Leo was a fine man and an extraordinary lawyer, and his death is an enormous blow to the firm and to each of us personally. He brought new blood to this partnership, and I think we have to give him lots of credit for the phenomenal success we've experienced since he came. Leo and I shared a vision for this firm that I know you all believe in, too, the vision of a little start-up and securities outfit that began twenty years ago with three guys—no gals at that time—in a little backwater known as San Mateo. We wanted that little outfit to grow in talent and experience and become a general-service business law firm of the finest caliber in the nation.

"In the eight years that Leo was with us, that pipedream started to look like it really could happen. I don't have to tell you that our client list is now the envy not only of the Silicon Valley firms but even of Wall Street, and we are really taking off in a big way. Leo wanted that for all of us, and I think we should honor him for the part he played in making it happen.

"But what does it mean to honor Leo, as I know we all want to do? I think it means figuring out what he would want for us now that he won't be here to help us out any more. I think every one of us should do some thinking and some pondering and work this out in our own minds, but I can share with you some of my thoughts about what Leo would want.

"First, Leo would want us to keep things going with the same momentum he created while he was here. He would want us to honor him by making this firm exactly what he wanted it to be—not just the finest firm of its kind serving Silicon Valley, which it is already; not just a boutique law firm with a few special skills in putting together venture capital deals or getting permits out of the SEC; but a full-service, nationally prominent, highly accomplished firm in every area of law that our clients can possibly need, a firm that takes a back seat to nobody, not even the big guys on Wall Street.

"I don't have to tell you guys that client confidence is the essence of this business. I haven't seen the paper yet this morning, but I can pretty well guarantee that the next few weeks are going to be tough. There's going to be rumor and speculation. Clients are going think we're losing momentum, doubting ourselves. I hope we will all undertake to be particularly conscientious, particularly excellent in all our professional dealings until things settle down again.

"These next few weeks are going to be especially hard on the younger people in Leo's group. They've got to provide continuity and keep the confidence of a number of our clients who have relied heavily on Leo up to now. Tom has agreed to step in and help Howard out. John is going to help Paula. I for one, and I know the rest of you agree with me, have the utmost confidence that with a little guidance, these two can and will continue to meet the clients' needs." Here Gerry found Paula and then Howard, and nodded encouragingly at each of them.

"Second, Leo would want us to find out what happened to him. I guess you all talked to one detective or another here yesterday. I personally talked to the lady detective, Nelson her name is. Unthinkable as it is, the police are speculating that one of us is responsible for Leo's death." The room, which had been quiet, became deathly still. "The police know their own business, of course. If they're right, I want to plead personally for the person who made this terrible mistake to come forward. But I have to tell you, I can't help thinking the police are wrong. In the long run I think we'll all be vindicated. Let's keep in mind that speculation is just that and nothing more until it's backed up by solid proof.

"So let's take great care to avoid internal suspicion and mistrust, which would be even more destructive to the firm than anything that's going to come at us from the outside. And let's help the police. Let's every one of us cooperate with the investigation to the very fullest extent possible without neglecting our clients. Let's do these things for Leo.

"Finally, in the days and weeks ahead, I kind of think Leo would want each of us to do some listening and some talking to each other, so that nobody has to go through this alone. I certainly encourage all of you to drop by whenever you feel like it, my door is open. Maybe you all can give me some help—I know I need it—and maybe I can help you out, too.

"The last thing I want to say may be a little corny, but try to bear with an old man. Along about four this morning I got to thinking about Milton, of all people. I want to read just a little bit of a poem called 'Lycidas' as a start to saying good-bye to Leo. 'Lycidas' was written for Edward King, a friend of Milton's who drowned, and the poem goes like this:

'Weep no more, woeful shepherds, weep no more,
For Lycidas, your sorrow, is not dead,
Sunk though he be beneath the watery floor;
So sinks the day-star in the ocean bed,
And yet anon repairs his drooping head,
And tricks his beams, and with new-spangled ore
Flames in the forehead of the morning sky:
So Lycidas sunk low, but mounted high,
Through the dear might of him that walked the waves,
Where, other groves and other streams along,
With nectar pure his oozy locks he laves,
And hears the unexpressive nuptial song,
In the blest kingdoms meek of joy and love.'"

The room was silent for a moment, and then he continued.

"That's about it from me today. I'm going to leave my secretary standing guard until about ten so we won't have any interruptions. I think you should use the time however you all see fit." Gerry got up and headed for his office.

"He's the soul of the firm," Connie said at Howard's elbow.

"Great speech," Madras said cheerfully. "Really, that demonstrates the kind of talent that got us where we are today. Well, back to the old billables, this one's for Leo."

"I do admire the water motif," said Peter. "After all, this is where the sharks swim."

"Come on, Howie," said Mary Belle. "We got our work cut out for us. You can eat your doughnuts while you go through the mail."

"It's kind of you to keep me on schedule," he said, but he got up obediently enough and followed her out of the lobby. "What did you think of Gerry's speech?" He hustled to keep up with her in the hall.

"Well, it proves that Leo had his talents, all right. Look how he managed to fool Gerry all these years."

"Mary Belle, you're all sentiment," Howard said, secretly relieved to hear somebody else pronounce that Leo hadn't been a saint. "I thought you liked Leo."

"Of course I liked him. Can't you tell a joke when you hear one?" Apparently he couldn't. He added that to his growing list of inadequacies.

At his office door he paused. "Take my calls until I tell you otherwise, will you please?"

"Howie, you know Mr. Vinelle has been trying—"

"Mary Belle, until further notice, take my calls." He closed the door on her startled face.

As he slowly munched the last butterhorn, Howard considered. He could see a chance for himself, two chances. Now that Leo was gone and he could legitimately look to Tom for guidance, maybe, just maybe, he could work his butt off and pull estate planning back from the precipice of disaster.

He realized that he had been staring at a green shape that was on the floor under his visitor chair. He walked over and got down on his knees to look at it. He picked it up. It was a heavy lead latticework disk about four inches across, with fleur-de-lis designs radiating out from the center. It seemed somehow familiar. He carried it back to his desk and sat down.

The second chance was trickier. Gerry wanted them to cooperate in finding out who killed Leo. He finished his butterhorn, threw the napkin in the wastebasket, and sat tossing the mysterious green leaded disk in the air just enough to feel its weight thud pleasantly in his palm. He still didn't see how he could help, but Inspector Nelson seemed to think he could. After all, there was one thing he knew; so did somebody else, but she might not be talking.

Time. What was this going to cost him in time?

He got Nelson's card out of his wallet and set it on the desk in front of him. That suit. Her eyes, amused, curious, reading Howard's face as he talked. Nobody else had looked at him since he had moved to California.

What the hell, he could do worse than get stuck learning about her and her job for an hour or two. The person who killed Leo was bound to be caught, deserved to be caught. Gerry seemed really to want that. He picked up his phone and started to dial.

As he dialed the last digit he suddenly remembered where he had seen the leaded disk before.

"Hello, Inspector Nelson? This is Howard Rickover."

"Yes. I'm glad to hear from you."

"Two things," he said. "First, has anybody told you that Leo was having an affair? Second, I think I've found the handle of your murder weapon. It's covered with my fingerprints."

12

Solo Sam

Howard did three things as preparation for meeting with Inspector Nelson. He wrapped the green disk in his slightly used handkerchief and put it in his briefcase. He went to word processing and flirted extravagantly with an operator until she gave him a printout of a document. He went home and ironed a clean shirt.

As he was fastening his seat belt to head for the police station, he glanced into his rearview mirror and saw an elderly woman in a bright pink pantsuit working her way slowly up his driveway behind his car. She came up to the driver's window and bent down.

"Hi," she said. "I'm Alice Pringle, your neighbor across the street."

He stuck his hand out through the window. "Hi. Howard. Rickover."

"I can see you're getting ready to go somewhere and I don't want to keep you, only I just wanted to introduce myself, and you're gone so much I haven't gotten the chance."

"Yeah, my life's a little crazy lately. Nice to meet you."

"Listen, I just wanted to mention a couple of things about our neighborhood since you're a newcomer and I've been here forty-two years." Shit. "We're a fairly friendly group, mostly homeowners, and we always try to look out for each other when we can. Picking up mail when neighbors are away, that sorta thing."

"Great."

"The other thing is we try to be considerate of each other whenever we can. It seems to make life pleasanter for everybody."

"Sure." He was willing himself not to look at his watch, he was almost certainly late by now.

"Anyway, there's one little favor I wanted to ask of you, if I could. A lot of us up and down the block are gardeners, including me, and we really appreciate it if the pet owners can kind of keep their animals from invading our precious flower beds and such."

"Oh, no. Has Stella been causing problems?"

"Stella, is that her name? She's a pretty little cat. The only thing is, she seems to have developed a special fondness for my rose garden, and I've got a Crimson Glory that's just about ready to expire from all the attention."

"Oh, I'm really sorry. Should we try mothballs?"

"Well, you know I hadn't tried anything yet, because some people object to having things put down that could make their pets sick. I know I wouldn't like it. But I'm beginning to feel a little desperate, and I thought I'd better talk to you about it."

"Absolutely. Mothballs are great. It'll serve her right. In fact, I should get them for you. Let me get a box from the store in the next day or two, and I'll bring them over and stick them in the flower beds."

"Aren't you nice? You know, sometimes you feel nervous when renters come into the neighborhood, they might be a little more cavalier than the rest of us. But I'm sure we'll all get along just fine."

"Thanks, Mrs. Pringle, I'm sure we will. I'll be over in the next day or two, okay? I probably should get going now."

"Of course. You young professionals are always so busy, I don't know how you do it. I don't think we tried to do quite so much when I was young." He started his engine. "I admire you for it, but I don't know if I envy you exactly. Nice to meet you," she called after him as he rolled slowly down the driveway and made his escape.

The spring sky was cloudless as he sped through the well-pruned streets to the police station. Translucent leaves wobbled on new stems in the faint breeze. Maintaining a police station seemed more a matter of civic pride than necessity in this sun-drenched, wholesome town. Murder seemed, well, histrionic.

Inspector Nelson met him in a room filled with police memorabilia. The mug shots attached to the peg board were yellowed. The shelf held several pairs of dusty handcuffs and a broken billy club. A large trophy with flaking gold paint proclaimed San Mateo second in the 1973 San Mateo County police and fire bowling league.

Her black blazer was a lint magnet, and one of the lapels was bent under. She touched her cold hand to his.

"Why did you decide to come?"

"I found the murder weapon, and I wanted to show off."

She said nothing.

"Also, I realized this is a perfect excuse for sharing an incredible piece of gossip."

She shook her head.

"And Tweedmore has asked us to cooperate. I think I can use the brownie points."

Her gaze was unreadable. "So what's the weapon? No, leave it in the handkerchief."

As he handed the disk across the table, he noticed that the handkerchief was gray as well as slightly used. "This is the base of one of our message spindles. I found it under the chair in my office this morning, and I was tossing it in the air when I realized. I sort of think this is the other half of what you found sticking in Leo."

She called for a technician to fit it to the weapon and dust for prints.

"Was it there last night?"

"I don't know."

"Does everybody have the same message spindle?"

"Regular old army issue, one for each lawyer. I checked our corner, nobody's is missing. At least he wasn't hoist on his own petard."

"Is the supply room locked?"

"No, and nobody keeps inventory that I've noticed."

"So everybody had access to the weapon, but who knew how to use it?"

"Is there something tricky about stabbing a guy?"

"The way Slyde was stabbed, yes. Your veterinarian mentioned that it was a skilled job, and the pathologist at the autopsy this morning was very impressed. The killer used a medical procedure called pericardiocentesis."

"A medical procedure for murder?"

"Well, a perversion of a medical procedure. Apparently if a person is in an accident, one possible injury is cardiac tamponade. That means the sac around the heart fills up with blood and makes it harder for the heart to beat. If you don't drain the blood quickly the person will die of a heart attack. So you do this procedure.

"You put the needle into the center of his chest, just under the sternum, here. Then you push it at a precise angle into the heart. You push it the right amount, the blood drains out. You push it farther, the guy's dead."

"Ugh, so who knows how to do that?"

"Your veterinarian can do it on race horses. His alibi is ironclad. The pathologist says it's a subtle procedure, and we're looking for a killer who used it in the middle of the day in a busy office on a big, healthy adult male."

"I don't know healthy. He just used a sun lamp."

"The pathologist said to look for somebody with extensive experience or very steady hands."

"Peter Bonifacio is going with a psychiatrist, don't they need medical training? But she's in L.A. Mary Belle teaches CPR classes, she's taught a bunch of people at the firm. Do you suppose they learn how to do it?"

"Can you find out?"

"Probably. But, well, couldn't you?"

"Yes, I can find out. But I'd rather not have everybody in the firm know I'm finding out."

He hesitated a long moment. "I'll try."

She made some notes. "While you're finding things out, any idea what the big favor was that Leo did for Peter Bonifacio?"

"No. Couldn't you just ask him?"

"Absolutely. And he'll give me the answer he's been rehearsing since I talked to him the first time. On the other hand, if I tell *him* what the favor was, he might be impressed. He might assume we already know whatever else there is to tell."

"Yeah, he might. And I might lose my job by playing Nancy Drew."

Her shrug meant it wasn't her decision.

"Look, I can't promise," Howard said. "If something occurs to me, I'll try it. But you'd really better pursue your other possibilities."

"Great. Now what's this piece of fantastic gossip?"

He handed her the document from word processing. She read, "'The Will of Leonard Makepeace Slyde.' Okay. You wrote his will?"

"I changed it for him. Look at Article III."

"'One-half the residue of my estate to Constance Valentine. The rest in trust to my children.' Who's Constance Valentine?"

"She's one of the associates, she was there at the party. One of your guys must have interviewed her."

"Here it is. White female, thirty-three years old. Forman's litigation department. Occasionally worked with deceased. Hadn't talked to him in two days, knew of no enemies, no motive. Expressed what Zatopa thought was sincere grief because Slyde's death hurt her chances for partnership. Why was he leaving her money?"

"Isn't it obvious?"

"You think they were having an affair."

"Don't you? And anyway, I have independent evidence."

"Why would he trust you with that information?"

"He didn't. I already knew by accident." He described the accidental meeting at Max's Diner. "A couple of days after that Leo called me in and told me to change the will."

"Any explanation?"

"He winked so hard his lip touched his eyebrow, and said, 'Cheap at the price.' Typical of his unwavering good taste. And then—"

The technician opened the door. "Sam, I ran the prints— sorry, I didn't know you were with somebody."

She introduced them.

"The parts definitely go together. Negative on the fingerprints. You going to be there for softball tonight?"

"Can't, I'm up to my eyeballs in this Slyde murder."

"Hell of a time to lose Jack, isn't it? Okay, I'll tell them you're having the Audubon Society over for dinner. Ansel Adams? Smokey the Bear?" He closed the door on her protests.

"What happened to Jack?"

"My partner. He's fishing for golden trout in the eastern Sierras. First vacation in eight years."

"And who's Sam?"

"They call me Sam here. It makes them comfortable, I suppose."

"Don't tell me you're a bit of an outsider yourself." She shrugged, busy over her notes. She was pretty even without enough sleep. "Not the typical detective."

"I need to make a living, I'm not big enough to be a lumberjack."

"Okay, I will mind my own business. Where were we?"

"You were describing the conversation with Leo about his will."

"Right. He asked me if I was happy with my job. I took that as a subtle hint that, if I wanted to keep it, I'd change the will and keep my mouth shut."

"And you did?"

"Absolutely."

"Well." She handed the will back to him. "If Slyde and Valentine were having an affair, maybe his secretary knew about it. How long ago did you change the will?"

"About two months ago. Maybe there's a date. . . ."

She waited, looked up. "Something wrong?"

"This isn't the will I wrote."

"I thought you said it was."

"No, this is wrong. It says 'The provisions of Paragraphs A and B apply only if my wife does not survive me.' I didn't write that."

"I don't understand."

"I can't believe this. Paragraph A says half to Connie. Paragraph B says half in trust. But this new paragraph C says A and B only apply if his wife dies before he does. And she didn't. She's alive. So there must be some other provision. . . ." He flipped rapidly back a few pages and then forward. "There isn't. This is really fucked."

He glanced up, saw her watching him. "Look, I heard those tapes, I know they think I'm a screw-up, but that's personality stuff. It's got nothing to do with this. Somebody else did this." He stared at the page for a moment, flipped to the next page, flipped back.

"Look, you can tell it was only this page that was changed. The words at the bottom are practically running off the end of the line so that the signature page won't have to be redone. Maybe Leo never saw it."

She looked it over and handed it back to him. He squinted at the page.

"Same type, it must have been done on the word processor. That means whoever did it probably had an operator's help. I've got to find out why this is here. I can't believe it's what Leo thought he was getting."

"Who benefits by the change?"

"Nancy Slyde, but in a totally roundabout way. Well, and maybe their kids if he had separate property. This will has no provision for distribution of anything— except maybe furniture—with Nancy alive. Which means Leo might as well never have written a will. Nancy gets everything under the rules of intestate succession. Valentine loses out completely."

"We can run tests, see whether the whole document was typed on the same machine."

"Won't that take time?"

"Not much."

"I'm going to talk to the operators today and see what I can find out."

"Who knows you came here?"

"Nobody."

"Keep it that way for now. Nobody talks if he thinks he's being spied on. More important, if it gets back to the killer . . ."

Howard imagined pushing open the door of his dark house. "Don't worry, I'm discreet. Leo said so. Anyway, what makes you so sure I'm not the killer?"

"Inspector's intuition. I'm right about ninety percent of the time." She grinned.

"Great."

"I may be hard to reach for the next forty-eight hours. Here's my number at home. I won't leave my name with your switchboard, and I don't think you should call me from your office phone. Could we plan to check in at some point? Say, Friday P.M.?"

"My house is a few blocks from here. We could do a quick dinner on your way home. If you have time."

She was writing in her notebook. "Seven-thirty?" They stood up. "You know, I get asked that question a lot, about being a cop. I think I did it because nobody expected me to, it made my future feel like I was going to live it instead of some other people. Then it turned out to be an incredible buzz. Why are you a lawyer?"

"At the moment I'm flattered you still think I am a lawyer. Sam. Sam. That's kind of cute."

"I see you have a death wish. Please don't indulge it while you're working with me."

13

In the Belly of the Law

He told himself he was excited because he hadn't had a chance to cook for anyone since he came to California. It would be fun to do some elegant finger food. Miniature quiches, say, or stuffed grape leaves. Suddenly he remembered the phyllo triangles in his freezer from the day he pretended to be sick. Roquefort and pistachio filling. Perfect.

There was only tomorrow night to buy the food and everything. Be good to go to the butcher on San Felipe, Bernini's for produce, but that was quite a drive. Better stick with something he'd made before that could be done ahead of time. And dessert. She was definitely on the thin side, she probably wouldn't go for chocolate mousse cake. And for only two people. What would be light and really impressive? He turned into the T&S parking lot just before seven.

He closed the door of his office, hid the will in a five-inch stack of interoffice memos, loosened his tie, and headed downstairs to word processing.

The T&S word processing room was located in the basement of the building. Here in the windowless bowels of Tweedmore & Slyde only the frantic pace and exhausted faces suggested any connection to high finance and doing deals. Frantic tapping was punctuated by a periodic high-pitched *wheep!* and illuminated by the faint green cast from the monitors. No client was intended to see the dizzying heights of paper, the industrial green sectional dividers, or the big dusty fan that failed to move the stale air. The operators wore blue jeans and T-shirts.

"Hey," said Howard, "did I screw up? Isn't this the day of the big party?"

"Right day, wrong workload," said Jill Espy, not breaking her rhythm. "I'll be lucky to be out of here by eight-thirty."

"That stinks. Aren't you and Jeff doing something for your birthday?"

"Supposed to be dinner, but you know how that goes. Even killing Leo hasn't helped." She stopped and rested her forehead on her fist. "God, that was tacky. I swear, my character degenerates a little more every day I work at this place. Hey, you guys, lighten up! Birthday cake!" She swung away from her word processor and led Howard into the kitchenette.

Howard was the only lawyer present and the only male in the group. He eyed the door periodically, fearing to see an upstairs face appear and catch him in the act of enjoying himself.

"Howard," said Liz, "I'm doing the Biscus will right now. And for about the tenth time, for your sake, I've decided not to kill Mary Belle."

"Don't be hasty. Is she being awful again? I'll talk to her, I promise, but I don't know what good it will do. My status with Mary Belle is at least a full step below yours."

"I swear that woman was a little uptight even before she got demoted, but now . . ."

"Oh, demoted, is that what you call it when somebody works for Howard Rickover? You know, I never thought about it. Who was she working for before I came?"

Liz glanced at the others. "You mean you don't know? Mary Belle was Leo's castoff." Everybody giggled.

"Wait, are you kidding?"

"What surprises you more? That Leo ever put up with Mary Belle, or that he gave her up for Candy?"

"Come on, you guys, Candy has a hard job. Still, Mary Belle is about fifty times more efficient. Who fired who?"

"Oh, Leo got rid of Mary Belle, definitely. There was a big stink about it. Apparently she really screwed something up, almost got the firm into a big malpractice action. That's why I don't see how she can be so superior all the time. So the next time Mary Belle gives you some shit, remind her why she works for you."

"Great idea, unless I want to keep living. Are we serving seconds?"

"Howard, what do you hear about Leo? Is everybody creeping around upstairs, feeling guilty for hating him all this time?"

"No, they're all just saying what a great guy he was and how much talent he had. What's even weirder is that everybody's working like it never happened. How's that for a company with heart?"

"Well, at least we know where we stand. If one of us dies tomorrow, don't expect the world to stand still."

"Well, the world might," Jill said, "just not Tweedmore and Slyde." Again, they giggled.

"It's so creepy that he died like this," said Rita. "It makes me feel bad for hating him all this time."

"I know," Howard said. "It makes him very human all of a sudden. Well, slightly human. Well, humanoid. Listen, speaking of Leo, did one of you make some minor changes in his will recently? He told me he had something minor that needed to be done, and I just wondered which of you did it for him." He waited. "Nobody? That's funny. Maybe he decided it wasn't necessary after all. Thanks for the cake, guys. I'll keep those wills and motions coming."

14

Uncle Howard

When he got back to his office, motions *in limine* five and six were back, as well as the Wisbiski will. There was a message from Jack Lincoln, with his home phone number: "Call at any time. I think you better, he sounds PISSED!" Also the half-finished research for tomorrow's emergency meeting with Bornzweig lay on one side of the desk, ticking quietly, Howard imagined.

He picked up his phone to call Lincoln, but sat with the dial tone wailing. Leo fired Mary Belle. Fired Mary Belle, it didn't fit. Her personality wasn't a subtle problem to be picked up on after several years. They said it was because she screwed up in a big way. In the four months he had known her, Mary Belle had never missed a trick. And something else, something that floated coquettishly around the edge of his consciousness. Yes. He hung up. Why didn't they fire her outright? Why keep a crabby, disgruntled employee on if she did something so bad she could never work for Leo again?

Somebody tapped gently on his door. Remembering Cal, who roamed the halls at odd hours looking for work recipients, he said nothing, hoping the person would go away. Another tap, louder this time. The door opened and Howard saw Liz the word processor, with a document in her hand.

"Thank God, I was afraid you were more work coming through the door. What's the matter, can't you read hieroglyphics any better than Mary Belle?"

Liz put the document behind her and stood there.

"Is something wrong? Are my arguments that bad?"

Liz made a sound that was half laugh and half sob. "Howard, I was just wondering . . ."

"Come on, Liz, you can tell Uncle Howard."

Whereupon Liz sat on the edge of a chair and began to cry. "I didn't kill him."

Howard got up and went around his desk and put his arm around Liz. "Good heavens, of course you didn't kill Leo. Why would anybody think you did?" Liz just sniffed and kept on crying.

"Liz," he said after a moment, "by any chance were you involved in changing Leo's will?"

Liz arched back against her chair. "Involved? What do you mean involved? I just did what he told me to. I didn't know this was going to happen. But I was so stupid . . ."

"Liz, you did what who told you to do? Leo? Who told you to change the will?"

"I can't tell you who. I promised not to tell. I absolutely swore and promised never to tell, but I didn't know *this* would happen."

"And now you're afraid the will had something to do with the murder."

She shot him a suspicious glance. "Aren't you? Why were you asking about it?"

"I was just curious, that's all. I'm the one who revised Leo's will for him, so I went to the vault and got it out, and I was just surprised to see that somebody else had changed it. No big deal. Maybe. But why did the person say he didn't want you to tell? Wouldn't the log book show it anyway?"

"No, that's just it. We didn't do it the regular way. He brought it to me in particular and asked me to make a minor change right away. It was graveyard shift, I was the only one around, he scared me half to death coming up behind me. So I made the change, and I happened to notice that the signature page had Leo's name on it. Then he told me not to bother marking it in the log book, and asked whether he could count on me not to mention it to anyone. To tell you the truth I was flattered that he trusted me to be in on something with him and Leo. I mean, usually the lawyers don't even speak to you, they make their secretaries do it. Then Leo got killed and all of a sudden I thought maybe Leo wasn't in on it after all, and, oh, Howard, I don't know what to do."

"Liz, did the person tell you why he was making the change?"

"He just said Leo wanted a quick change and didn't want to be bothered signing it again."

"Did you know what the change meant?"

"No, it said something about his wife, that's all I remember. Was the change really bad?"

"Liz, listen to me. No, the change wasn't inherently bad, although it's going to make me look like a complete fuck-up." She looked up, startled. "Because they'll think I did it, and it's a very unprofessional way of accomplishing something, even if Leo wanted it. But never mind that. Don't you think it's a little strange the way this whole thing happened? I mean, if the person asked you to help him because he was planning to kill Leo, don't you think he was a jerk to involve you in his dirty work? Doesn't he deserve to be caught?"

"Oh, no, I'm absolutely certain he—this person—didn't kill Leo."

"Well, in that case he should go to the police now and tell them what happened. Look, I know you did your best with the will, but the fact is, it looks like it's been changed. It's fairly clear that a lot of extra words have been crammed onto one page. Because of the change, a person who was going to get a lot of money is going to be left out. The will is going to be made public in a few days. That person is going to drag the whole thing into court. Eventually, the real story is going to come out anyway, and it's going to look terrible for you and this other guy, especially this other guy, if the truth comes out without you volunteering it. I think you'd better talk to this fellow, if you're sure you can trust him, and then if he won't go to the police you'd better. One way or another, will you go to the police?"

She nodded slowly, looking first at her feet and then at him. "Yes," she said, "you're right, I've got to. He'll see that." She smiled and stood up. "Howard, thanks. If I can be of help to you sometime . . ."

"I won't even hesitate, I promise. Let me know what happens."

He was flying through the revisions of motion *in limine* number five when there was a tap at his door. It was ten-thirty, hopeless. "Yes?"

This time it was Jill, the word processor, holding a document.

"Hi, come in, I've just about got another one ready for you. Can't you read that?"

"Howard . . ."

"Is something the matter?"

"Can I talk to you for a second?" She closed the door. "It's about Leo. There's something that's been bothering me."

She didn't look like she was going to start crying. "Sure, have a seat."

"Howard, this is weird, and I know I'm probably being paranoid, but do you have any idea what Leo and Cal might have been fighting about a couple of weeks ago?"

"Cal Forman? No, how come?"

"Well, it was a week ago Thursday, there was a huge

motion that had to go out, and I agreed to come in extra hours. Well, it turned out that the only time a machine was free was during the graveyard shift. So I was supposed to get off at eleven, but I just kept going until five A.M. I was so tired I was in a zombie state, but I wanted to have it delivered and off my desk, so I walked it up to Connie's office myself. I stepped off the elevator on six and heard this incredible yelling, bounding off the walls. It scared the shit out of me, and all I could think to do was get back on the elevator and get the hell out. So I punched the button and punched it and punched it. While I was waiting I kept hearing those voices, and I finally realized it was Leo and Cal."

"What were they yelling about?"

"Cal was swearing a lot. He said something about 'no goddamn morals at all.' He said, 'the morals of a fish, the morals of a sea urchin.' He was practically hysterical, you know how he gets. And Leo kept yelling at him to calm down. That's it, I can't remember anything else. But, well, don't you think that's a little weird?"

"Weirder than shit. Have you told anybody?"

"No. At the time I was so tired I was practically hallucinating, and I was just relieved that it wasn't somebody stealing all the typewriters. I went home and fell into bed and sort of forgot about it. Until Leo. You know what I mean."

"So, are you going to tell the police?"

"Howard, I don't know what to do. I am absolutely positive that Cal didn't kill Leo. But, well, what would you do?"

"Any chance they saw you?"

"Absolutely not. They kept screaming the whole time and I could tell they were over by Leo's office."

"Well, what about this? What if I call the police and tell them I know about this, but the person who heard it has to remain anonymous?"

"Would you? See, the whole thing is if Cal finds out I told them . . ."

"No problem. I'll do it. The only thing is, they may want to interview you directly. If that happens, I'll come back and talk to you about it, but I absolutely won't tell your name unless you say I can."

"Oh, Howard, I'm so glad you work here. I feel much better now. Want me to take that with me?"

"Uh, actually it isn't quite finished. I'll bring it to you later. Have fun."

As soon as she left he draped his coat over his chair. He left the light on and headed for the elevator. The swing shift ended at eleven and he wanted to be ready.

He parked his car on the street by the parking lot entrance and waited. Liz's car was a blue Civic, he hoped there was enough light to recognize it. At eleven-fifteen he saw her swing out onto Cabrillo and go left away from Daily City where she lived. He started to sweat.

At La Cadena she turned right, and he thought for a moment she was headed for the freeway. But at Perris Hill Park she stopped, shutting her lights off. He shut off his own lights and pulled in a few car lengths behind her. What if she did see him? he told himself. Liz wasn't a murderer. He hoped she wouldn't get out and start walking. He didn't have the courage to leave the protective shell of his car.

She didn't get out. After five minutes a car pulled up right behind her, and Bill Madras got out. He walked over to the passenger door and got in.

Howard's hands were suddenly cold. Bill Madras. If he tried to leave now they'd see him for sure. And shouldn't he stay to make sure Liz was all right? He lay down across the seat so they wouldn't catch his silhouette in a passing headlight.

After an eternity of imagining how his back would

feel as a bullet ripped through it, a car door slammed. Liz called out, "Bill? Bill!" Then he heard an engine start and a car drive away.

He raised himself just enough to see that Liz's car was now alone. She turned on her headlights, did a u-turn, and passed him on her way back to Cabrillo.

15

Double Your Fun

He was within minutes of finishing motion *in limine* number seven when there was a knock on his door.

"Go away!"

Cal Forman stuck his head in the door. "Howard? Did you say come in?"

"More or less. What's up?"

"Thank God you're here. I'm sorta in a jam, and everybody else is in court or out to lunch or some damn place. Please, please, can you help me out for a couple of hours before my client gets here? Here's what needs to be done . . ."

As soon as he left, Howard called Mary Belle on the intercom.

"Listen, special favor to enable the two of us to keep our jobs."

"What do you mean us, white man? What's the favor?"

"Please, keep everybody out of my office until this motion is back in word processing."

"Your work habits suck," she said, and hung up. He figured that meant "okay," and went back to his motion.

He ignored the knock ten minutes later. The door opened slightly, and he heard Mary Belle say, ". . . letting the people who work around here work."

Candy stuck her head in, her look of defiance fading into a lovely, if tense, smile.

"Howard? I know you're awfully busy, but I told Mary Belle you'd let me interrupt you for a teeny-weeny minute. It's terribly important."

The possibility that Candy Gilley was involved in anything important really was terrible, Howard thought irritably. "Sure, Candy, come on in, but we better make it quick, okay?" He looked at the document she held in her hand, trying to place it, but she closed the door securely and turned to face him stiffly with the document behind her back.

"Howard, this is very embarrassing because I don't know you very well, but . . ."

For one crazy second Howard thought she was going to start kissing him. He was actually relieved to see tears welling up in her eyes.

"Hey, tell me about it. Here, want a gray wrinkled handkerchief?" She took it and sat on the edge of one of his chairs.

"Howard, I think I'm in trouble and I have to talk to somebody about it. And you, well, you're so harmless . . ."

Howard laughed loud and long. "Hey, skip the flattery, okay? I don't think I can take it."

"It's not flattery, I really mean it. You are harmless. Do you remember that woman detective who was in here the day Leo was murdered? Well, I'm pretty sure she thinks I killed Leo."

"Thinks *you* killed him. Why would she think that?"

"I, uh . . ." She pressed the handkerchief against her mouth. "She thinks Leo and I were . . . involved."

"Candy, why do you think she thinks that? Did she ask you about it?"

"No, not directly. But after I talked to her for a whole hour or something the day of the murder she asked to talk to me again. I went to the station today and all she wanted to know was whether Leo was having any affairs."

"Well, were you and Leo involved?"

She nodded, her face pressed into the handkerchief. She looked up at Howard's astonished stare and buried her face again.

"Oh, it's horrible, I know. Nancy's such a nice person and everything. You must think I'm awful."

"No." Howard roused himself. "Who am I to judge? Let's just say I admire his taste more than yours."

She stared at him blankly, her nose red, and then smiled. "Oh, Howard, you're sweet. But what should I do?"

"Well, what did you do? Did you tell her?"

"Of course not. That would make me look guilty."

"Of adultery, maybe, but not of murder."

"Don't, Howard, I hate that word! And why is she asking me about it? If I told her, wouldn't Nancy find out?"

"I don't know. Probably not if you tell her in confidence. Especially if it has nothing to do with the murder. But, you know, she may not have been asking about you in particular. You were Leo's secretary, she probably just thinks you knew something about his personal life. I mean, do you know if he was having any other affairs?"

"Of course not." Her eyes flashed. "Leo was full of fidelity."

"Or any affairs in the past? I mean, now I'm telling this to you in confidence. I heard a rumor once that, and this was probably a real long time ago if it happened at all, that, well, that he and Connie Valentine were real good friends."

"Connie Valentine!" She managed a little laugh. "Leo absolutely hated Connie Valentine. He was scared to death of her. But I told him he didn't have to be scared of anybody, least of all her. It was embarrassing in a way. I mean Leo's so powerful and all, and her just a woman associate. Not even that good-looking, if you ask me."

"Did he tell you why he was afraid of Connie?"

"Uh-uh. But listen, Howard, what do you think I should do?"

"Well. I think you'd feel better if you told the detective about you and Leo. Only because you won't be scared it's going to come out sometime later and make you look like you aren't very honest. I really don't think that's going to make her suspect you of anything more. And if you want, I could make an anonymous call to her and make sure she can keep it in confidence."

"No! Don't do that. I . . . don't want to take up any more of your busy time."

"You know what else, Candy? I think you'd better tell her about Connie Valentine.

"Oh, Howard, you don't suppose *she* killed him, do you? A woman?"

"No, no, I'm sure she didn't, but I still think it's the kind of thing the police want to know about. Who are you protecting? Has Connie ever done you any favors?"

"I should say not. I'll definitely tell her. And, well, I'll probably tell her about Leo and me. Probably." She stood up. "Oh, Howard, thank you for all your help. I don't care what they all say, I'm glad you work here."

"There you go with that flattery again. Poor Candy. And you had to be the one to find him, too. You've had some tough breaks. Drop by in the next couple of days and let me know how you're doing, okay?"

Mary Belle opened the door without knocking and

glared at Candy. "Howie, Mr. Caenfetti has called twice in the last half hour. If you don't take it . . ."

"I'll take it. Put it through. See you, Candy."

Inspector Sarah Nelson was on the phone when Zatopa arrived. She gestured to the wooden chair beside her gray metal desk. She saw the big brown envelope in his hands, studied his face briefly as she talked.

"Right, I have thirty-one last names, some with two first names. Is there a master file for alumni? I see. That would include people who didn't actually graduate? Maybe the last five years then. I'll have the list delivered to you tomorrow. I appreciate it." As she hung up the receiver she said, "You didn't get anything."

He shrugged. "Nothing worth much. No calls from either phone after two P.M."

She was silent a moment. "So that means they were either incoming calls or they were local."

"He probably didn't take calls without somebody screening them. Most of these honchos don't."

"We've got to pursue this phone stuff. Can you start on it? I'm dealing with medical schools about this murder technique. And this evening I've got some witnesses to the hunting accident."

Zatopa sighed. "You want me to call all the numbers on these?"

"Going back two weeks. There's one other thing we might try first. I've done the messages in the waste-basket. Why don't you do the pile that was on his desk?" She tossed him a big clear plastic bag full of pink slips. "Then the Pac Bell records, then the phone log. You can use Jack's desk."

"You really think we're going to find your guy this way?"

"I think we'd better try."

*   *   *

By the time Howard left his office, there were only fifteen minutes before Bernini's closed. He loosened his tie and headed for Safeway.

He tossed the cookbooks into the kid seat of his shopping cart and flipped back and forth as he went down the aisles. Chicken marbella was for ten, so divide by three. Garlic, oregano he had, olive oil he had, prunes he needed. This dish was fun partly because the ingredients were so weird. He found Spanish green olives, capers, white wine, flat Italian parsley instead of coriander. Raspberries and lemon for the raspberry ice.

He slowed down and perused the vegetable bins thoughtfully, pinched a pepper, rejected the broccoli because of yellowness. Too bad there wasn't time to make it to Bernini's. But the Blue Lake green beans were crisp. He decided on a julienne of beans, red and yellow peppers, and zucchini. The romaine lettuce looked fine, he tossed the salad vegetables rapidly into the cart. Dressing: he had the champagne vinegar at home, and the mustard, and the corn oil (this was the advantage of a menu you could do in your sleep), but no egg yolks. He headed for the dairy case.

At the checkout counter he remembered the mint leaves for the raspberry ice, and made a glaring man in an expensive suit wait in line while he ran to get it. He stopped for wine on the way home.

He pulled most of the ingredients onto his dining-room table. Eight-thirty, this was going to be a late one. He changed quickly into his jeans, poured himself a glass of wine, and shoved the dirty dishes to one side. The doorbell rang.

"Mrs. Pringle." He looked around for his cat. "Is Stella doing something awful again?"

"No, dear, not at all. And I'm awfully sorry to keep

making a nuisance of myself. But I wanted to ask you a favor."

"Sure."

"I wonder if you could ask your visitors to park in front of your house instead of my place across the street."

"Absolutely. Only I'm pretty new here, I don't have many visitors."

"Listen, I may be a million years old, but I haven't forgotten completely what it's like to be young. Go for it. Enjoy yourselves. But you see, I don't get out as easily as I used to. If she'll just park in front of your house, then I can get up in the morning and enjoy my view."

"In the morning? Mrs. Pringle, believe me, I wish you were right. But I absolutely don't have a girlfriend at the moment, and there's nobody here at night except me and Stella."

"Well. My goodness. Who else is entertaining all-night visitors on this block?"

"I don't know," Howard said, laughing. "I hope it isn't somebody who shouldn't be."

"Well, of course it's none of my business anyway, only I do wish they wouldn't park in front of my rose garden. Heavens, maybe the neighbors all think it's me."

"If they do they'll be envious."

"Well, Howard dear, I'm awfully sorry." She clutched her chest in mock contrition. "I accused you falsely."

"Not to worry. I only wish your fears were more well founded. Listen, it's pretty dark. Why don't I walk you home?"

By the time he got back it was five after nine. As music from *Sunday in the Park with George* filled his kitchen he started on the raspberry ice.

While the sugar and water simmered cheerfully, Dot complained of the heat on the island of La Grande Jatte.

Howard pureed the berries in his food mill, discarded the seeds, added lemon. He combined the ingredients in his metal mixing bowl and put the bowl into the freezer. He set his timer for eleven-forty. Two hours to bring order to the whole.

He washed the chicken and tossed it into his big metal bowl. While George dotted red and orange onto a certain black hat, Howard brought the side of his cleaver down on clove after clove of garlic to remove the skin, then pressed the cloves into a separate mixing bowl. Why had he promised Huffman the trust papers by tomorrow? He was coming by the office at one, the motions *in limine* had to be on Forman's desk before then. Maybe if he was in the office by seven . . . Damn the Follies, he had a dinner to make.

By the time Dot stormed off the stage and left George with his black hat, Howard's hands were in the gritty marinade, carefully coating the pale chicken with the prunes, olives, and capers. Why was Madras screwing around with Leo's will? The guy might be a genius at mergers, but he obviously knew nothing about estate planning. It didn't fit. Leo would have come to Howard. Wouldn't he?

As the Boatman's dog sniffed bits of garbage from the park grass, Howard fished two dishes of questionable vintage out of the refrigerator and carefully put the chicken in their place.

As Dot moved on to Louis the Baker, Howard turned to the vegetables. Creating food wasn't as trivial as Sondheim was making out. But then maybe he was just a Louis, not a George. Two affairs. Leo had at least two. Busy guy, eclectic taste. Did Nancy know? She wasn't even there. Some other jilted lover.

He washed the peppers, zucchini, and green beans and spread them around his cutting board. This could take forever. He chose a bean and pruned it carefully until it was a suitable size. Using the bean as his template, he carved one red and one yellow pepper strip and a zucchini strip and piled the four vegetables in a little heap on the cutting board. At least he had a painterly eye. After stirring them a couple of times with his fingers he sliced a little of the width from each strip and piled them up again. Perfect. With a flick of his knife he whisked three of the strips onto the tabletop and started in on the beans.

The vegetables took a long time. While his fingers were flying over the strips, George's painting and its inhabitants passed into a different century. The beans would take longer to cook; he decided to parboil them. As Dot thanked George for the shade he plunged the beans into boiling water and turned over his egg timer.

George was propping up image after image at the cocktail party. Thank God you didn't need financial backing to do a dinner party. Still, you did need friends, something that had been in short supply since he moved out here. In a way, parties of ten or even twenty were more fun, you got to do more hors d'oeuvres, more elaborate desserts. Maybe if he got back to Boston for Christmas. He concentrated on making his fingers move faster.

While a critic accused George of being redundant, Howard turned out copy after copy after copy of red pepper, his fingers and the knife blurring in a well-rehearsed duet. The little heaps were beautiful, the uniform shape accentuated the differences of color and texture. Cal and Leo. Cal said he'd been in court all afternoon. Cal was no killer. Gerry was right, none of them were.

He segregated the zucchini and peppers in Ziploc bags and stacked them in his refrigerator. Putting them together is what counts. He lifted the beans from the pot with a slotted spatula and plunged them into cold water, their brilliant green fracturing and shimmering beneath the cold ripples. He rolled the beans in a paper towel and added them to the stockpile in the vegetable bin.

He spread the salad vegetables on the table. What was it about Sarah? Her dark eyes watching you, like she was trying to see your core. Why had she chosen him to be in on the investigation? Trusting him with all that confidential stuff. What made him special enough? While George contemplated his loneliness on the island of La Grande Jatte, Howard extracted the tender inside leaves of the romaine lettuce, picked the watercress from its stems, sliced the cucumbers and radishes, and placed them all in his frosted glass salad bowl. The orange slices would be for the last minute.

As Dot and George strolled in the green-purple-yellow-red grass Howard made the champagne vinaigrette dressing. He whisked the egg yolk and mustard and champagne vinegar for a minute, then drizzled the corn oil slowly into the mixture, fascinated by the sudden transformation of the watery yellow mixture into mayonnaise. Putting it together is what counts. As the last strains of the chorus faded, he popped the dressing into the refrigerator and glanced at his watch. An hour to go, the house looked like a garbage scow. So much for art, now we were talking work. Still, he had the new Gershwin album.

Forty-five minutes later the underwear had disappeared from the living room, the mold from the bathroom tile, the trash from the wastebaskets, the dishes from the sink. He securely closed the door of the study. Kleenex would have to do instead of toilet paper. The dust gorillas would have to stay. Fifteen minutes to go.

He ironed a shirt. He set out stemmed goblets for the raspberry ice, chose blue-and-white Florentine plates to put under them. For the phyllo triangles he chose a rose-and-white platter. The timer buzzed.

The metal bowl had frosted over, the raspberry puree had nearly frozen. As his electric mixer churned through the thick slush he calculated. She was coming at seven-thirty, chicken served at eight-fifteen. Before that, he needed to sauté the vegetables, the phyllo triangles should come out of the oven at seven-forty-five. He continued counting backward for every additional step. He needed to be home by six, six-fifteen at the latest. He switched his electric mixer to high speed and watched the puree become fluffy and pink. Then he returned the puree to the freezer, washed the beaters, and turned out the light.

Fifteen minutes later he reappeared in the dark kitchen, quickly crossed the room in his underwear, and pulled a bottle of Shadow Creek champagne from the paper bag on the table. By the light of the open refrigerator he placed the bottle on its side on the bottom shelf. After that the kitchen remained dark.

16

Balk

"Howard," Gerry Tweedmore said into the phone, "I think you should join Bill and me in the PelSol-Xylo merger discussions this afternoon. I know it isn't your bailiwick, but we have to make sure you develop some breadth even if we are in a crunch with estate planning. Why don't you sit in today and see how it operates?"

Why? Because he had to be in his house by six-fifteen, that's why. And the Brombeck estate plan had to be ready by five P.M. tomorrow. God, if this was Gerry's way of pulling him in to work on the merger documents . . .

By the time he got to Gerry's office, the discussion

with PelSol management was nearing its conclusion. "So it sounds like you two haven't decided in your own minds whether this SEC regulation is a problem or a solution," Gerry said to the president and vice president of PelSol, who were facing him across his desk. Madras sat on the couch off to the side. "Did you agree to the restructuring the investors wanted?"

"We agreed to everything already," the president said quickly.

"We agreed when they put a gun to our heads," the younger man said bitterly. He wore a short-sleeved plaid shirt and a beard.

Gerry turned to Madras and raised an eyebrow.

"The basics were agreed to before the last bridge loan," Madras responded. "No details, nothing in writing, but the umpire would definitely call a balk."

Gerry smiled at the PelSol people. "Well, I have some idea of what we're dealing with. I know from Bill that you're the kind of people who take the high road in business. That's the approach Bill and I feel comfortable with, too.

"Xylo's representative will be there this afternoon, and one of the four investors on your board. Let's all just see what the possibilities are and then meet back here at the end of the day. We'll do the best job we can for you. See you in there in a few minutes," he said cheerfully as the two men stood up to go. As the door closed behind them the light in his eyes blinked out, and his smile vanished.

"Why are we wasting our time with those clowns?" he said.

"They do good software, Ger. Just bad businessmen."

"Sloppy thinkers. We'll encourage the board to get rid of them. Now what's this accounting issue with the SEC?"

"It's a pooling issue."

Gerry nodded.

"The net result of all this stuff the investors want is that the stock ownership in the company goes from sixty percent common and forty percent preferred to forty common and sixty preferred. That violates one of the SEC's pooling requirements: You can't restructure ownership in the company in anticipation of the merger. We're stuck. If we do what we agreed to do, the pooling becomes an acquisition, Xylo takes a hit to earnings, the deal's off. If we don't do what we agreed to do, the investors won't vote the preferred in favor of the merger, and the deal's still off." Bill shrugged. "We're caught in a squeeze play, Ger; looks like we're out at third."

"Do you think this merger is in PelSol's best interest?"

"Absolutely. But assuming we find a way, we've still got the battle between these two and their investors."

"We have to presume we can control that situation. If this meeting turns up any hope on the SEC problem, let's get those two back in here right afterward and straighten them out. I want them taken care of today. Has Peter looked over the stuff you gave him?"

Bill nodded.

"He turn up anything?"

"Haven't talked to him."

"All right, see you guys in there in a minute. And Bill, I don't want those two interrupting. You have control?"

When Howard pushed through the swinging doors of the conference room only one other person was present. The man's coat was on the back of his chair, revealing a large gold watch and a monogram on the cuff of his cream-colored shirt. He offered Howard a hand and the appropriate number of white teeth in a tan face.

"Roger Loman, one of the investors in PelSol. You must work with Bill."

Howard took a seat near him. "That's right. Howard Rickover."

"Good. Bill's all right, if he weren't such a Giants fan. I hear Hammaker's still got rotator cuff problems."

Did baseball uniforms have cuffs? Fortunately, the doors swung open and Bill himself entered, herding the PelSol management in front of him. He wore a neatly fitting blue shirt, his tie swinging rhythmically as he walked. "Come on, Rog, admit it. Hammaker or no, Giants have the 'Humm, Baby!' spirit this year. Gonna be a great season. You guys sit here next to me." The software engineers sat stiffly and silently on the chairs indicated.

"So, Big Rog," said Bill. "Hear you got a new toy."

"Yeah, twin-engine Beach Baron."

Bill whistled.

"I was losing too much time in airports."

"Yeah, too bad flying's no fun." Their laughter did not infect the engineers, who sat stonefaced and deaf. A tall man in his thirties pushed an expensive briefcase through the swinging doors.

"Bill," he said. "Roger." He glanced without curiosity at Howard as he chose a chair at the head of the table. He tossed his pinstrip suitcoat over the empty chair next to him, revealing bright green dollar signs woven into his suspenders. This must be the investment banker representing Xylo. He snapped his briefcase open and started removing papers. "I hope we can keep it short this afternoon. I just got in from Tokyo and jet lag has me scrambled. We got any coffee?"

"Be here any minute, Lare, what's doing in Tokyo?" The doors swung open and Peter Bonifacio entered. He removed his suitcoat and squared the shoulders carefully on his seatback before sitting down between Howard and the investor. He nodded silently at the others by way of greeting. Howard shrugged his own coat off as discreetly as possible, hoping nobody would notice the stain on his tie. The doors swung open again, and Gerry Tweedmore entered. The meeting had begun.

"Gerry," said the man wearing dollar signs, "I'm Larry Masters representing Xylo. Xylo thinks we're spinning our wheels on this thing. As of today we're looking for new opportunities."

"I think you're wise," Gerry said. There were startled looks in his direction. "I don't know all the details yet, but it sounds like we may be at an impasse. I suggest we go at it this afternoon, rest on it if we need to, and wrap it up tomorrow if nothing's turned around. Fair? Now, just so we're all working on the same problem, I'd like Bill to describe this SEC matter."

Two hours later the only progress Howard could discern was the appearance of two creases in Roger Loman's shirt. Although Howard couldn't understand the proposals, the others seemed confident that they weren't making headway. Larry Masters apparently perceived the rotations of his minute hand to be the most interesting activity in the conference room.

Howard was fantasizing that he had just put the final touches on an already brilliant Brombeck estate plan when Peter shifted uneasily and cleared his throat. "Why—?"

"How certain are we that the SEC will use that single criterion to scrap the whole deal?" Roger asked. "Couldn't we get some kind of advisory opinion?"

"Not doable, Rog," said Madras. "They won't do an advisory on something that isn't a potential violation. It's like asking the umpire whether you should pop a fly ball or bunt."

Peter cleared his throat again. "I wonder if PelSol could decide not to do the restructuring and just adjust the common/preferred exchange ratio to reach the same result."

The investment banker was staring vacantly at Peter, formulating his next remarks. "I think your final effort should focus on the language 'in anticipation of.' Couldn't the effective date—"

"Wait a minute, Larry," Gerry said. "What about what Peter just said?"

"Didn't hear it."

Peter repeated his remark.

Larry flexed his dollar signs with a shrug. "Innovative, but it won't fly. Now my suggestion—"

"I think maybe it will fly," said Gerry. All eyes turned to him. "At least I think it's a genius of an idea. Tell us some more."

"Well," Peter said, "the goal is to redistribute the equity in PelSol according to some formula you've all agreed on. One way to do that is to restructure the company. But if this merger is going to be a stock exchange and the PelSol guys are going to end up with Xylo stock anyway, why not just adjust the exchange ratio so that the preferred guys end up with their percentage of Xylo and the common guys get their percentage?"

Everybody was silent for a moment. Gerry was grinning.

"Well," said Roger. "I suppose if we got our rightful percentages . . ."

"The SEC may declare it a de facto reorganization," Larry said.

Gerry nodded. "That's one tough issue, there are probably some others. But it's worth working on for another day, don't you think?" He glanced at Howard, who stopped blinking, fearful that any twitch might be interpreted as enthusiasm. "How about if Bill and Peter put together a rough sketch of the terms by tomorrow, say ten o'clock?" Thank God. It was a quarter to six.

Larry looked at his watch and stood up. "Looks like

we'll be here another night. Nice work, Gerry. Maybe there's some life in this deal yet."

"Very nice work," Gerry agreed. "But of course it wasn't mine." He nodded at Peter.

Larry glanced at Peter, then held his hand out to Gerry. "Well, I'm glad we've finally had the chance to do business."

As Gerry took Masters's hand, he nodded almost imperceptibly to Bill, indicating the PelSol management. Bill whispered to them as he escorted them into the lobby. Gerry and Masters stood talking quietly at one end of the conference table. Roger Loman, Peter, and Howard remained at the other end.

"So, where are you from originally?" Loman asked Peter as he loaded his briefcase.

"San Francisco."

"A native. So you're one of us."

"An interesting turn of phrase," said Peter. "Did you ever see a movie called *Freaks*?"

Loman shook his head, pulling his cuffs from under his coatsleeves.

"It's a story about circus freaks. At one point in the movie this beautiful young woman marries a dwarf. All the other freaks come to the wedding, and they dance around her, pinheads, guys with three arms, singing in these high-pitched voices, 'You're one of us, you're one of us.'"

Loman was silent for an instant, his smile carefully in place. "Well," he said cheerfully, "sounds interesting. I'll have to see if it's out in video. I tell you guys I finally broke down and got a VCR for the kids?"

"Big Pete. How," called Madras, pushing in through the doors. "This thing with Gerry should be quick. How about if you pop over to Burger King and get something for all of us. I'll meet you guys here in half an hour."

Guys?

"Wait," said Howard. "You need me here tonight?"

"Absolutely. Gerry wants you in on it. Gerry, we got Rickover, right?"

Gerry turned from Masters. "I don't think we'd better, Bill. I don't think Tom can spare him just yet."

Bill stopped for an instant, confused. "But you said. . . ?"

Gerry was already shepherding Larry Masters into the lobby. Bill stared after them with a puzzled frown. Then he rallied. "Okay, Peter. See *you* here in half an hour." As he pushed into the lobby he called, "Walt, Big Hans, bases are loaded. Let's duck into Gerry's office and knock it outta the park."

17

Don Howard

He had a fire going when Sarah rang the doorbell, and Ella Fitzgerald was singing Cole Porter. Although he had been expecting her, he found her presence in his doorway somehow startling. Her eyes weren't as black as in the image he had created, and he had omitted her freckles. Her hair was wet, the damp edges lay against the chocolate-brown polyester suitcoat.

She declined the champagne. He poured a glass for himself and brought her a Calistoga. "Anybody in jail yet?"

She smiled wearily. "I am. There must be a thousand phone numbers on Slyde's Rolodex. Why did they have to kill a lawyer?"

The phyllo triangles were puffy and perfectly browned. She took one absentmindedly.

"How about you? Any news on the will?"

"Yeah, and I got some other stuff."

"Great." She held up a red vinyl binder. "Could we sit where I can take notes?" She took another triangle.

He seated her at the dining table where they could talk while he sautéed the vegetables. By the time he set the chicken on the table she was smiling at him in astonishment.

"How did you do all this in two days?" She was making notes in her big red notebook. "Okay, first a woman named Liz says she changed the will. Won't say who told her to, but at midnight on day of discussion met with attorney Madras at park. Apparent argument, left in separate cars. P.D. not to contact Liz at this time. Second—"

"Would you like salad now or after dinner? It's romaine and orange slices with a few other things thrown in."

"Either way." She was looking at her notebook, comparing something.

"Hold on a minute, I'll do the dressing."

"No thanks. Plain is fine. Okay, second, deceased and attorney named Cal Forman in heated argument in early A.M. four to six weeks before murder." She looked up; her glasses were charmingly big on her face. "Who's Forman? Did we interview him at the party?"

"He was only there for a minute, I think. He was in the middle of a trial."

"Third, Candy Gilley was having affair with deceased." She chewed a bite of the chicken thoughtfully. "Says deceased not having affair with Valentine. Says deceased disliked Valentine."

"Actually, she said he was afraid of her. Here, take some more of the sauce. I hope it's not too weird. It's made with olives, prunes, and capers."

"Thanks. Okay, afraid of Valentine. Any reason you can think of for Gilley to make that up?"

"I don't know of any. Maybe Leo told her that to throw her off."

"Mm. Anything else?"

"That's it as far as our investigation goes. I personally found out an amazing thing, which is that my pain-in-the-butt secretary is Leo's castoff."

"What do you mean 'castoff'? They were lovers, too?"

"God, no. But the word processors told me she used to be Leo's secretary and got fired. Maybe that's why she got crabby. Maybe she used to be a saint."

"Could be." She flipped back a page. "This thing with Madras looks interesting. Was he close to Leo?" Howard shrugged. "Why would Leo want him to change the will?"

"To tell the truth, I'm surprised Leo didn't come to me directly. I guess Madras could be lying. But why Madras would want to change the will I don't know."

"I agree it looks like Madras was involved, but maybe that meeting you saw was planned long before Liz talked to you. I think I'll have him and Liz watched for the next couple of days."

"Let's leave me out of that part, okay?"

"Then Cal Forman. I'll get an appointment to talk to him. Then Connie Valentine. I think it's time to get her explanation about the will. What else? Find out anything about Leo's big favor for Peter Bonifacio?"

"Not yet."

"Same with the murder technique? Fine, why don't you concentrate on that for the next day or two. If you have the time. I'll take care of the rest of this." She pulled off her glasses and rubbed her eye with the heel of her hand. "You ever want a cut in pay, I'd say you have the makings of a real snoop."

"I was pretty lucky. Here, let me take that for you. I'll get dessert. It's raspberry ice."

"Thanks, Howard, but I don't eat dessert."

"This isn't really dessert. It's just water and raspberries. It has about two calories in it.

"I guess I'm full."

"Oh. Okay, then. Coffee?"

"I'd love to, but I need to get this surveillance set up."

"Want to use my phone?"

"The numbers are back at the office. Thanks for dinner. See you."

Her hair still wasn't dry.

"Mr., um, Tweedmore's office."

"Hi, Candy, this is Howard. You working for Gerry now?"

Her voice was muffled. "Yes."

"Candy, I don't think you have to whisper, this isn't anything to do with what we were talking about earlier. I just wondered if you'd do me a favor."

"Sure," she whispered. "What?"

"Do you think you could arrange for Peter's secretary, Sally, to join you and me for lunch today? I know Peter's out of the office, and I'd sort of like to get to know her better."

There was a pause. "Oh, Howard, I think that's very romantic. Sure, I can set it up, but remember, the rest is up to you."

At Vivaldi's around the corner, Howard stood back to let the women enter the booth. Candy jabbed him and pushed him in before her. Sally St. John was yet another gorgeous T&S woman. She had long black curly hair, and today she was wearing bright red pumps that made her legs look long.

After they ordered, Howard sank down into the booth and sighed. "Boy, this whole thing with Leo's pretty weird, isn't it?" Candy jabbed him under the table. He turned to Sally. "How's Peter taking it? I know they really liked each other."

Sally nodded. "I think he's taking it pretty hard."

"He told me once that Leo had done a big favor for his career."

"Oh, absolutely. Bringing Peter over to work with him and all."

"Maybe we should get some wine," said Candy. "You guys want some wine?"

"Oh. You mean Peter didn't always work for Leo?"

"No, that's been less than a year. He started in litigation, and he was pretty eager to make a move. Leo helped him switch."

Candy was motioning for the waiter.

"I see," Howard said. "And I guess it worked out pretty well."

"Well, actually—"

Candy jabbed him under the table again. "Waiter, we'd like a bottle of wine. What do you think, guys, white or red?"

"Nothing for me, Candy," said Howard. "I have a rough afternoon."

Candy stared at him in disbelief.

"Nothing for me, either," said Sally. "Thanks."

Howard turned back to Sally. "Was there a problem working for Leo?"

"Oh, all right," Candy told the waiter. "Just bring me a Crystal Geyser."

Sally glanced at Candy. "Oh, it probably doesn't matter. Promise you won't tell anybody though, okay? Peter really liked working for Leo and all, but . . . about two months ago he started looking for a new job."

"How come?"

"Howard," said Candy, "Could I talk to you for a minute?" Howard kept his eyes on Sally, who shrugged unhappily.

"I don't even know. It's just that I'm supposed to cover for him when he's out at interviews."

"Was he asked to leave?"

Sally nodded quietly, almost imperceptibly. "I'm pretty sure he was."

"Just for a minute, Howard, okay?" Candy said. "Sally, could you keep our places?" She followed Howard grimly into the entryway.

"Howard Rickover, you don't seem to have much flair for this sort of thing. So far, all you've talked about is murder and her boss losing his job. How do you think that makes Sally feel? What's going to happen to her when Peter goes?"

"I'm sorry, Candy, I guess you're right. I just thought it was something we could talk about."

"Not to mention talking about Leo right in front of me."

"I'm sorry, Candy, I really am. I guess I'm just nervous."

"Well, I don't think you're getting very far. She likes chocolate and animals, why don't you talk to her about that?"

"I will, Candy, thanks for the advice. Shouldn't we go back in there now? Maybe you can help me keep things going."

She tried, but frankly, Howard was no Don Juan. Right now his idea of romance was arranging to borrow a Red Cross manual.

18

Hillsborough Grill

"Howard, come in," Gerry Tweedmore said. "Sorry I couldn't see you earlier, but we had a closing this morning that was pretty darn complicated. Just when you think you've seen the whole gamut, the client thinks of something different to throw at you." He smiled wearily and rubbed the side of this face. "Sit down. How goes the battle in estate planning?"

"We're doing pretty well. The clients are being surprisingly understanding. Actually, I came to talk to you about Leo."

"Glad you did. How are you feeling about all that?"

"Fairly freaked out, like everybody else, I guess. The only difference is that I decided to do something about it. That's sort of why I'm here."

Gerry stopped rubbing the side of his face and raised his eyebrows, inviting Howard to continue.

"When Sarah Nelson, the inspector, interviewed me after the murder, she asked whether I knew about some big favor that Leo did for Peter's career. At the time I didn't, but now I think I found out. Leo got Peter out of Cal's litigation group into copyright and trademark, right?"

Gerry nodded.

"So I called Nelson this morning to let her know. But while I was waiting for her to call back, somebody told me that Peter was asked to leave the firm about a month ago. I'm sure Nelson will want to know why. I thought maybe you could tell me."

Gerry rubbed the side of his face again. "I don't know that it's appropriate for me to talk to you about this."

"Oh. Of course. I don't mean to butt in. It's just that . . . Well, maybe when Inspector Nelson calls back, I'll tell her she can ask you about it."

"That might be best. I'm a little surprised you have the time for this, anyhow. I know you won't neglect Tom and the clients."

"No," he said quickly. "I won't." So much for trying to impress Gerry. "It's just . . . well, like you said a couple of days ago, helping the police seems like one of the things we can do for Leo. This didn't seem like that big a deal."

Gerry was tapping the desk lightly with his pen. Behind him on the bookshelf Howard could see his textbook, *Tweedmore's Corporate Taxation*, from his days as professor at Stanford. Did he keep it there on purpose? "Heck, I guess you're right. And half the firm probably knows about it, anyway. I'll tell you what. Can you treat this information about Peter like it's subject to attorney-client privilege? Nobody can hear about this except Inspector Nelson, does that sound fair?"

Howard nodded.

"Well, Peter wasn't asked to leave. He just got in a bad spot and everybody came to a mutual decision. See, Leo took him on to do copyright and trademark. Which was great for a few months, but then the work dried up. We didn't really need another guy in corporate, and Leo already had all the litigation help he needed. There wasn't much for Peter to do to pick up the slack. So we all agreed he'd start looking, but there's no deadline. He'll have a job here as long as he needs one."

"Why couldn't he just go back to Cal's group?"

"Cal had already hired somebody to fill the spot." Gerry pulled a document over from the corner of his desk and set it in front of him. "I'm not sure Peter wanted to go back, anyway. That answer your question?"

"Yeah." Howard stood up. "I'll let Inspector Nelson know. Thanks."

"You know, it's great that you want to help the police. I hope we all will. But I don't like to think of you running yourself ragged trying to do two jobs at once."

"No. It's nothing like that. This just seemed like a little thing I could do more easily than she could."

"That's fine, then. Would you ask Emily to come in for a minute? Thanks. See you."

He saw Madras heading into the john and followed him.

"Big How. Keeping up with the dead?"

"Barely. Bill, do you think we're doing enough to solve Leo's murder?"

Madras stiffened, his face to the speckled wall. After an instant he said cheerfully, "Hey, I don't guess anybody's done enough until they find the guy. Why? You need some extra responsibility?"

"No. Of course not. But, well, doesn't Gerry want us all to be working on it?"

"Gerry? Sure. The way he wants us all to do *pro bono*."

"I didn't know we did *pro bono*."

"We don't. Get it?" He walked to the sink and turned the water on. "See, every year or so the subject of legal services for the poor comes up. All the partners say what a fine thing it is. They encourage everybody to do absolutely as much *pro bono* as is compatible with getting our other work done. So we do. Which is zero." He turned off the water and turned to Howard with a paper towel in his hand. "I guess you could say Leo's sort of *pro bono* now. How art the mighty fallen." He shook his head as he threw the towel at the trash. "See you, How."

He was surprised that a homicide inspector had an address in Hillsborough. On the way over he suddenly realized. She probably had a husband, even kids. God, why hadn't he thought of that before? He imagined making conversation with some big, hearty stockbroker while a kid gummed a Zweiback and whined to be let out of his highchair. In French, whined in French, because this was the Peninsula. Maybe the food would be good.

Why was he spending another whole evening on this lousy investigation, anyway? It was turning into a huge time sink. Even if he had some talent for it. What was it getting him? It was pretty obvious Gerry's call to action had been bullshit from the very beginning. He was terminally naive.

Time to bail out, while he still had a law practice to attend to.

He arrived at a home containing a family that was probably very like the one he had imagined. Inspector Nelson lived in an apartment over the garage.

Well, he guessed it qualified as an apartment. It was actually a big room with a cubbyhole attached. The cubbyhole contained an unmade bed. The room had a white metal freestanding sink with a corrugated counter that looked like the toy his sister had when she was a kid. There was a hot plate sitting on top of a brown motel room refrigerator, and a card table with two folding chairs. Bread and Cheerios and a few cans sat in wooden boxes that had been turned on their sides.

There was a brown velveteen overstuffed chair that looked like a lot of dogs had slept in it, and a teak couch with faded green foam rubber cushions. A lot of what looked like camping and ski equipment was stacked

along the walls, along with a CD player playing
Beethoven's violin concerto. The walls contained several
nature photographs matted in metal frames.

The front wall of the room was floor-to-ceiling cur-
tainless windows, with a sliding glass door that opened
onto a wooden deck. Outside, he saw a hammock and
chaise longue and two kinds of bird feeder.

Sarah was wearing a shiny, mustard-colored dress
with a loose brown jacket.

"Listen," he said, "I hope you aren't offended, I felt
desperate to wear jeans tonight."

"Of course not. I just got home. Sit down a minute
and I'll change."

He chose the sofa. She reemerged from the cubbyhole rolling up the sleeves of a lavender and tan plaid
flannel shirt. The faded jeans hugged her butt. She was
barefoot.

"You like grilled cheese?" she said, bending low and
pulling a brick of cheddar from the little refrigerator.
"Otherwise, there's a deli about a mile from here, it'll
only take a few minutes."

"Grilled cheese is fine," he lied, and she turned on
the hot plate. He accepted Calistoga in the bottle.

"I have some news on the Bill Madras front," she
said, stirring butter in the pan. "Guess where he spent
last night."

"Liz?"

"Nope. Try a better neighborhood."

He thought a moment. "I don't know."

"Would you believe Portola Valley, consoling the
widow?"

"Come on. You're shitting me."

She smiled at the sandwich she was making.

"All night? With Nancy?"

"The tail didn't see who opened the door. But there

was a Ferrari Dino in the driveway. Madras got there about eleven and left this morning at six."

"This is unbelievably gross. I mean, Leo was a creep and all, but he had kids."

Sarah shrugged.

"And she's probably about ten years older than he is."

Sarah laughed at the sandwich, a little snort low in her throat.

"And he's repulsive. Isn't he? Don't you think so?"

"Oh, I don't know. On a scale of one to ten, with ten being a slobbering pervert, I'd say he's about a nine."

"I knew he was making an impression. Holy shit. I think you've got your guy."

"Well, there are problems. We have no reason to think he knew the murder technique. Also, he told me he was out that afternoon with a client and got back shortly before the party began. That would make it hard for him to have had time to kill him."

"But it has to be. It explains the will perfectly. Madras was trying to void the amended will so he and Nancy would get everything."

"I admit it has possibilities. I want to follow them both for another day or two. We'll have the Slyde house watched around the clock to verify who is there at night and who drives the Ferrari. I need to check her background, see if she could have taught Madras the tamponade stuff. And we need to check out his story about the client. Mind if we use paper plates?" She set his sandwich on the card table. "Go ahead and eat it. It won't be good if it's cold." She lifted the other sandwich with a spatula and plopped it into the hot skillet.

His sandwich was burned on one side, and he had to wait while the cheese cooled. In her jeans and bare feet she looked relaxed and easy, her hair seemed natural instead of ungovernable. It was the suits that created the discord.

No point in withdrawing his help now. There probably wasn't much more to do, anyway. "I can talk to
Madras about the will. It would make sense for me to be
concerned about it. I can just drop in on him without
giving him a chance to make something up."

"We'll see. So tell me"—she flipped the sandwich—
"what did you find out about Peter?"

"This is definitely boring after your news." He explained what he knew while she put her sandwich on a
plate and joined him at the table. He couldn't see if her
sandwich was burned. If it was, she didn't care. She was
munching with relish.

"Well," she said, "I guess that qualifies as a big
favor, even if it didn't work out. But what he said still
bothers me."

"How so?"

"He said, 'I love his guts.' What do you usually do
with people's guts?"

"Hate them."

"Exactly. And from what you say about Leo's reputation, that's a more likely sentiment. If this thing with
Madras doesn't fall into place soon, maybe I'll talk to
Bonifacio again. Also, it's time to go to Connie Valentine
directly. That wasn't much food. You want another one?"

"No. Thanks. That was fine."

She took his plate and threw it into the plastic garbage can under the sink. "You want an apple? Or a car-
rot?"

"Thanks, it'll be good for me to eat less for a change.
Can I ask you something? Was that thing ever alive?" He
pointed to the corner of the room.

"Oh. Yeah. It was a Christmas tree."

"This is May."

"I know. I missed the time you could put it out with
the garbage, and I can't seem to get to the dump on a
Saturday."

"I knew there was an explanation." He nodded at the walls." Did you take the photographs?"

"Um-hm."

"I've done photography a little. Mostly people. Where was that?" He pointed to a photograph of a pale-green ice chunk floating in a blue-black lake.

"That's Precipice Lake. It's in the Sierras, Sequoia National Park. The bird's a snowy owl, that was in Alaska. The monkey flower was here in the foothills."

"Is this all backpacking?"

"And some snow camping."

"You go with friends?"

"Once in a while. I go alone mostly. It's sort of people versus not-people. My whole job is listening, watching people, trying to understand people better than they understand themselves. Being alone on weekends gives me a chance to forget all that. I spread out and blend in with the rocks and trees. It makes me feel human."

"So the people make you feel inhuman, the rocks make you feel human. Maybe I should be spending more time with rocks."

She smiled. "What do you do for fun?"

"I cook. I go to ballet. There's a program up in the city tomorrow night I'm pretty excited about."

"Surely people don't like ballet."

"Of course people like ballet, Sarah, why do you think they pack themselves into those tiny little seats for huge sums of money?"

"In Chevy Chase it had résumé value."

"Chevy Chase sounds like a fun institution. But Chevy Chase doesn't own the ballet."

She shrugged.

"Did you say Chevy Chase, as in rich D.C. suburb?"

She nodded.

"And I don't get to ask, right?"

"What don't you get to ask?"

"How a woman brought up in a rich D.C. suburb ends up chasing murderers in California."

"Didn't we already discuss this?"

"You mean about living your own life." He considered her silent nod. "Not to belittle your narrative ability, Inspector Nelson, but I'm missing that hint of illuminating detail that brings a story to life."

She squinted as if to bring him into better focus.

"I can't help it," he said. "I think you're at least as mysterious as this murder you're trying to solve."

She shrugged. "I suppose it's as interesting as ballet. Want a glass of wine?"

"Did you grow up rich?" she asked when they were seated on her balcony. He shook his head. Night was blackening the space between pinpricks of stars, and the San Francisco Peninsula shimmered below them in the warm air. The wine tasted a little like soap.

"I did. I come from a family of Right People, we were brought up to do Right Things. In my case that meant marrying a rich investment banker or at least becoming a rich investment banker.

"For a long time I did what was expected. I was good at school, I went to Brown and studied economics, but at the same time I was good at literature, as Right People should be. I got a reputation for staying up all night to produce insights into *Dead Souls* or *Tristram Shandy*. I had an affair with a spoiled brat who probably turned out to be an investment banker somewhere down the line. I was on track.

"Then in my sophomore year a friend died. She fell from a second-story window in the middle of the night and landed on her head. None of the explanations made sense. It was probably a freak accident, except that the window ledge was more than a foot wide and it was hard to see how somebody could fall out. People talked about suicide, but who would try to kill herself by jumping from a second-story window? Homicide seemed out of the question, partly because her roommate was asleep in the room, partly because who would be stupid enough to push somebody out a second-story window?

"She lay in a coma for three days until her family decided to pull the life support. The second day I went to see her. . . . This happened at the end of May, during finals. I called home. I told my mother about seeing her in the hospital, and when I finished she said, 'Sarah, I hope this doesn't mean you're neglecting your studies.'"

"That's all she said?"

"Sensitive, wasn't it? That one remark triggered a dramatic change in my life. It summed up everything my parents had ever said to me. My feelings weren't just unimportant, they were dangerous because they might interfere with the accomplishment machine.

"My world unraveled like a big sock. I remember typing out my last paper of the semester with tears pouring down my face. I thought I was crying for Beth; it took me weeks to figure out I was partly crying for myself.

"I slowly realized that all the work I had ever done was intended to get me love and acceptance. I had never done one thing because I wanted to do it. And the big joke was it didn't work. I didn't just feel lonely. I felt like the only human being in the universe.

"I spent the summer at home working for a broker and hiding in my room. When I went back for my junior year I couldn't work. Identifying my motivation destroyed it, and nothing took its place. I came to a stop, I believed I would never do anything again. I've been shot at twice since I became a cop, and the terror of being shot at was less than the terror I felt that winter, sitting in my room, doing nothing, looking down on that dirty snow.

"At the end of the semester I got the hell out of there. I had a friend living in L.A., so that's where I headed. I got a waitress job at an IHOP, which was all right in some ways. I didn't have to ask myself why I was doing it, I was doing it to eat. It was physical and not cerebral, I liked that. I felt useful in a way. Hungry people, I brought them food. But you had to act friendly, and I wasn't feeling friendly.

"A lot of cops hung out at this IHOP. The owner gave them free coffee to keep them around. I got to know a couple of them, and one of them took me on police ride-along one day. The next day I did it again. The next day I applied to the police academy.

"It was a short-term thing, until I could figure out what I really wanted to do. After a couple of years it had gotten better instead of worse. I liked being responsible for my own life-and-death decisions out on the street. I liked being outside all day. I didn't have to smile when I didn't feel like it. I felt useful. Most of all I loved the adrenaline rush."

"You *liked* the adrenaline rush?"

She smiled at the glitter below them. "Sometimes after a scary chase you can feel it all down your arms, a tightening sensation. . . . For the first time in my life it was fun to do the thing itself.

"I've been doing it now for six years. Detective work is even better than street work, you get more time to think about motives. You get to piece together puzzles. You get shot at less. You get to watch from an unmarked car."

"These don't sound like the pleasures of Chevy Chase."

"There were no pleasures in Chevy Chase. Just the big myth that we were a Happy Family full of Right People, when the truth was that none of us could stand each other."

"What does your family think about you being a cop?"

"I imagine it embarrasses them. They dislike me for making them look like failures. At least I'm out here in California. They can tell their friends I'm in law." She lowered her voice and raised her eyebrows. "'Well, you know, our Sarah is in law.'" He laughed, she was silent for a moment. "So what about you?"

"Not much to tell. My father never liked me much and then he died. But he had a loyal brother, so now my uncle stepped in and doesn't like me much. When he can spare the time."

"Why a lawyer?"

"God, who knows? My uncle's a lawyer, when he got ready to pull strings I guess those were the ones hanging over his desk. That's not right, I'm oversimplifying. I'd like estate planning if I could be good at it. It could work into managing some sort of foundation for the arts." They watched the lights for a moment in silence.

"You know," he said, "what I'd really like to do is have a restaurant up in the city. I don't want to manage it. I don't even want to cook every day. I just want to decorate it and put fun things on the menu and have interesting people come. Lovers. Famous playwrights. Maybe the mayor. I want lots of wonderful things to happen there. People to suddenly get to the bottom of things.

"Like, your family could come. Something in the wine, the candlelight, would allow you to say 'It's all just a big lie. We don't even know each other.' And they would say, 'We know, it's so lonely, what a relief.' And then you could all start over."

She kept her eyes on the lights below them. "Those'd be some special candles."

"I guess. It would be like three weeks of backpacking all in one evening."

"And what would you get to the bottom of?"

He should have expected it, a detective to the last.

"Oh, I don't know," he said cautiously. "Anyway, I don't have the money to open a restaurant, we'll all just have to stay confused. So, how did you get from L.A. to San Mateo?"

"Not a chance," she said. "Too long, too boring, too late."

"Well," Howard said, and stood up. "I guess we're on hold while you're putting the nails in Madras's coffin."

"Absolutely not. I'd still like to know about this tamponade stuff. Having one reasonable-looking suspect doesn't mean we should slow down. Give me a call late tomorrow and I'll let you know what we've got."

He paused in her doorway. "Thanks for letting me make contact with a human being tonight. These last few weeks have been tough."

"I've made them tougher, haven't I? I hope we can wrap this up in the next few days so you can get back to your real work."

And not see her again. "I guess I'm not in a hurry."

He couldn't find the deli she had been talking about. He stopped for a Big Mac.

19

The Once and Future Litigator

Howard snapped a card into his Rolodex and picked up motion *in limine* number four. Mary Belle entered without knocking.

"Listen, I think we've got problems."

"Hey, I know we've got problems, Mary Belle. Which one is troubling you? The motions *in limine*? The Caenfetti trust. He's fired us and gone to Brobeck." She shook her head impatiently.

"I'm afraid this is a new one, Howard. And it's my fault. You know the Broll probate? You remember one of the sons lives in Frankfurt? Well, the notices went out like they were supposed to, only the Frankfurt Broll won't find out about the hearing until about two months after it's over. I put the wrong postage on it."

"You mean, like not airmail?"

"That's what I mean. The whole notice is screwed up, and we're too late to renotice it in time for the court date."

"Well. How long ago did this happen?"

"Tuesday. I can't believe I didn't catch it for two days. I feel like a real fuck-up."

"Hey, don't worry about it. Call the court and get a new hearing date. It's only a matter of a few days. Then we'll renotice it with a cover letter from me, saying we screwed up on our overseas notice. Do you have time to call the court today? Can you draft the letter?"

"I'll do it right now, Howard. I'm really sorry."

Apparently she was sorry. He got to be Howard for a whole day.

At four-thirty he was waiting for a call from word processing that motion *in limine* number six was done. Probably either Jill or Liz was working on it. He called Jill.

"Jill, I don't want you to say anything, but do you have a minute to listen?"

"Yes."

"I called that detective and told her about Leo and Cal. She said she was going to follow up on it, she'd get

back to me if she needed more details. She said she
didn't need to know who overheard it, at least for now.
And she told me to thank the person for coming forward.
Isn't that pretty perfect?"

"Yes. Thanks."

"Now I need a favor, I think it's a little one. Do you
remember telling me at your birthday party about Mary
Belle screwing up some big case? I'd like to know what
case it was. Do you know?"

"No."

"Could you find out for me?"

"Yes."

"That would be great. I don't mean to be cloak and
dagger, but I really don't want anybody but you to know
I'm asking. And I don't want Mary Belle to know anybody's asking. She's enough of a pill already."

Jill laughed. "Would you believe I noticed? Don't
worry. I'll take care of it."

"Thanks a lot, Jill. I'll let you know if I hear anything
else from the detective. Are you doing my motion *in limine*?"

For two days he had been terrified of picking up his
phone and finding Caenfetti on the other end. He was
extremely relieved that it was Gerry Tweedmore. Gerry
wanted to stop by Howard's office, if that was all right.
He was carrying a file.

"Howard, I've got a little trial coming up in two
weeks, I wondered if you'd like to handle it with me."

"A trial . . ."

"Straight trial work. Discovery is closed, of course.
I'll tell you why I'm thinking of you. I know you came
here to do estate planning, and I expect that's going to
work out fine. But you've been doing some litigation,
and I hear you've done a pretty good job. I don't see how

it could hurt to get some real trial experience just in case you need litigation for backup somewhere down the line."

So Gerry thought estate planning would go to hell without Leo pushing it. Howard was half afraid of the same thing.

"Well, certainly there's nobody I would like to do a trial with as much as you, Gerry . . ."

"I've talked to Tom about it, it's definitely going to be hard on him. But he has your interests in mind, and he agrees with me that it might be good for your career. He's agreed to keep estate planning afloat by himself for the next couple of weeks."

"Do you think I can learn the material fast enough?"

"I'm sure you can. It's going to take some work, and you'll have to make time for it. The way I handle something like this is I triage. Do you know what triage is?"

Howard shook his head.

"You sort all your responsibilities into three piles. One pile is the matters that can make it for a couple of weeks with no attention at all. Set those aside and forget about them until after the trial. One pile is for matters that are in such bad shape that even working on them for the next two weeks can't save them. Hopefully, you haven't got any of those.

"The third pile is things that will be all right only if they get attention in the next two weeks. When you get that pile stacked up, see how much of it Tom could step in and handle. The rest you're stuck with. Hopefully there won't be much. Then you can give pretty much your full attention to the trial.

"You certainly won't have time for extras. For example, I think your extracurricular stuff will have to go on hold for a bit. What do you say?"

What could he say? Gerry was considered the best teacher in the office, the exact opposite of Leo. Where would he get the energy to prepare an entire trial in two weeks?

"Well . . . if you're sure Tom doesn't mind."

"Good. Let's get some coffee, and we can get started this evening."

Jill knocked on his door. The yellow square stuck on the front of his motion *in limine* said "CompuStar."

He arrived breathlessly at the opera house at five minutes to eight. His uncle had told him Sandra was "a looker," which Howard translated as "not visibly deformed." It was perfectly okay with him. He placed himself in the same category, and was much too tired to battle a disadvantage. Anyway, they were box seats, and the music was going to be great. Evelyn Cisneros was doing *Swan Lake,* and they were doing the Joffrey piece, "Round of Angels." He took the steps two at a time, looking for the maroon-and-black bag she would be holding in her left hand.

She radiated good health and sophisticated sex. Her dress was something tight-fitting, low-cut, and black that rustled with irritation as she turned to the sound of her name.

"Yes," she said as the bell rang. "You're miserably late. We better move on it."

She led Howard up the stairs and into the box as the lights dimmed. Theirs were the two seats in front. At the first intermission she planted her bare arms firmly on the balcony and leaned out to survey the crowd.

"I'm sorry I was late," he said to her profile. "Things at work got pretty crazy at the last minute."

"No harm done," she said coldly. "Now we have a few minutes to be seen." Her manner let him wonder whether her remark was self-mocking. "My father didn't tell me what you do."

"I'm a lawyer."

"I thought about being a lawyer. It was what my father wanted, of course. But then I took the MCATs for a lark and decided I couldn't waste the scores."

"Then you're in medical school."

"Stanford. I'll do neurosurgery." As she swung her head her black ponytail brushed her naked shoulders. "But tell me about you. What kind of law?"

"Estate planning. Oh, and trials apparently."

"If I were a lawyer I'd definitely do trials. Medicine has no equivalent. So I dabble in Savoyards in my spare time. Whatever spare time is for a medical student."

"Savoyards. Is that the Gilbert and Sullivan group on campus?"

She looked at him for the first time. "Maybe you've seen me. I was Yum-Yum in *The Mikado*."

As it happened he had seen her, the night Peter was there. She had been good.

"No," he lied. "I don't go to theater much."

"Well," she said, "you'll have another chance. I just got the part of Josephine in *H.M.S. Pinafore*."

"Really," he said. "How about the ballet? Have you seen the Joffrey piece before?"

"Wasn't Robert talented? I play tennis with his niece, which is how we managed to get these incredible seats. Unfortunately, I just haven't been able to use them much this season, now that I'm doing my residency and working with the Physicians for Social Responsibility."

"Really. What are you doing with them?" What were they doing behind that curtain, resanding the floor? She was describing the talks she had given after touring the Bikini Islands when the curtain rose.

Joanna Berman danced "Round of Angels." By the second intermission he was feeling expansive. Maybe they could start over. He bought her a drink at the bar.

"Do you mind if we stand over here by the stairs?" he asked. "I love to watch all the fancy clothes."

Somehow they had gotten onto whether she owed it to society to have children. Suddenly she said, "Would you look at that?"

A woman in her sixties with bright round spots of rouge on her cheeks was working her way toward them in a full-skirted green dress with a gigantic sequined bow across her chest. What the hell, it was a chance to connect. Their heads were bent together giggling when he saw Sarah.

She was smiling, almost shyly, her shoulder against the speckled wall by the far exit. She was wearing jeans, and her fists were deep in the pockets of a brown corduroy bomber jacket. The roaring chatter of the crowd accentuated her stillness. She followed their gaze to the woman in green and back again, then pulled her hand from her pocket and wiggled her fingers hello.

Grinning foolishly, feeling the heat rise into his face, he wondered what disturbances in the natural order had brought this police inspector to this particular ballet. He wanted to believe he was somehow responsible.

He raised his eyebrows and turned his palms up to say "What are you doing here?" She smiled and shrugged just as Sandra wrapped her hands around his elbow and leaned toward him. He felt himself blush as Sarah's calm gaze appraised Sandra. He responded to Sandra's remark and turned back to see a bomber jacket disappearing through the door.

"Listen," he said, covering Sandra's hands as a prelude to disengaging them. "I'll be back in a . . ." The lights blinked. "Oh. Never mind. It's not important."

Sandra, still on his elbow, steered him back to their seats.

"Come with me to a party," she said as they made their way up the aisle after the performance. He was staring stiffly ahead, searching the perimeter of his vision for Sarah.

"A party? I don't think—"

"Linda Joffrey might be there, she could introduce you to this Cisneros lady. And I want you to meet some friends of mine. You look tense, you could use some fun. Doctor's orders." She hailed a cab.

The party was in a mansion on Nob Hill. He followed her up a staircase into a dimly lit, loud room.

"Look there's Matia."

"Who?"

"The blond in the corner who looks like a Greek god. Matia!"

The Greek god's eyes bounced off Howard like a handball off a cement wall. "Where have you been, Sandra? This has been a bloody bore. Come on, Tony has a new song he's dying to inflict upon you." He took her by the elbow and pushed her into the crowd.

Howard found a spot by the bookcase where he could see when the phone was free. Whoever owned this place was big on Garcia Marquez. He picked up one of his novels and started thumbing through it.

"Ah," said a voice behind him. *"Cien Años de Soledad."*

It was Matia, apparently banished by Sandra to keep Howard company. She was standing in a crowd doing some kind of joke with balloons. She bent to hold one balloon at each knee and shouted, "Kneesles!" The crowd barked its approval.

"Yeah," said Howard. "I guess so. Only it looks like this guy found a translation."

"I never read translations. I think it's disgusting to have some nobody's interpretation stand between myself and the artist."

"I guess I see your point. I've often wondered if *Light in August* would have made sense if I'd read it in the original."

Matia frowned. "But of course Faulkner wrote in English."

"No shit. Maybe I better stick to translations. Would you excuse me, I see the phone's free. And tell Sandra I said thanks. For everything."

Sarah didn't answer.

He called a cab and escaped down the steps into the dark.

20

Four to Tango

She called him the next evening. "Howard, it's Sarah. Can you talk?"

"Sarah. Hi."

"We got the results of the tail. The Ferrari is definitely Nancy's. The only other people in the house are two little boys and a nanny-type person in her sixties."

"Well, what do you think? You think that's conclusive?"

"I hope so." Sarah laughed. "Unless he's kinkier than I like to think about."

Howard was silent. She was going to take him up on his offer to talk to a murderer.

"Howard, you don't need to talk to him unless you want to. I think there are good reasons to see him myself, tomorrow."

"No. I want to do it. But I'm nervous. What if we're wrong and he just laughs at me? What if we're right, and he decides to kill me in the office, too? Never mind, don't answer that, I know he won't."

"I think we should wire you for sound. That way, I can be in the parking lot and listen, just in case."

He considered. "You know what, I think it would give me stage fright. I'll be all right. I'll be fine. Listen, about last—"

"Ope. Hold on a minute." He heard her cover the receiver. "Howard, I've gotta run. Do we need to talk again before you see Madras?"

"No. No problem. I'll you tomorrow night."

Zatopa dropped the stack of résumés heavily onto Inspector Nelson's desk. She looked up.

"Nothing, Sam," he said. "The only one who even talks about medical training is the veterinarian. Oh, and that Mary Belle Strick lists her CPR certification."

"No luck with prior experience?"

"About a third of the people don't have any. The others all seem to be U.S. Attorney or some business law firm. Nobody's been with a firm that does medical mal, at least according to those books you told me about. One guy has done insurance defense, but that may just be fender benders. I've got the firm's phone number. I can call and ask."

"Thanks." She nodded, rubbing her eye. "You'll be pleased to know that Bonifacio's girlfriend was right where she was supposed to be when Slyde was killed. L.A.P.D. confirmed that she was on a thirty-six-hour rotation in UCLA hospital that started at seven A.M. on the day of the murder and didn't end until the next night. They interviewed the interns who worked with her."

"Something will turn up. I hear you're getting grief about that surveillance."

"Some. We have to keep on it, though."

"I think what's bothering the boss is it's only about half effective, anyway. I mean, we can't follow him into the law firm every morning."

"Yeah," she said. "I know what's bothering the boss. The same thing is bothering me."

"How come he's letting a civilian get this involved? I think we're skating out over the edge of the canyon this time."

"Maybe we are. Look, Andy, it's late. Don't bother making that last phone call tonight. Why don't you get some rest? I need to make sense out of this autopsy report."

Madras wasn't there. His secretary, Linda, said he was due any minute. Howard said no message.

At ten-thirty Madras's office was still dark. Howard stopped at the bookshelf a little way down the hall and flipped through something incomprehensible.

At eleven the door was closed. He could hear Madras talking on the telephone. His heart pounded in his ears all the way back to his office, where he dialed Madras's extension. Still busy. A few minutes later, still busy. A few minutes later it rang and he hung up.

"Mary Belle, I'm going to see Bill Madras for a few minutes."

"So? You need a map?" She didn't look up.

"No, just, well, in case you need me, I'll be in Madras's office, all right?" She shrugged.

When he got over there Madras was on the phone again. Linda was watching him curiously.

"Why don't you hold on a minute?" she said, and glanced at her telephone console. "I think this one is short."

"Thanks. I'll be right back." He went for a drink of water. Why had he let Sarah drag him into this? Hadn't done a damn thing all morning, being led around by his gonads. But there was more to it than that. Would Madras think fast? What was he going to say?

When he got back, Linda shook her head.

"Still talking. Oh, wait. There. He hung up."

Howard knocked on the door and Madras called out. He stuck his head in.

"Bill, have you got a minute?"

Madras glanced up and then continued working on a document in front of him. "Hey, Big How, wish I did," he said to the document. "Can Linda take care of it?"

Howard lowered his voice. "Uh, actually, it's about Liz."

Madras looked up from the document and frowned. "Liz who?"

"Liz Christ. The word processor."

"Don't know her."

"Uh, I'm pretty sure that's not right. I know about the will."

Madras stared at him blankly for a moment, then put down his pen. "Come in. Close the door." He watched Howard perch nervously on the edge of a chair. "Now, what's this about a will?"

"Leo's will. I know she changed it. And I know she's been talking to you about it."

Madras squinted at him for several seconds. "Yeah," he said, "All right. She told me what she did for Leo, I advised her to come clean. Maybe it won't even cost her her job."

"You told her to come clean?"

"Is there an echo in here? Well, first I told her to let it go. I mean, the main thing is that's what Leo wanted, he just went about it in a screwy way. But she's worried about you, thinks you could be in trouble for it, and, hey, she's right. So I told her to come clean and say Leo told her to."

"*Leo* told her to change the will so that it's only effective if his wife is dead?"

"Hell of an echo. She just inserted whatever language he gave her. At least that's what she says and I assume it's true. Why else would she do it?"

"Well, how about because you told her to?"

Madras barked a laugh. "Listen, pal, I don't know why I'm even talking to you about this. I don't know why I'm talking to *Liz* about this, except that she's a good kid. So if you'll excuse me. . . ."

Howard inhaled deeply, the way he'd been taught to do in speech class if you think your voice won't come out.

"How about Nancy Slyde? Is she a good kid?" He saw the muscles of Madras's jaw clamp and ripple. Then Madras whistled.

"Hey, Big How. You've done your homework."

"I'm just wondering what Nancy Slyde has to do with this."

"Well, we can't have you wondering. No, we can't. You want something to drink?" Howard shook his head, Madras buzzed Linda on the intercom and asked for a Coke.

"The fact is, Nancy is more than a nice kid. She's a nice piece. Also rich. I met her on the firm retreat last year. She got lonely when Leo was off on his business trips, so we started keeping each other company.

"A few months ago she started asking me questions about Leo's will. I didn't know a damn thing about it. He told her he didn't want one because he was superstitious. She thought he was lying, wanted me to find out. There's something about Nancy girl that makes you want to keep her happy, so I finally checked. She was right. There was a will, and you know what was in it, since Liz says you wrote it for him." Howard nodded.

"It was funny, she didn't care at all about Leo screwing Connie, but she was very upset about the bucks. Kept bugging me about it. I figured out that I could insert that one sentence, Leo would probably never notice the change, and *boom*! all the money was Nancy's again. Not bad for a venture capital man." Madras was smiling with satisfaction when Linda came in with the Coke.

"Well, Nancy thought I was great for thinking it up, and she wanted me to do it. I figured Leo was only thirty-three, in a way it didn't matter what the hell was in his will. I mean, Nancy and I might not be together forever anyway, and whenever I wanted I could change it back.

"This girl Liz sort of has the hots for me. So I got her to change it, I said Leo wanted it that way. I gave Nancy a copy and forgot about it. We went back to talking about more interesting things. Like me.

"Until last Thursday. When Leo got blown away, I freaked. I mean, what if Nancy had something to do with it? Which she couldn't have, I guess, I mean they say it had to be somebody who was there that afternoon. But I was scared to change it back, Liz would know it wasn't Leo this time. I was stuck." He shrugged, he was grinning. "What the fuck, it might as well be Nancy's money as Connie's. Nancy was his wife."

"But aren't you afraid somebody will think you killed Leo? I mean, now you get Nancy and her millions."

"Not a bad plan, is it? Only to tell you the truth, Nancy's a little old for me."

"You don't love her?"

"Well, yeah, I love her. I mean, I was screwing her, wasn't I?"

"You stopped?"

Madras looked away for a moment and scratched his forearm. "Well, I mean, now that Leo's gone and all. . . . I can't have her getting the wrong idea." He looked back. "Anyway, no matter what anybody thinks, I didn't kill the guy. If I have to I'm sure I can prove it. But I won't have to prove it, because nobody knows anything about this stuff."

"Well . . . but what if. . . ?"

"Right, let's do the what ifs. What if Liz tells somebody? She won't, but even if she did, she thinks we were both helping Leo. What if Nancy tells? You think of a reason for her to do that, let me know. What if you tell? Now, why would you want to do that, especially now that Liz insists on taking you off the hook?

"But reason or no, How, suppose you go ahead and try telling somebody we had this conversation. I'll deny it, I'll say you misunderstood me, I'll make you look like an unbelievable fuck-up. They'll listen to me instead of you any day. Hell, now that Leo's gone, I've got more billables than anybody here. By the time I'm finished telling my side of the story, whatever anemic little trickle of a career you have here will be finished."

He smiled at Howard, picked up his Coke by the top, and sucked noisily.

"So, Big How. What else have you been wondering about? I want to clear up any little doubts or worries right now."

"None. You've made it all pretty clear, I guess." Howard stood up.

"Good. You're off the hook, you can forget about it. I assume that's why you're bothering with this."

Howard shrugged.

"Unless you've got the hots for Liz. Or that broad on the police department." He watched Howard's face and smiled. "I see. Yeah, she's not bad." He winked. "Go for it. Just remember to leave me out, okay?"

Later, Howard blessed him for those last remarks. They mitigated his anguish over the decision not to be wired for sound.

Connie Valentine's secretary watched the lights on her console until Connie was off the phone, and then opened the door for Inspector Nelson.

"Good morning, Ms. Valentine. Thank you for taking the time to talk to me."

"Well, in fact"—she glanced at a large clock on her wall—"I haven't much time to give. I'm due in a deposition in seven minutes. Perhaps we should get to the point."

"Yes," Sarah said, and sat in a tan chair with pink threads. "Can you tell me why you were made a substantial beneficiary in Mr. Slyde's will?"

If Connie Valentine revealed surprise, it was by showing too little affect rather than too much. Her eyes remained on the clock face for an instant, then recentered on Sarah's face. No other muscle moved for at least thirty seconds. Then she sighed and let her eyes flick down to her blotter and back again.

"No. That is, yes, I know the reason. Please excuse me, this is very . . . unexpected."

"You didn't know you were a beneficiary?"

"No. I didn't know, and I wouldn't have agreed to it. It isn't fair to Nancy."

"Were you and Mr. Slyde personally involved?"

"Is Nancy going to find out about this?"

"Not from me. But of course you know the will is going to be made public in a matter of days. She will probably have her suspicions."

"Why did he do this? Of course, it's very sweet of him. . . . Yes, Leo and I were involved. Not very smart, I know. But you may know this yourself, Inspector, it isn't always possible to be business and nothing else."

Sarah smiled. "How long had the affair been going on?"

"About a year."

"Was it still going on at the time of his death?"

"Yes. We both knew we should break it off, of course. For a lot of reasons. I just couldn't do it." She shrugged and smiled, almost shyly. "I guess I'm just drawn to power." She paused. "Inspector, I see what you're getting at. But even if I had known about the will, I wouldn't have wanted the money. I make plenty of money of my own. I wanted Leo's company much, much more. Oh, dear. By trying to be nice, Leo has put me in kind of a bad spot, hasn't he?"

"It does give you a motive."

"But surely there are other beneficiaries. Each of them has just as much motive as I have. Or are my morals more suspect because I'm the other woman?"

"I wouldn't think so. Tell me one other thing if you can. Did Mr. Slyde have any reason to be afraid of you?"

Connie Valentine raised her eyebrows and tilted her head. "None, I assure you. Leo Slyde had less reason to be afraid of me than anybody I can think of."

"Well, you may have preferred to be discreet about your involvement with Mr. Slyde, but he obviously didn't share your preference. I think they said the will would be made public in a week. You may want to consider how its provisions will affect the people around you and be prepared."

"I certainly will do that. I know you didn't come here as a favor to me, but I still appreciate the warning."

Sarah stood up to go. "I like your office. It isn't the standard Tweedmore and Slyde issue."

"No"—she smiled—"it isn't. This stuff is all custom-made, a little smaller than standard, did you notice?"

"You know, I did feel a little . . . off, somehow."

"That's exactly what's supposed to happen. I figure this is my domain, why not make it my size? These big, macho guys come in here to push me around, and they're thrown off balance by it, they feel out of their element, unwieldy. A simple trick, but it seems to help."

"Well, whatever your methods they must be effective. I understand congratulations are in order."

"Yes," said Connie Valentine, and Sarah saw the

polished eyeteeth. "T and S's first woman partner. I can tell you it feels very good."

Howard took the Steele will to word processing and stopped in at Burger King for another savory lunch. When he got back there was a book on his chair with a note.

> Howard—
> Here is the Red Cross CPR manual that we got in class. I really recommend that you sign up for classes yourself, and not try to rely on this alone. Let me know if you have any questions, I took some notes during the classes that nobody can read but me.
> Have fun.
>
> Sally

He set his burger and fries out on the Burger King bag and started flipping through the manual. It was a spiral-bound looseleaf entitled *Red Cross CPR Module*. He checked the index for "tamponade" and "pericardiocentesis," the buzzwords Sarah had given him. It was obvious that nothing nearly as medical-sounding as those terms was anywhere in the manual. Next he turned to the chapter entitled "Single Rescuer CPR" and started to read. It was set up like a decision matrix: If he's not breathing then do one thing, if he's breathing get this other information, etc. No reference to any invasive procedure. The manual stressed again and again the need to get professional help as soon as possible. Dead end.

Somehow, he'd like to get Sally to look at her notes to see whether anything like tamponade was mentioned, but it seemed unlikely. He'd take the manual home and go through it completely, but the answer seemed obvious. Whoever learned to do pericardiocentesis learned it from something more sophisticated than a CPR course.

They had agreed that he would phone Sarah at eight P.M. He told her every detail he could remember about the Madras conversation. When he finished she said, "Shit."

"What do you mean, shit? Aren't you impressed with my interrogating abilities?"

"Mm. You think he did it?"

"Well, I'm not so sure. He didn't seem very shy about telling me all the rotten things he was doing. Why tell me all that stuff and not tell me that he murdered him, too?"

"I agree. That's one reason I said shit."

"What's the other one?"

"We checked out his story about being with a client. The client confirmed it. I was hoping the client was lying, but now this . . ."

"I'll tell you one thing, the guy definitely has class. He reminds me of a frat brother I used to have who ate spaghetti through his nose."

"You had a frat brother?"

"Yeah, my uncle told me I should join a fraternity so I wouldn't be lonely. Guess how well it worked." He wished she was there, on his sofa. "Anyway, I guess this means we should keep looking for other suspects, right?"

"Absolutely. I've got an appointment to see Cal Forman tomorrow."

"Listen," he said, "before you go. About the other night, I don't want you to think . . . I mean, not that you care, but . . . That's not the kind of person I spend much time with."

"What kind of person? Beautiful women in expensive clothes?"

"Yeah. Sort of."

"Thank God I'm ugly. Maybe we can be friends."

"I didn't mean that." He heard her snicker. "Why are you so mean to me?"

"It goes with being ugly. What about the ballet?"

"Yeah, what about the ballet? After our conversation the other night that was the last place I expected to see you. What were you doing there?"

"Curiosity. I wanted to see if Chevy Chase owns the ballet."

"Does it?"

"Not clear. I mean, *Swan Lake*. Who cares if people can diddle around on their toes? Hey"—she blocked his protest—"I'm a cop. My idea of culture is a season subscription to mud-wrestling. But that other thing, 'Dance of Angels,' even I could tell that was about something. I suppose I'll go back eventually and find out what. In the meantime, I have something new for our investigation list."

"I'll bet it's the same thing I thought of. We go back to watching Nancy."

"Exactly. Let's see if there's anybody else at your firm who likes to keep Nancy happy."

21

Sharks Bearing Gifts

Inspector Nelson heard a muffled "yes" in response to her knock, and cracked the door open. Cal Forman waved her into his office with his whole arm, several times, without looking at her, his chin holding a phone receiver against his left shoulder. "Um-hm. Um-hm. Um-hm."

As soon as she was inside his office he stopped gesturing and held his hand suspended above his right ear.

"Yeah. Dave? She's not—Dave. Dave. She's not going to take you to the cleaners, we aren't going to let that happen. Dave. Are you listening to me? Finish up your business over there, nothing's going to happen in the next few days you have to worry about. I'll call her lawyer." He motioned to Sarah to take a seat in a gray and tan plaid arm chair, still without looking at her.

"Yeah, I know him. He's not too bad. Finish up your business, as soon as you're back we'll sit down and go over this. When you getting back? Saturday when? You wanna meet then? No, I don't mind. You got my home phone? Fine. Dave? How's London? It's gonna be all right. See ya." He hung up and stared at the phone.

"Right." He looked at Sarah for the first time and grinned broadly. "Ms. Nelson, is it? I'm Cal Forman. What's up?"

"Mr. Forman, I'm with the San Mateo police department. I'm here about the Leo Slyde murder. It was reported to our department that you and Mr. Slyde were arguing violently one morning a couple of months before the murder."

"Hell, yes. Only once?" And Forman laughed wildly. "I can't believe they only heard us *once*. We must have been whispering the other times." He laughed again, loud and long, until Sarah felt herself blushing. He looked pleased.

"I take it then you argued quite a bit?"

"As often as I could spare the time. You want to know if I killed him? The answer is no. I was in court."

"Yes, I know that. But this particular occasion that was reported to us took place at about five o'clock in the morning. Can you remember what you were arguing about?"

"At that particular time, no. Five in the morning. That probably sounds stranger than it is. Leo and I both work pretty long hours sometimes. When was that, January? Was that when Peter left? Or when he wanted to come back? Yeah, I think that's what it was."

"Peter Bonifacio?"

"Yeah. Smartest guy we ever had in the department. And we lost him. Damn shame."

"And you blamed Leo for that?"

"It's not a question of blame, Leo just did it, that's all. You want the story?"

"Please."

The phone rang and he got up and opened the door. "Lisa? Take my calls, will you please?" He wore a tan linen suit with a pale-blue shirt. He came back and sat down.

"The thing about Peter, he's very, very bright, but he's not much good in court. He gets a little too excited. See, Peter originally thought he wanted to do corporate law. But after a month or two we realized he was brilliant at taking a body of law, boiling it down to the essence, and presenting it to the court. Finest legal writer this firm has ever seen. So he decided to do litigation.

"But he wasn't comfortable in court. He'd go, but he didn't ask to do it, kinda hung back. For the first couple of years he didn't get much experience. One day we were going to court on a summary judgment motion, and I told him it was his. I was just gonna sit there.

"Well, it started off okay. For a first-time major court appearance he wasn't doing bad. He was nervous, but who wouldn't be?

"Then the judge started asking some questions that were kind of off-the-wall, and by the way Peter answered them you could tell he was getting frustrated. That's not good. The first rule of courtroom practice is that the judge is brilliant, maybe you just haven't explained yourself very well. But the client didn't look worried. I figured we'd get through it okay.

"Then Peter was referring to some of the evidence, and the judge, Judge Reed here in San Mateo County, interrupted him and said, 'But that's hearsay, isn't it?' Well, the lawyers on the other side started nodding, and to tell you the truth I was sorta nodding, too, it did seem like hearsay if you didn't think about it much. And Peter lost control.

"'Hearsay?' he said, grabbing the table, and his eyebrows went all the way up to his hairline. 'Did I understand your Honor to say HEARSAY?'

"I jumped up and started pulling Peter by his coatsleeve. I couldn't even slow him down.

"'You are a judge? Your job is to discern subtle legal distinctions, and you think a statement by a party to the contract that he will accept eighty cents on the dollar is HEARSAY?'

"Well, the judge came down on his bench with the gavel like he was going to break it in two and screamed 'Out of order!'

"'Your Honor,'" I said. 'We beg your pardon. We really, really beg your pardon. We submit on the papers.' And I got Peter outta there before the judge slapped sanctions on him. The client was so white he almost fainted, and the next day the judge issued a one-sentence ruling denying our motion."

"Was it hearsay?"

"Of course not. But what good did that do us? Well, we held Peter back a few months and then sent him in again. Different judge, up in San Francisco. That one was fine. For a while everything was fine. But then a few months later he did it again. Called Judge Demeroux 'gormless,' which he is, and which really pissed him off because somebody had to tell him what it meant. That time Peter did get sanctions, and we lost the client.

"That was a couple of years ago. So after that you can appreciate we didn't send Peter into court very often. Hell, we were afraid he might wind up in jail. So instead he loaded the bombers. We put him in teams. The other guy'd do all the court appearances, and Peter was in charge of the law. He did the research, wrote the briefs, told the mouthpiece what to say. We tried some successful lawsuits that way. Very successful.

"Then about eight or nine months ago Peter shows up in my office and tells me he's switching departments, going to work for Leo. I could not believe what I was hearing. Trademarks or some damn thing.

"I tried talking to him, tried to figure out what was going on in his mind. He was five years out of school, another two, three years at most to partnership, and by switching he was practically starting over again. I didn't get any straight answers, he wanted to do it and so he did.

"So Peter went over to Leo's group, and about six months later I get this little knock on my door. Peter comes in and clicks his pen a few times and asks me for his old job back. The trademark work wasn't developing the way Leo had hoped, and Leo had no more use for him.

"I asked him what promises Leo had made to get him over there in the first place. He said no promises, he just didn't think he had any alternative. I asked him what in the hell he was talking about.

"So it turns out Leo and Peter had this secret meeting. Once a year the partnership meets to talk about senior associates and make decisions about new partners. Very secret and hush-hush, even though it's all bullshit. So after the one last, let's see, a year ago February, or anyway just before Peter left, Leo went in and closed Peter's door. He sidled up and slapped him on the back a few times, and told him the partnership had decided he could never be a litigation partner because he didn't know how to handle himself in court. In another year or two he was on his way out."

"Leo wasn't supposed to tell him that?"

"It wasn't true. It was just a big damn lie. I've got a whole department full of people who can handle themselves in court. Knowing what to say is much more difficult. We needed Peter. We'd be a better department today if we still had him.

"So then Leo told Peter how sorry he was, and by the way there might be one last chance for him. Leo needed a trademark guy, no court appearances at all, just advising the clients and doing the searches or whatever the hell they do. But it all had to be very confidential. Leo would be in big trouble if the partners found out he was leaking information out of the meetings.

"You wanna know what was really going on? Leo had some kind of short-term crunch over there and didn't think we'd lend him an associate. See, that's the kind of guy Leo was. Can you imagine doing something like that to a young person's career?

"Unfortunately, I just couldn't take Peter back. The people in our department were sour on him for leaving, and he made a very bad impression with some of our clients while he was working for Leo. I'd hired another guy, the veterinarian, to replace him. All I could do was express myself fully to Leo, which I did. As you know."

"I take it you aren't particularly sorry to see Leo out of the partnership."

"Hell, yes, I'm sorry. We were partners for several years. If you're gonna swim in shark-infested waters, it doesn't hurt to have one shark swimming on your team. He may take a little bite now and then, but you'll manage to keep afloat."

"Did Peter realize what Leo had done?"

"We sorta figured it out together. He told me what Leo said, I told him what a big damn lie it was."

He was silent a moment. "Lousy shame. But Peter'll land on his feet. Hell, he's been in worse positions. He very nearly became a goddamn horny monk!"

She waited, smiling, while his laugh subsided.

"Wait a minute. You don't think Peter killed him."

She said nothing.

"Bonifacio?" He raised his eyebrows and slapped the leather on the arms of his chair, enjoying himself. "The guy who almost became Father What-a-Waste? It's a good thing I was in court. You'd really be after me." He laughed wildly. "Am I wrong? See, when I get mad you know it immediately. I swear, carry on, my kids think I'm one hell of a wild man.

"Now, after my stories about Peter you might have the wrong impression. He does get sorta crazy in court. But outside the courtroom, in the six years I've known him I've never once seen him so much as raise his voice. He gets mad, he just hunches down in his suit and clicks his pen a few times. Does that sound like a guy who'd walk right into Leo's office in the middle of the day, with about thirty-five people within shouting distance, and kill him there on the spot?

"But what do I know? I'm just a lawyer, and plenty of people tell me I'm not even good at that. Well, Ms. Nelson, what else?"

"Any idea who might have killed Leo?"

"Nope." Cal swung his head back and forth like a huge bell. "Not at all. No idea." The bell sounded at every swing. "Nope. Nope. Leo was bad, but he wasn't bad enough to kill. At least not in my book. Evidently somebody disagreed with me." He giggled. "Yes, sir, somebody didn't share my assessment.

"Leo represents a real Silicon Valley type of individual. Somebody told me once, 'Don't get caught in the desert with Leo and only one cup of water.' I'll tell you something." Cal shook his index finger rhythmically and gently. "That guy missed the point. He should have said, 'Don't get caught in the desert with Leo and only one oasis.' Leo Slyde was a very thirsty bastard."

He laughed, softly this time, his eyes locked onto hers, then dropped his hands into his lap.

"Well, Ms. Nelson, what else? That it? Good luck."

That morning Howard filled in the squares on his monthly chart for every day up to trial. When it turned out that some of the squares weren't big enough, he walked over to the bakery for a butterhorn just to calm down. Then he started on the four hours he had allotted himself for reading the deposition transcript of the plaintiff's real estate valuation expert and preparing cross-examination.

After two hours his notes were barely legible even to him. Every couple of pages he would realize that he'd been concentrating on how far behind he was instead of the content of the transcript, so he'd have to flip back and start over. He was irrationally relieved to hear a loud knock, then see Candy Gilley swing open the door, saying ". . . not his keeper, Mary Belle. I'll ask him myself."

"It's all right, Mary Belle," he called through the open door. "I forgot. Candy and I do need to talk for a minute."

"You bet we do, Howard Rickover," she said, slamming the door. "All I've been hearing for the last two days is gossip about Connie and Leo having some big affair. I'm sick of it."

"Wait a minute, I had nothing to do with spreading rumors. I've been cloistered in here, I haven't even *heard* any rumors."

"Yeah, well I've heard enough for both of us. I told you, Leo hated her. I even remembered, it had something to do with his island."

"He hated Connie because of his island? What did she have to do with his island?"

"That's all I remember. He said something else, but, to tell you the truth . . ." She giggled suddenly. "I was having a little trouble concentrating. Right while he was telling me, he was—"

"Stop! I don't want to hear this."

She hesitated, frowned, and then shrugged. "Have it your way. But I'm telling you, it was fantastic. He got that little Mazda for half what it would have cost another man. Anyway, they weren't having an affair, and if I hear one more person say they were I'll freak." She dropped into his chair and started crying.

"Well, that is pretty awful, I guess. But, in a way, as long as you know it isn't true, what difference does it make?"

"It's so insulting to me."

"But they don't know anything about you. And you want to keep it that way, right? I mean, do you want them gossiping about you and Leo the way they're gossiping about Connie?"

"Of course not." She sniffed. "It's disgusting."

"I agree. So be glad you and Leo had something private, special, just for the two of you. Let them waste their smirks on something that never happened. Here. Use my handkerchief. Oh, wait. You know what? I think it's been in here since you used it last time. Tell you what, how about a Kleenex?"

Mary Belle brought him three letters as soon as Candy left. "If you keep sending women out of your office with red eyes, I'm going to change my opinion of you."

"I didn't know it could get any worse."

"It couldn't. I was thinking of revising it upward."

Poor Candy. He just hoped she never found out about the will. Stinking bastard didn't care who he hurt, right up to the last.

22

Sally's Imagination

"Inspector Nelson. Do have a seat. How kind of you to come." His voice was gently mocking, but not, she thought, unkind.

"I don't know what it is about you, Mr. Bonifacio, I can't seem to stay away."

"By all means, indulge yourself. Would you like some coffee? I understand several people have tried it today and lived."

"Perhaps I'll skip it for now. Do you mind if we close the door?"

"Go right ahead. Sally has a boring job, I like to provide opportunities for her imagination." His office was spare. The only paper on his desk was a thick document he was marking with a red pen. There were a black pen and a pencil leaning awkwardly in a leather pencil cup. As she closed his door she saw that the coat that hung on a hanger had been buttoned, twice.

"I guess I should offer my condolences," he said as she sat down.

"Why is that?"

"I can only assume your investigation is going badly, if you're back to see me about that hunting fiasco again."

"I didn't come about that, although I admit I still

think about it from time to time. I talked with Cal Forman a couple of days ago." His hands were in his lap, she heard his pen click, twice, just below the burnished desktop.

"I see."

"I think I know now why you loved Leo's guts."

"I made an awful mistake using that phrase in connection with Leo. Do you read O'Neill? *Long Day's Journey* is one of his best."

"No, but I do listen to what people tell me. You'd be surprised how it helps."

"And now that you apparently know how Leo assisted my career, you suspect me of having killed him."

"You must admit that certain details keep pointing in your direction. The most recent is a motive, which you took some pains to conceal."

"Would you really have expected me to tell you? As you say, it could suggest a motive, and I hardly see the point in that. But that's not the main reason I didn't tell you, now that I think about it. You see, the entire episode is nearly unbearable to remember, much less to repeat. Coming somewhat late to the law, I was particularly eager to succeed here. As you now know, I proved to be fatally deficient."

"Well, I know that you've decided to look for another job."

"Is that what Cal said? How kind. In fact, I am now a thirty-six-year-old failed associate from Tweedmore and Slyde, facing Herculean effort to salvage my reputation and become a partner at a second-rate firm. I don't chat casually about that sort of thing, even to a charming detective."

"You must be furious."

"After talking to Cal, I admit I was irritated."

"Most people would be enraged."

"I'll tell you something that it cannot possibly be in

my interest to tell you. I am capable of a certain anger at times. For example, my . . . shall we say 'colorful' outbursts in court, directed at certain intellectual midgets. People who hold themselves out as being able to dispense answers when they don't know the rudiments of how to think. I myself worried a little after the hunting incident, whether it was some unconscious attempt to get even for the way Leo assisted in my demise. I might have believed it was, I half hope Leo thought so. But the fact is, I can't shoot well enough. *Certainly* not while falling into a ravine." He laughed, one spare little burst of sound, and shook his head. "And I made no attempt, conscious or unconscious, to stab him in his own office in the middle of the day. The very thought makes me call for my beta-blockers." He rapped his knuckles heavily on his wide chest. "I ultimately think you will realize that any lawyer in this firm would be more capable of such a feat than I would."

"I don't know what you mean."

"In spite of my rantings in court, I'm . . . hesitant, I guess you would say. Reluctant to act, constrained about confronting people. Perhaps it follows from my religious training. I thought this job would change that, require of me a certain, well, boldness. I thought that, in order to make partner here, I would necessarily become a little less unacceptable in the process. But, of course, that didn't happen."

"Do you at least like the work?"

"The analysis is fine. Unfortunately, I don't spend much of my time doing that. And there is too much of all of it. The much-touted pleasures of a job well done are very hard to experience. In order to do a marginally passable job, I've allowed the rest of my life to shrink to the point of nonexistence. On the whole, I hate it."

"Then why go to another law firm?"

"Why indeed? Theoretically, I am now free to do

whatever I like. Unfortunately, I have never figured out what that is. I can tell you, however, the possibilities do not include going to prison for a crime I didn't commit. Though it is a living, I suppose. Tell you what, if I'm still here in six months, let's talk."

"What were you doing when Leo was killed?"

"I haven't convinced you. Well, I'm flattered in a way. Let's see, what was I doing? I don't recall precisely what time the murder took place. I was here. I had just gotten back from Santa Barbara. I was almost certainly flirting with my secretary, Sally, about her red dress. I really like her red dress. Shall we ask her?"

"No need. By the way, your remark about the beta-blockers reminds me. Somebody mentioned that you have a fiancée in L.A. with medical training. Peter's neck suddenly became shorter; he rolled his shoulders.

"That's true. And I assure you, if I seem to be flirting with the women here at the firm from time to time, it means nothing, it's merely a joke." He turned his chin awkwardly, trying to escape from his tie. "It's, well, I like to think it's in the tradition of Woody Allen."

"Of course. I didn't mean to imply otherwise. I was just wondering, has she studied CPR?"

"CPR? Yes. I saw her use it once. Why do you ask?"

"Something about the way the murder was committed. I need to get an explanation from someone."

"Well, I'm sure there are people close at hand who could help you. I mean, why would you rely on—"

"Oh, no, of course not. I was just thinking out loud." She stood up. "I do appreciate your time, Mr. Bonifacio, and I'll try not to need it again."

"Please, Inspector, investigate me at your convenience," he said, walking her into the hallway. "Next time something more thorough, perhaps." From behind her typewriter, Sally laughed.

23

Lucky DeLuth

It was nine-thirty at night, and the jury instructions were going, well, they weren't going at all. Howard sat balancing the big red BAJI jury instruction book on the edge of his desk and staring at an instruction that read: "If evidence is offered in this case against one defendant, you may consider it in regard to that defendant only. Evidence offered against one defendant may not be used to determine the liability of any other defendant."

He couldn't decide whether that belonged in his case or not. If one of the defendants was a corporation, didn't the jury *have* to consider testimony against its officers in order to decide whether the corporation was liable? He kept reading the instructions before it and after it, trying to understand the context in which the instruction should be used.

And this was the easy part. Soon he would be out of the formbook entirely, trying to forge little nuggets of law culled from dozens of reported cases into an impermeable shield he and Gerry could carry into court on Tuesday. Only the little nuggets were resisting the heat of his intellect, refusing to meld into the comforting, shiny surface he had envisioned as he conducted research in the law library. Suddenly he had tens of cases to support all his inessential points, with naked gaps through which the opposition could send a full-dress regiment. And his fluorescent light was flickering, and his foot was falling asleep. As he flipped the page for the thirtieth time, the word CompuStar caught his attention.

It was written in the margin of his monthly chart, and for a moment he couldn't place it. Ah yes, Mary Belle's demise.

He walked out into Mary Belle's secretarial station and got out her files listing. Nothing under CompuStar. Then he checked the list of closed files and found dozens. Apparently the firm had lost the client entirely. All corporate stuff, with the exception of a single lawsuit, *DeLuth v. CompuStar*, billing attorney Gerry Tweedmore. And then a *John DeLuth Stock* file.

He copied the file numbers and went into the storage room for inactive files. He found the light switch. Maybe he could just pull the files now, as a kind of break, and then reward himself with looking through them when the first set of jury instructions was in word processing. Well, maybe he should take a quick look to make sure they were the right files.

It took a long time to piece together the story. After he did he certainly didn't believe it.

When she opened the door to her apartment something was wrong. Her dress wasn't ugly. It looked like something Katharine Hepburn would wear, with tailoring that led your eye from the wide shoulders to the narrow belted waist, and a V-shape across her hips where the skirt started. The pale, rough silk made her skin glow. She looked stunningly seductive.

Surely this couldn't be for his benefit. She seemed oblivious to any transformation in herself as he watched her cross from sink to table and back again, putting food on the table. Maybe it was like monkeys at a typewriter. If you bought enough random dresses one was eventually bound to look good. Especially if you were working with that body.

Certainly there was no transformation in the cooking. She dislodged an egg from the pan on her hot plate and handed it to him on a chipped turquoise dish. The egg was edged in black lace, and the yolk bobbed in a milky puddle. But he had foiled her. He opened the pastry box and pulled out a buttermilk doughnut.

"So tell me," she said, peering into the box. "Why are we interested in your secretary?"

He braced himself to taste the coffee. It was strong and rich.

"I told you the gossip about how Mary Belle got fired as Leo's secretary and ended up being mine. She was supposed to have made some huge mistake that cost the firm a lot of money. I found out it had to do with a client named CompuStar. Last night I read the file and it doesn't make sense. Do you know about founders' stock?"

She dipped her doughnut into her coffee. "Sure. Mine was sturdy peasant."

"Give me a break. People who come to work at these little Silicon Valley start-ups get options to purchase what is called founders' stock at a cheap price. It's supposed to be an incentive for the person to stay with the company and make it wildly successful so that the stock will dramatically increase in value. Since the goal is to keep the person with the company, they dole it out in little amounts, like one hundred shares a month for one hundred twenty months or something like that. But the guy gets a big tax break if he makes an 83b election. . . . Never mind. For tax reasons, the stock option plan usually says that the guy gets all twelve thousand shares immediately, but the company has the right to buy back all but one hundred shares after the first month, all but two hundred shares after the second month, and so forth. The repurchase stuff is just a formality. The lawyer handles it if the guy leaves, everybody knows the intent is that the guy only gets part of the stock if he leaves or is fired before the one hundred twenty months are up.

"So. This guy DeLuth was CompuStar's V.P. of marketing, he got his stock for, I don't know, pennies a share, and he lasts for about eight months. Then he gets fired, and he gets this severance pay and stuff, including a stock certificate for eight hundred shares of the company. They're probably pissed that he got any stock when he was such a lousy V.P., but it isn't worth much anyway and they're just glad to get rid of him.

"Two years later, when the stock is valued at about a hundred dollars a share, this guy DeLuth pops up and starts demanding all of his one hundred twenty months' worth of stock.

"So the first thing in T and S's file is this polite demand letter from DeLuth to the president of CompuStar, and this scribble in Leo's handwriting in the margin that says 'Get rid of this jerk.' So Peter Bonifacio gets it and looks at DeLuth's option plan. It says the company had to send a notification of repurchase within ninety days of termination. He goes to the file for a copy of the letter of repurchase, and guess what? Leo never sent one, he sort of forgot. Only details like this are beneath Leo's contempt, so really Mary Belle sort of forgot.

"So the next thing in the file are some letters going back and forth to DeLuth's lawyer offering to buy DeLuth out for ten thousand dollars even though his claim isn't worth a penny yada-yada-yada, only DeLuth isn't going away and pretty soon he's threatening to file suit. The tone of the file is getting more and more anxious, Bonifacio is saying we have problems, would somebody please pay attention, and then CompuStar gets slammed with a lawsuit for one point four million dollars. They bring in Gerry Tweedmore.

"After that, Peter does all this fact and legal research, looking for some kind of defense, because it's obvious who is responsible for costing the client all this money. Peter considers and rejects all these legal theories: Maybe DeLuth wasn't really terminated if they kept him on the group health insurance; maybe he said something that made the company think it didn't have to give formal notice. None of it's going anywhere.

"Then Peter found an angle that allowed the company to claim DeLuth never properly exercised his options in the first place. So now DeLuth not only loses the extra stock, the company is going to countersue to get back the eight hundred shares he did get.

"You can tell from the file Gerry's pretty excited. I even remember Gerry and Peter talking about it. They draft up the answer and cross-complaint and give it to DeLuth's lawyer and notice DeLuth's deposition. And then T and S's malpractice carrier pays DeLuth eight hundred thousand dollars.

"Wait," said Sarah. "Somebody pays DeLuth?"

"Exactly. You get this great cross-complaint on file, and the next piece of paper is a settlement agreement for eight hundred K, and the next piece of paper is a Xerox copy of an eight hundred K check from the carrier. File closed. Mary Belle, perpetrator of all this suffering, packs her stationery and ends up working for a flunky. Me."

"I don't understand."

"Me neither."

"Maybe the defense was no good after all."

"Says who? Gerry thought it was good. Bonifacio thought it was good. Who else was there to have an opinion? It certainly never got to a judge."

He reached into the box and pulled out a maple bar. Sarah got up to get the coffeepot.

"Doughnuts," she said, her back to him. "I had you figured for a muffin type."

He paused in midbite. "Wait. Do I want to know what's a muffin type?"

"Sure." She shook the last drops from the coffee cone and set it in the sink. "Muffins are cultivated, like pâté and polo. Doughnuts are unrefined, like fucking and football. Want more coffee?"

"Thank you for clarifying that," he said, holding out his cup. He pushed the box across the table. "Need a football?"

She reached into the box, suppressing a grin. "Well. All right, I suppose the insurance settlement is odd, but what's it got to do with Leo's murder?"

"Two things about this file bother me. First, what made these guys give up all of a sudden? I don't know what that could have to do with Leo's murder, but it's weird. The second thing is that Mary Belle doesn't just sort of forget things."

"She did with this stock letter."

"I don't believe it. First of all, Mary Belle doesn't make mistakes. Mortals make mistakes; Mary Belle catches the mistakes that mortals make and announces them over the paging system."

"Come on, Howard. . . ."

"That's my less persuasive reason for thinking Mary Belle didn't do it. Take it or leave it. My strong reason is that *once* in the time I've known her she did make a minor mistake, and she got positively humble about it. She pointed it out to me, she apologized, she didn't pick on me once for a whole day.

"That's Mary Belle's character. She's sarcastic, she's hostile, but she's fair. She wouldn't take it out on other people if she made a mistake. And yet the universal opinion in the office is that Mary Belle went from being slightly abrasive to being an unbearable jerk after she got demoted. And I told you what she said about Leo. If your employer kept you on the payroll after you cost them eight hundred thousand dollars, wouldn't you be grateful?"

Sarah put her chin on her fist and tapped idly on the table with her other hand. In the morning light her eyes were flecked with green. "Did she deny making the mistake?"

"No."

Sarah tapped some more. "If Mary Belle didn't make this mistake, why is she pretending she did?"

"Exactly. Aren't I pretty clever? One of two things is true. Maybe I'm wrong and she did it and just has bad character. The other possibility is that she didn't do it, but Leo had something over her and forced her to say she did. So if I were investigating Leo's murder, I'd want to know what Leo had over Mary Belle."

"And how would you find out?"

"I'd ask her."

Sarah collected the stray chocolate sprinkles from the bottom of the doughnut box and licked them off her finger. "Be careful."

24

Unreal Estate

In the first shock after Leo's murder, Howard had agreed that the least he could do for Nancy was compile a list of Leo's assets for the executor. He had not foreseen himself, six days before trial, on a hard wooden chair at Security Pacific. A bank officer had been sighing heavily at Howard's elbow for upward of three hours while Howard furiously listed little bits of Silicon Valley stock, most of which were undoubtedly worthless.

He also found the deed of trust for Montgomery Island, made out to Leo and Nancy as tenants in common. It was banded together with an appraisal valuing the property at $5.2 million U.S. dollars. Howard whistled softly. No wonder Leo was always talking about the island, it must be the size of Manhattan. There was also a sales agreement, which said all cash, $3.9 million U.S. dollars, seller a guy named Lyman Mink.

Howard flipped back to the appraisal and looked at the date. October 4, 1986, less than a month before the sales agreement was signed. He set the two documents side by side.

Lyman Mink. Lyman Mink. Where had he heard that name before? Howard felt the bank officer's eyes on him, willing him to keep writing. He banded the documents back together and dropped them into the box. Lyman Mink was either a fool or very grateful. After the trial, maybe he'd try to find out which.

He heard his office door open.

"Mary Belle, would you knock? What if I have a client in my office? What if I'm changing my clothes?"

"With these picture windows? You want to shoot the moon at greater San Mateo, what difference will one measly secretary make? I promise not to lose control. Word processing wants the jury instructions."

"They're on the chair, under the DeLuth file." He saw her freeze, then reach under the file and pull out the jury instructions.

"There was a cross-complaint in DeLuth I wanted to take a look at."

"Hope it helped." Her stringy red hair covered her profile. She reached for the door.

"Mary Belle." She paused, her back to him and her hand on the knob.

"Give it a rest, Howard."

"I don't think you screwed up the DeLuth repurchase."

She turned and stared at him. "That's nice. Why don't you tell the partners? They still seem bent out of shape about it."

"I'm not saying there wasn't a screw-up. I just don't think you did it."

Her eyes narrowed, she scratched her left nostril thoughtfully. "What do you care?"

"You just don't make careless mistakes like that."

Her laugh ricocheted around the office. "Forget it, Howie. It's just compared to you that I look competent. You finished with DeLuth? I'll get it out of here."

Half an hour later she buzzed him on the intercom. "I'll be back in a few minutes, I need a Coke from Burger King."

"Fine."

"Can I bring you something?"

He stared at the intercom. Mary Belle offering to do him a favor? "No, Mary Belle, I guess not. Thanks for asking." He continued to stare at the pink box after it fell silent.

Later that afternoon, she dropped a letter into his in box for his signature. The client's name was misspelled. Howard considered it the biggest insult he had received since joining the firm.

He sat in a cone of light on the floor beneath Mary Belle's typewriter. He hadn't even found the switch for the hall light. Apart from his own occasional rustling of tissue paper, the only sound in the surrounding blackness was the directionless roar of air being blown through the ventilation system.

He was looking through Mary Belle's chronological files from her tenure with Leo. Candy had shown him Mary Belle's system for dealing with the details of stock issuance to officers. As he had expected, the system was both simple and nearly foolproof. He had learned that there were two copies of every letter of repurchase. One went into the officer's file. The second was Mary Belle's personal blue tissue carbon copy, which she filed along with her other correspondence in chronological order. It was a hopeless long shot, he knew. But he had to verify that Mary Belle didn't have the blue tissue copy of a De-Luth repurchase letter.

Part II of 1985 was back in the farthest corner of the metal cupboard under Mary Belle's desk. As he backed his torso carefully out of the little space, a voice said, "Oh, my my." He banged his head on the cabinet.

"Hi, Mary Belle. What brings you here so early?"

She set her purse and cigarettes on the stand next to the typewriter and shook her head slowly.

"Howie, we've got problems. You just couldn't leave it alone, could you?" She was looking at the shiny black cover of the chron file. He didn't bother to ask what she was talking about.

"Now things are going to have to get ugly," she said sorrowfully. "Let's discuss this in your office."

She started backing him slowly toward the crack of light that beamed under his door. "As usual, you don't begin to know what you're messing with." She almost pushed him against the closed door. As the door swung open, her eyes locked onto those of Inspector Sarah Nelson.

25

Defying the
Surgeon General

Mary Belle looked from Inspector Nelson to Howard and back again.

"Well, well, well," she said. "I guess you do know what you're messing with. I underestimated you, Howie. I didn't think you'd be any better at causing trouble than you are at practicing law."

"I take it you remember who I am, Ms. Strick?" said Sarah.

"I remember."

"I wonder if you'd tell us both what Mr. Rickover is messing with. We know there's something very wrong with the DeLuth case. We've read the file, we know you took the blame. What we can't understand is why. Was it personal loyalty?"

Mary Belle's laugh made Sarah jump. "Oh, my, no," she said. "I wasn't that bad off. I took the blame because I had no choice. As Leo well knew."

"Why did you have no choice?"

"Oh," she said, and pushed the air with the palm of her hand. "You want me to go through that little dance now? With him here?"

"I can leave," said Howard.

"Oh, who cares? I could use cup of coffee, though. And an ashtray. Hang on." She left.

"Howie," said Sarah. "Howie. That's kind of cute."

They waited in silence for several minutes until Mary Belle had wreathed them in smoke.

"All right, how did I get my ass in a sling? When I came to work here seven years ago I was under what you might call a cultural disadvantage." This time her laugh didn't even make Sarah blink. "I'd run away from my stepfather's dump in West Virginia. I didn't have a high school diploma. My boyfriend Lenny and I traveled with a bunch of bikers, we'd been in some shit.

"I ditched Lenny and got myself to the Bay Area where I was staying with a cousin who didn't owe me any favors, and, oh, my my, I needed a job." She stubbed out her first cigarette and shook a second one out of her pack. Howard saw Sarah glance at the window to confirm that it didn't open.

"Long boring story, I got a job here as a file clerk, which I could do in my sleep, and Leo kept losing secretaries. He was this totally disorganized hot-shot kid right out of law school. He worked around the clock and expected his secretary to keep up with him, so they all quit. Hell, I could type, so after about the fourth one quit in three months I told him to hire me. I told him I couldn't be any worse than the other four, and he agreed. I decided then that I was going to be the best secretary in the business, and I didn't let Leo get in my way." Howard braced himself for her laugh and then relaxed when it didn't come.

"I was his secretary for over six years. We worked together constantly, seven days a week sometimes. It was like a marriage, except ours worked, his and Nancy's never did. They were crazy times."

She concentrated on her ashtray as she stubbed out her second cigarette. "Leo worked so hard that he was out of his mind all the time, smart but sloppy, always on the edge of disaster. That was my job, to keep him one step ahead of disaster. I supplied the details. I got the papers typed, I found his errors, I got his stuff to court on time, I got him to Japan on time, I kept his little army of flunkies pumping the shit out so that he could be off making new deals. I don't kid myself. You look at any one of the things I did, it was boring. But the volume of it, and the stakes, that made for a challenge, oh, my, yes. I got a reputation for pulling all-nighters, I'd get us a pizza and some Coke, and I'd be out there shooting it back just as fast as he could throw it at me. I'd finish up at five A.M., go home and take a shower and head back to put in a day's work.

"Mind you, it was costing me to live that way. I started chain-smoking, I got an ulcer and had to stop the pizzas. I was going with a guy and we talked about getting married, but he wouldn't put up with the hours so I told him to get lost. I could take care of myself, I bought my own place, I figured the hell with him. For the first time in my life I felt like I belonged to something. We rose through the ranks together, Leo and me, he became a partner. I have to say I admired him. We talked sometimes, I told him my background. I knew his was sort of similar, and he was a whiz kid, an SVM at thirty. I was sure he realized I was valuable, irreplacable, and that was enough to keep me going."

She sat back for a minute and closed her eyes, her lips pressed together as she inhaled the smoky air, deeply. Sarah glanced at Howard but didn't speak. Mary Belle exhaled through rounded lips, opened her eyes, and sat forward again over her ashtray.

"About eight months ago Leo called me into his office right after Peter and Gerry had been in to see him. It was about DeLuth, he wanted the letter of repurchase. Now, we have done literally hundreds of these letters, and I was surprised that I actually remembered a name going back almost two years. I couldn't think why, but I remembered the letter. That was one reason I knew it had been done. The other reason I knew was that I set up a foolproof system for this stuff. Candy showed it to you, right? Is she screwing it up?" Howard shook his head. "See, it really is foolproof.

"So, sitting there in Leo's office I was a little surprised that a copy wasn't in the DeLuth stock file, but it was no big deal. I told him it was probably misfiled, and anyway I had a backup copy in my chron file. You know what a chron file is. I start with January first every year and stick a copy of every piece of paper that goes out from my desk into the file, and then at the end of the year I toss it in the back of a cabinet and start a new one.

"We had some hearing going on at the time, opposing a TRO, so it was a few days before I got around to looking for the letter. I got out a two-year-old calendar and the file to figure out about when the letter was typed, and that was how I remembered.

"See, January twenty-eighth is my birthday, and every year I take the whole week off. So I printed out this repurchase letter at least a week ahead of time and gave it to him to sign. I asked him about it a couple of times. Finally, the day before my vacation, he said he couldn't find it, but leave him a note and he'd look for it on Monday.

"Well, no way could he be trusted with that kind of responsibility. I printed out a whole new letter and took it in and made him sign it. I got it into the out box, and he came by with his coat on and said he'd walk all the stuff to the mailroom himself. I figured it was his time he was wasting. I couldn't take it, I had to get out of there. So I stuck my copy in the chron file and that was that.

"So I remembered this as I was sitting there, and I started to get nervous. Maybe Leo had dropped the damn letter on the way to the mailroom, he was certainly capable of it. I decided to go directly into the chron file for the other copy.

"I told you all my chron files are in a cabinet under my typewriter, along with a lot of other things I never look at. I pulled my chair away and sat down on the floor, thinking it might take awhile to find a chron file from two years ago. There it was, right on top. I figured, well, something's going right. I flipped through January a couple of times, I didn't find it. But I knew it was there. So I finally undid the metal clasp, pulled all the pages out of the file, and started turning the pages from one stack onto another, one at a time.

"I still didn't find the letter. What I found was a scrap of paper between two other letters, right up by where the holes were punched, showing me that a page had been torn out.

"I reached up onto my desk and got a cigarette, and sat there looking at that little scrap of paper until the cigarette was long gone. I would never, and I mean never, remove a piece of paper from any file by ripping it out. Nobody knew that file existed except Leo and me. The conclusion was inescapable. Leo ripped that page out of my file.

"I finally decided he had gotten impatient and was so damn sloppy that he ripped the letter out. Which made no sense, mind you. Leo never had time for any detail like that. If he really wanted it faster he'd just yell louder. But nothing else was remotely possible.

"It was pretty late at night when I was looking through this stuff. I remember waking up in the middle of the night and thinking 'Leo's setting me up. Leo wants to make me look like a fuck-up.' I was so upset I finally went into my living room and sat in the dark. The more I woke up the calmer I felt. Leo wouldn't do that to me. Not my hero. And there wouldn't be any point. If the letter never went out, the client wouldn't give a good goddamn who didn't send it, Leo was responsible. I finally got back into bed and went to sleep.

"Leo was out at a client's in the morning. As soon as he came in I went to talk to him about it. When I walked in he was dialing his red phone, and he held it away from his ear like he wanted me to hurry up and get out. I asked him if he had the DeLuth letter.

" 'Don't know,' he said, and glanced around at the piles of paper on his desk. 'Did you give it to me?'

"I said, 'Leo, can that call wait a minute? We've got a problem.' And I started to explain about the scrap of paper in my file. He wouldn't listen, he interrupted.

" 'Sorry, Mary Belle, you know I can't stand these details. Either you sent the letter or you didn't. Have you got a copy?'

" 'I have a piece of a copy,' I said, and held it up. I saw him freeze, just for a second, and I knew I was in deep shit. Then he saw the scrap was blank and he relaxed.

" 'That's cute. But like I said, if you mailed the letter I need a copy. If you didn't'—and he winked at me—'good thing I'm your lawyer.' He picked up the red phone and started dialing it again to let me know the audience was over.

"That was it. A couple of days later he called me in, didn't even ask about the letter. 'Mary Belle,' he said. 'How are ya? Listen, I saved your ass.' It seemed the DeLuth matter was heating up, CompuStar management was asking lots of questions, he needed to get me off the desk for a few weeks until things blew over. I was going to word processing. 'But listen, I told everybody what a great secretary you are, your future here is secure. I even got you your same salary. Just one thing, I don't want you talking about this to anyone, okay? It could jeopardize our position while we're trying to work a deal. Everybody fucks up once in a while, just don't deny it. It'll make you look bad and I'll be embarrassed I stood up for you. Do we understand each other?'

"I told him to shove it. I told him I knew what he was trying to do, and it wouldn't work. You know what?" She grinned, stubbing out her cigarette. "I swear to God I hurt his feelings. He told me he was just trying to help me out because of all our work together. He wanted me to think it over for a day or two. In the meantime, I was off his desk.

"I slammed out of there expecting never to go back. It didn't take me long to realize what Leo had figured out. No matter what I told people, who would believe me? King Leo walking his own mail to the mailroom? King Leo, down on his hands and knees rifling my chron file? And why? *I* wouldn't believe a story like that. And let's face it, I was good at my job, but not popular."

Mary Belle fished around in her flattened cigarette pack and drew out a last cigarette.

"Second, what was I going to do for a job? I'd had exactly one boss for six years, and I couldn't afford to let any employer dig back into my past prior to that time. I had no family. I was stuck."

She shrugged. "The rest is public history. Leo's malpractice carrier paid CompuStar for 'my mistake.' I became the highest paid word processor in history until Howie showed up, then I became the highest paid flunky's secretary in history.

"I still couldn't figure out why he was setting me up. Until I met Candy Gilley. Suddenly it became clear. Leo wanted somebody a whole lot more like family than I was." Her laugh ricocheted around the office. For a moment nobody moved.

"By the way," she went on. "I didn't kill the creep, even if he did stick a knife in my gut. I already have to live with myself for wasting six years on the man, I certainly wouldn't risk the rest of my life just to kill him. I'm not even particularly glad he's dead. By the time he died I was only mad at myself. I was this eager little puppy dog slavering for approval, willing to turn my whole life over to Leo just for the privilege of belonging, just to have him like me a little. I lie in bed at night and get the creeps just thinking about it. Leo being dead hasn't changed that at all.

"So. There you have it. If you think you can hang me for murder, lock me up. Otherwise, I have work to do." She got up and disappeared out the door, the smoky air swirling furiously in her wake.

Later that afternoon, Howard and Mary Belle went over his trial notebook. She got up to go.

"Mary Belle, one more question." She paused in the open doorway. "You ever heard of Lyman Mink?"

She squinted the left side of her face. "Mink. Mink. Oh, him, that awful little friend of Leo's with all the pinkie rings. What do you want him for, you don't have enough trouble?"

"We ever do any work for him?"

"Not directly that I know of. He was involved in the Trillobyte Memories securities case. One of the directors, I think, and we represented the company."

"Oh. I remember. Connie's case."

"Yeah, another one of those start-ups that blew a few million and went belly up. You need to get ahold of Mink?"

"Cal told me there's pleading in the Mink file I should take a look at. Any way to get our hands on the file?"

"It's probably in storage at Bekins. When do you need it?"

"I *need* it about four days ago. Can you get it for me by the end of the day?"

"Hey, if we pay enough I can probably get it for you four days ago. Bill it to the trial file?"

"Thanks, Mary Belle. Will you close the door?"

Ten minutes later, from the pay phone at Burger King, he set up a meeting with Sarah for seven P.M.

26

Howard Revisited

"So he set her up," said Sarah, staring into her half-empty glass of amber wine. She was slouched at his dining-room table watching him grate Parmesan. "But what did happen to the letter of repurchase? Why hadn't that happened before? Or since?"

"I know. But what's the difference? This isn't a professional liability case, as you so delicately informed me after Madras spilled his beans. It's a murder case, and I don't see any way to test Mary Belle's story further. It may as well be true, we can't prove otherwise."

"You think it's true?"

"Yeah."

"Then we'll leave it, for now at least. Any word on the CPR stuff?"

"Sally's notes don't have anything about tamponade, and she's pretty sure they never mentioned it. I don't see where else to go."

"Then we're at a standstill?"

"Practically. There in my briefcase is one other angle that probably won't amount to anything. Remember Candy said Leo was afraid of Connie stealing his island or something? Well, the other day I came across the real estate purchase file for the island. There's an appraisal right in the file that says it was worth one point three million more than he paid for it."

"Sounds like he got a good deal."

"I'll say. If I got that good a deal on this place the seller would pay me a million to move in. Why would anybody give that good a deal?"

"So?"

"So, he bought it from a guy named Mink. I found out today that Tweedmore and Slyde only did one piece of work for Mink ever, a securities fraud case that came up about three months after the sale of the island. It was handled by Connie. It turns out I sat in on Mink's deposition the first week I was there, and something weird was going on." He shrugged. "I don't know. Connie and Mink, Mink and the island. I thought there might be something. . . ."

"Let's take a look while we eat."

"It's sort of a two-handed dinner." He set a big platter on the table. She squinted through the steam.

"Not as fancy as last time. I must be losing status."

"I can't believe you had the nerve to say that," he protested to her laughing face. "You wouldn't eat anything last time, you may recall. And I think fettucine al pesto measures up to a grilled cheese sandwich."

"Very unfair. I'm not the one who writes Betty Crocker fan mail. I showed you some of my best pictures."

"Hung them up just for me no doubt." He lifted a big tangle of pasta onto her plate. "So, is this a good time for you to tell me why you left the L.A.P.D.?"

"I wasn't getting along with somebody."

He waited in vain. "There you go again. Jabber jabber jabber. A boss?"

She nodded. "I was their youngest woman sergeant, and for two years I had the very best assignments. Detective in burglary, inspector in homicide. I was too candid in my opinions of somebody, and suddenly the rumor mill said I was going to be running traffic school. Then a friend of mine got shot. It rattled me."

"Like that woman in college."

"I don't know. Anyway, the guy I was living with was on the police force, I just couldn't get any distance, any perspective. I decided it was time to retreat and reconsider." She grinned. "So I come to sleepy little San Mateo and this fat homicide drops in my lap."

"Leo would be flattered, I'm sure. So, the guy you were living with. Is he still in L.A.?"

She nodded. "We talk sometimes." They were silent for a moment, their forks scraping the stoneware plates. "How about you? Are you in a serious relationship?"

He shook his head. "I've only been in one, when I was in Florence. Mostly a lot of serious crushes that never go anywhere. It's been like that all my life. When I was in sixth grade we had math class right before dancing. One day this girl I had an incredible crush on caught me cheating on a math test. She said, 'I won't tell if you promise not to dance with me.' "

He realized he had never heard her laugh out loud before. It felt like a reward. "That's the most sincere insult I ever heard," she said.

"I don't know. I could probably think of some others. You want espresso?" She didn't answer. Her head was resting on her palm, with her fingers cupping her face. She tilted her head a little, appraising him. "You take a lot of trouble to appear ineffective. I wonder why."

He opened his mouth and then closed it again, astonished. He couldn't bring himself to offer an answer that wasn't as good as the question.

"Jesus," he said finally. "That's how you solve murders." He returned her gaze for a moment, then got up to clear the table. "You want espresso?"

"You have any real coffee?"

"Espresso *is* real coffee, you cop."

"It looks weird."

"All right. All right. I'll make you some real coffee."

"I like your place," she said, touching a ceramic parrot perched on the countertop. "You have things here that matter to you."

"Yeah. Some of it's a little tacky, like my Vatican toothpick holder. Did you see that?" It was gold-painted plastic. Pasted in one of the windows was a hologram of the Pope blowing kisses. "All this stuff reminds me of people and places. The parrot comes from Florence. My friend Nina gave me the penguin over there by the fireplace. And that silver candelabra in the corner was my grandmother's. Isn't it spooky? I'm hoping a spider will find it soon and complete the atmosphere." He led her into the living room. "You really think you'll go to the ballet again?"

"When the time is right. Could you tolerate a ballet with a mud wrestler?"

"Now who's pretending? Here's the file."

After an hour in front of the fire, Howard said, "I'm getting some idea of what Hillman, the plaintiff, says happened. Mink had a two-and-a-half-million-dollar investment in Trillobyte Memories, and right before the company is about to ship this portable computer Mink says he wants out, for personal reasons, nothing to do with Trillobyte at all. Mink finds Hillman and talks him into investing two and a half million so that Trillobyte will give Mink his money back. Hillman talks to Mink and the company guys, and the product is great, the company has a great future. Two months after Hillman invests they start shipping the product, it malfunctions, the whole company goes down the tubes and takes Hillman's two and a half million with it. Hillman says Mink and the company officers knew what was coming and lied to him about it, and that's fraud (which it would be) and Mink and Trillobyte owe him his money back."

"So what happened to the case? Has it gone to trial?"

"Nope. Settled. See, here's the Settlement Agreement and Mutual Release. Let's see. Mutual release, dismiss the lawsuit, yada-yada-yada, one hundred fifty thousand dollars to Hillman, all of it paid by Mink. Which is not surprising. Trillobyte's assets were all tied up in bankruptcy court. Hm. A hundred and fifty thousand."

"What does that mean? Fraud or no fraud?"

"Well, definitely it means Hillman found no hard and fast evidence of fraud. One hundred fifty thousand dollars of his two-and-a-half-million loss is lousy. On the other hand, Mink was out one hundred fifty thousand and his legal fees, that's quite a bit for a totally trumped-up charge. Let's see, did they ever finish Mink's deposition? No. I'd say Mink had something he didn't want Hillman to find out about, and Hillman wasn't convinced he could prove fraud. Well. What's in that for Mink to feel grateful to Leo about?"

"Maybe we better ask Connie. There's probably nothing to it, but there's something else about Connie that keeps bugging me."

"What's that?"

"Does Connie seem ambitious to you?"

"Is the Pope Polish?"

"So how come she's sleeping with one of the guys she works with?"

"Uh, Sarah, how about because she *is* ambitious?"

"That's what I'm having trouble with. It seems like a dumb, dumb way to try to make partner. What's that going to do to her reputation with the rest of the partnership? And what assurance did she have that Leo would carry through with any promises he made, anyway?"

"Well, maybe she just liked the guy. You heard what she said. She's just drawn to power."

"No she's not. Not if it's somebody else's power. It

doesn't add up. Anyway, I want one more shot at her. And this time I'd like you to be there."

"How come?"

"Lots of reasons. You might know whether her explanation about the case makes sense. And if nothing else, it'll definitely be more fun." She stood up and started snapping sheets of notes into her red notebook.

"Sarah," he said to her back. Perhaps she didn't hear him.

"This was fun, too," she said, turning. She was close, her face tilted up toward him. She was smiling faintly, remembering something, her dark eyes enjoying his face in the flickering firelight. If he touched her hair . . .

She picked up her notebook. "Will you call me in the morning about the Valentine interview? Say around ten. See you."

27

Nightwatch

When Inspector Nelson couldn't sleep she sorted slides.

She was sitting on her sofa with a beige plastic binder balanced on her knees. One by one she held the slides up to the light and squinted at them through the specially designed magnifying glass that hung from a cord around her neck. She tossed most of them onto the pile of slides and empty bright yellow Kodak boxes at her feet. Occasionally she inserted a slide into one of the plastic pockets in her binder.

She filled the last pocket on a page, removed the page from the binder, and held it up to the light. These were of a great blue heron, taken over a period of days. Standing in the red-and-yellow dotted marsh. Ankling the shallow water. Stabbing its powerful beak at a squirrel. Taking off, its graceful dark legs dangling uselessly behind. In some of the close-up shots you could see water beaded on the feathers of the heron's neck and the tiny, distinct barbs that made up each feather. You could also see the furious yellow eye.

She returned the page to the binder and put the binder on top of a crate. She filled a paper bag with the dozen or so empty yellow boxes and the discarded slides. Then she stood in the middle of the living room and stared in the direction of her bed.

After a long moment she turned out the light. She felt her way across the room in the dark and out onto her deck. The lights below her at this hour were sparse, the moon cold and luminescent in the cloudless sky. She leaned both hands on the wooden rail, her elbows locked to support her upper body, and let the chill night air blow through her. Then she closed her eyes and dropped her head onto her fists.

"Damn," she whispered. "Stinking ballet."

Her phone rang.

Howard went to bed around one. Stopping by his living-room window to close the drapes, he saw a car parked across the street in front of Mrs. Pringle's rose garden. Now where had that come from? She'd probably blame him for it again, on the grounds that he was a renter and less than a million years old. What the hell, maybe it'd be gone before she got up in the morning. He went to bed.

He woke up with wet sheets clinging to him like a shroud. The acid green clock numerals said three-fifteen. Somebody was in the house.

What had he heard, a creak, a footstep? Molecules

were racing and colliding in the dark. His ears strained for a repeat. Many seconds passed. Nothing.

He put his hand out from beneath the covers and snapped on the light. A dream. It had to have been a dream. That damn car across the street. Take it easy. He reached onto the floor for his robe, still straining for any sound. Take it easy.

When he had warmed up inside his robe he headed for the kitchen. On his way through the living room he parted the drapes to see if the car was still there. A man was crouched near the hedge looking in at him.

He backed away from the window to the telephone, feeling in the dark for the right buttons. "Somebody's looking in my window."

"Your address?"

"Four twenty-four San Felipe."

"Your name?"

"Howard Rickover."

"We're on the way."

He hung up the phone and stared at the front door, his back to the wall. He couldn't remember locking it. He watched the doorknob, waiting for the metal to catch some faint light as it turned. Should he turn the lights on? The hedge rustled. He should get a knife. What if another guy was in the kitchen? He pressed his back into the wall opposite the front door and stood frozen, watching, he didn't know how long.

A car door slammed, he heard footsteps in the driveway. There was a knock. "San Mateo Police, Officer Pitlack. Mr. Rickover?"

He opened the door and stood blinking at Sarah. Officer Pitlack was standing behind her.

"I'll leave this to you, then, Inspector," said Officer Pitlack, and Sarah stepped inside.

28

Howard the Confessor

"Jesus. Sarah. Did you catch him?"

"He's gone."

"I thought . . ." He pointed to the kitchen.

She drew a gun from beneath her jacket. "Wait here." When she returned her gun was out of sight, and she shook her head. "Nobody."

He exhaled, pulled his robe tighter around him. "Did you see him? Is it the guy who killed Leo?"

"No, Howard. I owe you an explanation."

"About what? The guy in the bushes?" He backed up and sat heavily on the sofa.

"That man you saw was hired by the department to keep your house under surveillance."

Rage burst upon him, took his breath away. He put his face in his hands until he could talk. "Why was he two feet from my window?"

"He heard something and the house was dark. He wanted to be sure you were all right."

"Guy's a fucking idiot." He looked up. "What if I'd had a gun? What if I'd had a heart attack? Why didn't you tell me?"

"I didn't want you to think you were in danger."

His response was partly a gasp, partly a squeak. "Have I misled you? I won't even watch movies where this kind of shit happens."

"That's why I didn't tell you."

He stared at her a moment, and then his eyes hardened with comprehension. "Oh. You were afraid I'd quit." He looked at his hands for a long moment. "You know what, I have a feeling I've been really stupid about you." He looked away again, considered. "What else have you withheld? What have you been lying about?"

"It's not—"

"I've wondered why you took me into your confidence so easily. Spilling your tapes. Loving my guts. You think I killed him."

"No."

"Then it's something worse. I'm your decoy. You're billing me out as your star witness to every jerk you talk to in this case, then sitting back to see who takes the bait."

"How could I do that when you work with them every day? Don't you think somebody would have given me away by now?"

He stared at her coldly, immobile.

"Look," she said. "What I've told you is true. I have left some things out." Still he said nothing. "The main thing I haven't told you is something about me. About why I left the L.A.P.D."

He didn't even blink.

"The person who got shot. It was my fault."

"What person? The cop?"

"She wasn't a cop? She was a witness."

"I thought it was some guy who was a cop. What is going on, Sarah? It's, what, four o'clock in the morning? I'm sitting here in my bathrobe scared completely shitless. I find out you're the one who did it to me. Now you decide it's time to unburden yourself of some personal sorrow. What does this mean?"

"There's more of an explanation about the man outside than I've given you. I think you should know the rest."

She was still standing just inside the closed door, her corduroy bomber jacket over the mustard-colored dress.

For the last two weeks he had colluded with her, dreamed about her, encouraged her to disrupt his life completely. Only now did he realize he knew nothing about her. The dark eyes that had assessed him so calmly looked sorrowful, anguished. He was conscious of feeling pulled once more in the direction she wanted him to go. He resisted, savoring a moment of control. Then he chose the dangerous course.

"I should. Let's have some coffee. Let's let me get dressed. Let's turn on the heat in here."

"Before I was assigned to homicide," she said, her hands around the coffee mug, "I did undercover work." He had seated her at the dining-room table, where the light from the kitchen illuminated her face. He kept his face hidden in shadows.

"There was a drug case, we had a witness. Not an eyewitness, we needed her for background information. I cultivated her friendship for ten months, and in the end I got what we needed.

"What we didn't know at the time was that she had some other, specific information that she believed put her and her son in danger. One week she disappeared, went underground. I closed out my investigation and went on to homicide.

"Then about three weeks before the drug trial, the district attorney suddenly realized what this witness knew and had to have her testimony. They came to me, because they knew if anybody could find her I could.

"I found her all right. She was glad to see me. She threw the door open, hugged me, she had tears in her eyes. Then I served her with the subpoena.

"She came apart completely. She cried. She slapped me. Her son stood in the kitchen doorway, watching us.

"She testified at the trial. She had no choice. Six weeks later she was shot."

"Killed?"

Sarah nodded slowly. "Kid's an orphan." She was looking into the dark living room.

"I started screwing up after that. Took some stupid risks. Started popping off to that department big shot I told you about. I don't know if I was trying to get killed or fired. My friends pushed me to take a leave of absence, and I decided to come up here to sort things out."

"So the guy on the lawn out there," he prompted after a moment. Her eyes searched the shadows in vain to find his face.

"The man on the lawn is exactly what I told you he was. You got more involved in the investigation than was safe. Think about the conversation with Madras. It went too far, I'm sure he knew exactly what you were doing. Who knows what some of the others figured out? I've already gotten one innocent person killed. I didn't want you to be the second."

After a moment Howard shook his head. "Still doesn't add up, Sarah. If you were so worried about my skin, why suck me into the case in the first place? Why play those tapes? Why not just leave me alone?"

"I may quit this job, Howard, but I haven't quit it yet. I had to know who killed a man, and I couldn't find out alone. Three hours in Leo's office and I knew that solving this murder required inside help. Whatever clues existed were hidden in a mass of detail I'd never be able to decipher."

"But why me?" The words sounded strange as he spoke them, he had rehearsed them so many times.

"You were perfect. You were nonthreatening, I knew people would talk to you. You were smart. You were intuitive. You—"

"What makes you think I'm intuitive?"

"In a ten-minute police interrogation, you figured out that the police officer had problems with her family. I didn't think I was talking about that. But let me finish. You were on the outs with the law firm. That gave you a motive for getting involved in something where you could feel more appreciated. You were truthful, naïvely so." She considered, then smiled slightly in spite of herself. "And I liked you. I thought it would be fun."

"Shit. And the tapes?"

"They were meant to entice you. Make you feel special. You realize I didn't play them all."

He closed his eyes and shrank back deeper into the shadows. "God, I bet you were good at undercover."

"Yeah," she agreed quietly, biting her lower lip. "Undercover, out in the open, one of the very best." Her smile was bitter. "Those years of training in Chevy Chase were good for something."

"Yeah. Except you probably grew up in the Mojave."

"No. I told you the truth about that."

"And you trot it out whenever you want somebody to feel special."

"No."

"I suppose you'd have told me about Chevy Chase even if you thought it would make me less likely to help."

She considered. "Probably not. But see how I'm changing. I'm telling you all of this."

"You had to. I saw the guy."

"Can you possibly suppose I didn't have a hundred stories to explain him?"

"I should have thought of that, Sarah the old pro."

"You know I can't even see your face?" She waited a moment, then leaned toward him. "I've been looking for a reason to tell you all this. In the last two weeks I've finally recognized this job for what it is. I can choose not to do it any more. But I can't choose to do it without using and betraying people sometimes. Nice people, people that mean something to me. It's built right into the job description.

"I probably can't convince you that I respect and like you. I admire your integrity. And I was right, you are fun. I just hope I haven't had the power to damage your ability to trust people." She looked at her hands, and when she spoke again her voice was businesslike. "Listen, whatever you decide to do now, we need to keep the tail on you for another day or two. What do you want to do about the Valentine interview?"

"I don't know. I need to be alone for a while. Really alone. Nobody creeping around my window, all right? I'll call you later about Connie."

He watched her walk down the driveway. There was the faintest quickening of dawn over the rooftops.

"Sarah," he called in a loud whisper.

She turned.

"Tell the guardian angel to keep away from Mrs. Pringle's rose garden."

29

Death in the Fast Lane

"Come in, Howard," said Gerry. "Emily, close the door, will you? We don't want to be disturbed. Have a seat. Let's see, I asked you to bring the cross-examination of their real estate valuation guy, what's his name?"

"John Fishback."

"Fishback. Right. And then you've got our expert, Newman, his direct. Let's take a look."

"Actually, Gerry, here is most of Newman, but it's in pretty rough shape." He reluctantly handed several sheets, partly typed and partly handwritten, across the wide, burnished surface of Tweedmore's desk. Tweedmore glanced at it and raised an eyebrow.

"Couldn't get Mary Belle to type it for you, huh? Well, that's all right, I'll let you decipher it for me. And is this Fishback, too?" He shuffled through the papers, squinting at the handwriting.

"Actually, Gerry, no. Fishback isn't in there. I've . . . it's outlined, but . . ."

Gerry dropped the papers onto his desk and leaned back into the soft leather. His temple was resting on his left fingertips and he scratched his hair thoughtfully, staring at the pages.

"You know, we've got a trial in three days, and this stuff I've given you is at the heart of the case. I guess you know that?"

Howard nodded, staring into Gerry's eyes like a rabbit staring into headlights on a freeway.

"This is your first trial, and I think you ought to be taking it pretty seriously. The client does. I do." Howard said nothing in the pause that followed. "So, what in the heck seems to be bogging you down? Are you choking up? You aren't doing any estate planning, I hope, because if you are, I'll call Tom and tell him—"

"No, it's not Tom. It's, uh, a combination, I guess. I sort of underestimated the amount of time some of this stuff would take, the jury instructions, and then . . ."

The light in Gerry's eyes blinked off.

"I hope we haven't misunderstood one another. A trial is just about the most demanding thing you will ever experience. I guarantee we're going to have about three nasty surprises, and that's if we prepare everything absolutely, completely, fanatically. If we try to take the slightest chance anywhere, we're going to get caught with our pants down, the judge will know it, the other side will know it, and we'll deserve to lose.

"As of now, you don't have time for estate planning,

and you sure don't have time for anything else. Do we understand each other?

"Before, I told you to triage. Forget about that now. Now you have one case, one concern, and that's this trial. If you can't live with that, tell me." The leather squeaked as Gerry leaned forward in his chair for emphasis. "I'm an old guy, but I can still get the work out when I have to. If you want out, tell me now."

"No. I want the trial. I'll get the work done, I promise. I'll have the Fishback and Newman examinations by tomorrow afternoon. That'll give me the whole weekend to fix them up. I'll have the jury instructions Saturday morning."

"I'll mark you down for tomorrow at two P.M." He tossed the handwritten pages back across his desk without looking up. "Tell Emily to bring me my messages."

As Howard slunk back to his office, he recalled wistfully the way Leo had handled the MacAffee screw-up. Which reminded him, he was due at Sarah's office in exactly twenty minutes. Howard swore.

Connie looked startled when Howard followed Inspector Nelson into the police station room with the old bowling trophies. Then she frowned.

"I thought you had a trial in three days."

"I do, Connie, this is the last thing I'm doing on this."

Connie turned to Sarah. "Inspector, I'm sure this is terribly important, but Mr. Rickover and I just don't have time to interrupt what we're doing in the middle of the day." She stood up. "If you need some time with us, I suggest you get in touch with my secretary at the end of next week—"

"Please sit down, Ms. Valentine. I'm afraid this can't wait until next week, and I won't take much of your time. By the way, Mr. Rickover isn't here to answer questions, he's here to ask them." Connie shot Howard a startled look.

"Fine, I've got five minutes now that I've come all the way over here. Just what seems to be troubling Howard?" She flashed her eyeteeth as she sat down.

Sarah continued. "Ms. Valentine, I understand that you were the primary lawyer handling the case of *Hillman v. Trillobyte and Mink.*"

Connie raised her eyebrows. "And?"

"Were you also involved in Mr. Mink's sale of real estate to Leo Slyde?"

Connie Valentine's smile held steady, but Howard thought her eyes darkened.

"No, Inspector, I was certainly not involved in any real estate deal. You see, a firm like ours is divided into departments, and real estate is something I have nothing to do with. I'm sure Howard can give you the names of—"

"But you did know that Mr. Slyde bought his island from Mr. Mink?"

"I may have heard that, yes."

"And you also knew that he bought it for one point three million under its appraised value?"

"Inspector, how could I possibly know anything of the sort? I've told you, I had nothing to do with his real estate deals. Just because Leo and I were, friends, that doesn't mean we spent our time discussing the details of his personal business."

"Just what did you and Mr. Slyde discuss, Ms. Valentine?"

"Good heavens, Inspector, apart from his real estate transactions and his dental appointments, what didn't we discuss? We discussed everything that mattered to him. The office. His family—"

"And where did these discussions take place?"

"We had them in restaurants, not here, of course, we went to the city. Howard saw us there."

"But you can't have carried on much of an affair entirely in restaurants. Where else did you meet? Motels? Your home?"

"Yes, both."

"In motels. What motels?"

"Hotels up in the city. Stanford Court."

"And how did you register at the Stanford Court?"

"I don't remember, we didn't go there often. If you persist in this offensive—"

"You have an eight-year-old niece who lives with you, don't you, Ms. Valentine?"

"She's nine."

"Did she and Mr. Slyde get along well?"

"They got along all right. There was . . . some jealousy, you know, but I think that's fairly common."

"Yes. And you also have a housekeeper, isn't that right, a Mattie . . . Retinger?"

"Apparently you know I do."

"And if I asked your niece, Alexandra I think it is, she would certainly recognize Mr. Slyde, wouldn't she?"

Connie stared at Sarah and was silent.

"In point of fact, Ms. Valentine, Alexandra has never seen Leo Slyde, has she, except maybe at a firm picnic?"

Connie looked away for an instant, looked through the 1973 Bowling Championship trophy, exhaled slowly. "I want you to leave Alex out of this."

"All right, let's talk about Mrs. Retinger. Would she recognize Mr. Slyde?"

They were both silent for a moment. Sarah was watching, waiting, but Connie stared into the corner and didn't speak.

"Ms. Valentine, we've taken a wrong turn here somewhere, and I'd like to go back to the beginning. Did you and Mr. Slyde have an affair?"

"No."

"And yet you did have personal business with him,

didn't you?" Connie said nothing. "Ms. Valentine, Mr. Rickover saw you and Leo Slyde at a restaurant called Max's Diner on or about February eighteenth of this year. Did you or did you not have personal business with him?"

"It . . . wasn't exactly personal. It had to do with a case."

"Did it have to do with *Hillman v. Trillobyte and Mink?*"

"I can't tell you what it had to do with. Attorney-client privilege."

"Ms. Valentine, Leo Slyde was murdered four days before you came up for partnership review. You claimed to have complete confidence in his support, yet you lied to us about having an affair with him. He left a large sum of money to you in his will for some reason that you're not talking about. It may interest you to know that his real lover—yes, Mr. Slyde really was having an affair—says he was afraid of you. That you were one of the few people he really disliked. I'd like to ask you again. What was your personal business with Leo Slyde?"

"I tell you it's attorney-client privilege, I am ethically bound to keep it in confidence."

"But who's the client?" asked Howard. "Not Leo."

Connie didn't answer.

"The client's name isn't privileged," he pressed. "Is it Lyman Mink?"

She was glaring at him with malice. "It's Mink. And since you know so much about the privilege, you know he's the only one who can waive it."

"He isn't in a position to do that," said Sarah. "I'm afraid Mr. Mink is dead."

"What?" Howard said.

"How do you know that?" Connie asked.

"We tried to contact him about the sale of the island. I have the death certificate."

"What did he die of?" Connie asked.

"Accident. He choked in a restaurant called Nero's up in the city."

"Well." Connie stood up. "Under the circumstances—"

"There's no privilege," said Howard. Both women looked at him. "If he's dead there's no privilege. This just came up in a contested will I'm handling. The attorney-client privilege doesn't survive the client's death except for certain stuff related to his will. It's in the Evidence Code."

Connie turned to Sarah. "Of course you realize I can't rely on what he says in a matter—"

"You don't have to," said Sarah. "I'll get it for you." She called for someone to bring the Evidence Code. Howard found the section and handed the book to Connie. After several moments she looked up.

"It does appear to say that there's no longer a privilege. I'll need time to research the case law—"

"There isn't any case law," said Howard. "It's sort of unambiguous. Look at the commentary after nine fifty-four."

Connie set the book down and pushed it away from her. "I'll need to have you sign a statement that you won't reveal what I'm about to tell you."

"That's impossible," said Sarah.

"Who else is going to find out about what I say?"

"Anybody I choose to tell." The toughness in her voice was startling. "But I can tell you that my interest— my only interest—is in finding and prosecuting Leo Slyde's murderer. I won't use or reveal the information you give me for any purpose except that one." She paused. Still Connie said nothing. "You can force me to get a subpoena. Think carefully before you do that."

"All right," Connie said. "I'll tell you about my business with Leo. How in hell did you ever pick up on the Trillobyte file?"

*   *   *

"I went to Tweedmore and Slyde with the intention of becoming not just a partner, but their most successful and richest partner. My father was a tough Madison Avenue marketing guy. He wanted boys, to the extent he wanted anybody, and he let my sisters and me know it. When I was ten he left my mother and we were suddenly poor. My mother was very bitter, she felt she deserved a man to take care of her. I thought she was a pitiful fool. The way to be taken care of, I knew, was to take care of myself. That's what I live by. I've never gone out of my way to screw anybody. But I'm always looking over my shoulder.

"To make partner I sacrificed everything. I've streamlined my life. I sleep five hours a night, I can eat garbage or even nothing at all. Hard work, brains, and political savvy, I've always known I had plenty of all three. Within a month after I started everybody else knew it, too. For a while things were fine.

"But then I started getting shit from Leo. The greasy little creep was coming on to me. I had read in *The Managerial Woman* or somewhere that you're supposed to keep your sense of humor and handle a come-on that way. Which I tried. But he wouldn't let up. I had the feeling he wasn't even attracted to me, he just wanted to prove he was king of the mountain. He wanted to take me down a peg or two, I wasn't being meek enough. Eventually he implied that my success at the firm depended on it. I wanted to squash him like a bug and I couldn't. It was getting to me.

"Around that time I was working on, as you somehow guessed, the Trillobyte case. If you know anything about that case you know that one big question leaps out at you. What made Mink decide to sell? At the time of the sale he told Hillman he had personal reasons, and when he started the lawsuit he stuck by that. He and the company officers all told the same story. Their machine had it all in one little portable box. Monitor, keyboard, a hundred twenty-eight K of memory. Customers were screaming for it. There was solid evidence from the marketing plan, their ad campaigns, their components purchases, that they really believed they could get thirty percent of a multimillion-dollar market within six months after they started shipping product. Every officer in Trillobyte had a fair amount of his personal fortune tied up in the company, and nobody but Mink made a move to sell. It looked to me like Mink made a lucky move, Hillman made an unlucky one, and Hillman was a crybaby.

"I worked primarily for Trillobyte, they were our client. But we had a deal that I would also represent Mink as long as there wasn't any conflict of interest. I didn't interview him in depth until his deposition came up. About three days before the deposition I sat him down to go over his story in detail, and of course the main question was 'What personal business?' And he told me generally about some real estate syndicate he was very heavily into, said he needed the two and a half million to keep the whole syndicate from going down the toilet. I asked to see records, he said he'd bring them to the deposition. It sounded pretty vague, but I had gotten so confident with all the very persuasive evidence from the company that I made one of the biggest mistakes of my entire career. I didn't push him for details.

"So we get into the deposition, we go through all the preliminary stuff, he sounds fine. They ask what did he need the money for, and all of a sudden he's giving them vague bullshit and refusing to answer their questions. They've already deposed the main corporate guys, they know their case is garbage as well as I do, they're hardly even listening to themselves talk anymore. Then all of a sudden Mink is dancing around like he's standing in a hot skillet, and they're leaning forward in their chairs with their goddamn tongues hanging onto the carpet.

"So I call a recess, and I get Mink in my office, and I ask him where is the documentation for the real estate syndicate. He stonewalls and he stonewalls, and I convince him he can kiss his two and a half million good-bye if he doesn't level with me." She opened her hands and shrugged. "So he levels with me."

She sat back in her chair. "Leo, as I knew, was corporate attorney for Trillobyte. That meant he did their incorporation and their dealer agreements. That is, his flunkies did them. Well, when the officers were getting ready to ship product they felt magnanimous, standing on the verge of untold wealth. They got sentimental and offered Leo some founders' stock at a very competitive price. Leo, ever willing to make some easy money, plans to buy the stock, but he doesn't know much about computers. So he gets one of Trillobyte's computers from Mink, the guy who introduced him to Trillobyte. He gives the computer to this computer jock named Wendy Hite for evaluation. Well, Wendy looked it over for a few days and then called Leo. She told him the computers were going to fail in the field because something called plated-through-holes in the circuit boards were defective. I don't know what else she told him.

"Well, as Leo told Mink, at first he thought he would just politely decline the stock offer. Then he thought of his poor pal Mink twisting in the wind and losing two and a half million bucks, and decided Mink should know.

"The rest is public record. Mink drummed up a personal financial crisis, got Hillman on the hook. Within weeks Trillobyte starts shipping product. Exactly as Hite predicted, there are massive field failures. Trillobyte is in bankruptcy before they ever know what hit them. And Mink is, well, grateful.

"Now comes the real estate deal. Mink owned this island, part of an archipelago off the coast of British Columbia. I saw it once on a business trip. You can only get to it by seaplane. It's about a mile across, sandy beaches and then high granite cliffs. The whole island is covered with Douglas Fir. Surrounded by narrow channels hundreds of feet deep, so you get tremendous swift currents from the ebb and flow of the tide. An old wood lodge with a year-round lodgekeeper, and an icehouse and smokehouse for hunting and fishing. It's a beautiful, beautiful piece of real estate. Leo had been there and he wanted it.

"Six months after Trillobyte failed, Mink quietly sold the island to Leo for more than a million under value. That's where half of Hillman's two and a half million went. It went into Leo's pocket, and the two of them were guilty of about forty different disgusting things. Fraud, breach of fiduciary duty, ethical violations for Leo, my God. It was rotten. Rotten for Hillman, rotten for Trillobyte, potentially very rotten for the law firm. But it was sweet for Connie Valentine.

"I went back into the deposition room that day, and I told them Mr. Mink was ill. They screamed and yelled and I told them I'd be in touch. Then I got rid of Mink and sat down in my office and figured out what to do.

"To my credit, first I figured out what to do about the lawsuit. You remember the deal was I would represent both the company and Mink as long as there was no conflict of interest. This was the biggest conflict of interest ever imagined by a whole roomful of legal ethics professors.

"Obviously Mink—and Leo—had screwed not only Hillman but the company, as well. Who knows what would have happened if Trillobyte had known about the problem before they shipped? At least they wouldn't have destroyed Trillobyte's reputation the first time out of the chute. Also, Trillobyte truly was blameless as to Hillman, and they deserved to be out of the lawsuit immediately at Mink's expense. But Mink was my client, had told me this dirt in confidence, and I could not reveal it.

"Well, I saw what had to happen. After I got that squared away in my own mind, I started thinking about Leo. I started thinking about Leo and my future at Tweedmore and Slyde, and I gave old Leo a call. I asked him to join me for dinner, somewhere nice and private up in the city. I could hear him smiling into the telephone. He thought little Connie Valentine had decided to be accommodating."

Connie sank back into her chair and folded her hands against her chest. "I ask you to imagine the pleasure it gave me to tell Leo why he was there. That's when Howard saw us, by the way. Leo hated it that he saw us.

"I told him there was only one way out of this mess, and it had to happen quickly. Mink *had* to settle the whole lawsuit at his own expense before they got a court order to resume his deposition. I told him I thought I could do it for half a million, and Mink would also have to pay out all legal fees, including Trillobyte's. I told him I didn't want to hear where the money came from. I didn't bother to describe the alternative. Leo was smart enough to know it included a trip to the California Legal Ethics Committee.

"Then, with no allusion to his slimeball advances, I told him one more thing. I told him it wouldn't do for him to hold this against me when it came time for partnership. I told him the only way I could be sure he hadn't held it against me was for me to make partner. I told him I fully intended to work my ass off and deserve partnership when the time came, and all he'd have to do was stay out of my way. And really, Inspector, I had every confidence that he would stay out of my way.

"That was it. I called Mink into my office and told him the same thing about settling the case. He agreed, I got the best deal I could for him, and you know the result. A hundred and fifty thousand dollars and Mink was very grateful to pay it. I put Trillobyte aside and never told anybody about it, until today."

"Do you have any evidence for any of this?"

"No. Never saw any written Hite report if there was one. For that matter, Leo never explicitly admitted what he had done. But if this thing has to be dragged up again, and I very much hope it won't be, apparently there is some kind of appraisal that shows the deal Leo got on the island. And I can find Wendy Hite. She was in a confidential relationship as Leo's consultant, but a court order would overcome that."

"And what about the will?"

"I never knew a goddamned thing about that will. I've thought about it. One possibility—which I don't believe for a minute—is that Leo committed suicide and wanted to leave me with a motive. The other possibility—and knowing Leo, this is more likely—is that Leo thought he was immortal and didn't care what the hell was in his will. He was just dicking around with it to convince Howard he was having an affair with me."

"Why would he want to do that?"

"He probably figured I was going to tell somebody I'd seen them together," said Howard, "and the gossip would be out of control. Maybe he was afraid the real reason for the meeting would eventually come to light. So he shut me up. By talking to me about Connie formally, professionally, he put me under an obligation not to violate a client's confidence. And it worked."

"Anyway, Inspector," said Connie, "with partnership approaching, I was one of the very few people who was better off with Leo alive."

"You were actually sort of pleased about this Trillo-byte thing."

"You bet I was." Connie stood up, planted her hands firmly on the table, and leaned toward Sarah. "Be-fore my father left, he taught me the words 'gelt' and 'schmuck.' I figured out for myself that if you don't have any you are one. I've never asked for a handout from anybody, I just want to be allowed to win fair and square. If I beat Leo at his own rotten tactics . . ." She shrugged and smiled broadly, her eyeteeth reflecting great stars of light. "I guess that means I'm pretty good at the game.

"I don't have time for any more of these tête-à-têtes. If you want proof of what I've told you, leave a mes-sage—a discreet message—with my secretary. If you want anything else, get a subpoena."

As her heels clicked down the hallway, Sarah and Howard sat in silence. Finally Howard said, "I think I believe her."

Sarah was resting her chin on her open palm and swiveled her head to look at him. "Me, too, more or less."

"I also think Leo was a bigger creep than we real-ized."

"More dishonest, certainly."

"I also think you can be one mean mama when you want to be. I wouldn't want to be on your shit list."

Sarah snorted softly, rubbing her eye. "Speaking of shit lists," she said. "You don't owe me any explana-tions, but I'm interested."

"Why I came?"

She nodded.

"After you left I sat around thinking about what a miserable shit you were. How it was going to be your fault if I screw up this trial on Tuesday. And that got me thinking about the trial. You might not know what a trial feels like. Just saying the word makes me so anxious I can't hear. But the more I think about it, I actually feel sort of disconnected from it. It can make me miserable, but it doesn't have much to do with me.

"So just as Mrs. Pringle shuffled out onto the porch this morning and bent over to get her newspaper, I realized. I do feel connected to this murder investigation. Who killed the guy? I really have to know."

She nodded.

"I don't know what I think about you yet," he continued. "I guess I'll have to worry about that later."

"Want a grilled cheese sandwich while we go over some stuff?"

"How about tortellini at my place?"

Heading back to the police station at eight-thirty, Howard pulled over across from the T&S office and stopped the car. "Do you mind, just for a second?"

The pink granite building was dark except for the top floor, which blazed brightly. As they watched, light flared up in the conference room, and two people, too distant to be recognizable, came around by the windows and sat at the conference table.

"You know what that is, Sarah? It's a giant law machine that pulls in human beings, sucks out their brains, and spits out the carcasses. It's a factory. All that thick carpet and fancy art is camouflage. See, there go all the little lawyers up the conveyor belt. Then there's a rattling and a roaring and a banging inside the big furnace there. Then, see, over there on the other side those big stacks of green money are piling up, and all those bones in the garbage bin. The end product isn't even legal services. It's plain old green money.

"It's been bugging me for weeks now, what makes people do it? At first I thought a few very shrewd guys were making a lot of money off of other people's naïveté.

"But you heard Connie today. I mean she's a *partner* now, she shares in all that wealth, and I don't get the feeling it's going to change her life much at all. Cal Forman told me once that partnership is nothing but a license to keep going. They're all being ground up. There's no lock on the door, why don't they just run away?

"Listening to Connie today, it suddenly came together. She's getting even with her asshole father. And Peter, he keeps trying to make himself less unacceptable, who knows what that's about? And then Madras. He's a workaholic, I think he works until he collapses so he won't have to think."

"I'd say it's working," said Sarah. "The guy's about as reflective as a black hole."

"Maybe that's what they're all doing. Money's just the excuse. Or a way of keeping score. It's how Connie's going to beat her old man, who's probably been dead for a hundred years and doesn't give a fuck.

"What will these people think when they're on their deathbeds, listening to the ticking of their expensive wristwatches and wondering what they've done with their lives? Are they going to think 'Oh, boy, they really accepted me'? 'Oh, boy, I guess I showed him'? Are they going to realize that all they've ever done was to try to distract themselves by clawing their way up some mountain that doesn't even amount to a smudge in the universe?"

"Who says they think anything?" Sarah said. "They probably just die."

"Sunny Sarah. Geltschmuck. Death in the fast lane."

Up on the sixth floor a light blinked out.

"Yeah, well, everybody has their little problems," Sarah said. She was staring into the dark beyond the windshield.

"You know, Sarah, I don't mean to be gloomy or anything, but I don't think our investigation is going very well. We've churned up all these incredible suspects, but the more we look the less likely it is that any of them killed him. Am I wrong?"

"No. You're not wrong."

"So, uh, what happens to our investigation when we run out of things to investigate?"

"As they say in the bizworld, it goes on the back burner. I mean, it's not like we're going to sit idly and pine. You've got a trial and a career to think about. I've got about seven other investigations going. So I forget about this one."

"Just like that?"

"I try." She was silent for a minute. "I got a call today. L.A.P.D. wants me back."

"I thought you were worried about the lousy assignment," he said quickly.

"Somebody left, somebody came. That won't be a problem now."

"Oh," he said. He was embarrassed that he didn't sound more enthusiastic. It was scant comfort that she didn't seem to notice. "You think you'll go back, then?"

"Don't know. In case you weren't listening this morning there are some other problems. And I can't decide anything until this Slyde thing is resolved." She was tapping the tip of her forefinger against her front teeth.

"I was listening. You have to find some way to live with your own conscience. What happened in L.A. was horrible. And I can't say I like the way you jerked me around." They were silent a moment, staring out through the windshield. "You know what, though, in a certain way it turned out okay for me. I mean, it's the whole reason I'm out here in the dark looking up at that glittering crazy house instead of killing myself to be part of it. As soon as this trial's over I'm getting way the hell out."

"To do what?"

He shrugged. "I don't know. Maybe estate planning in the middle to slow lane until my restaurant gets going." He sighed. "I just have to go back in there tonight and be a speed freak for another three days. I hope I can do it."

30

Tribulation by Jury

On the morning of trial Howard met Gerry in front of the building. Howard had slept from one to four A.M., then been in the office for three hours trying to improve the plaintiff's cross-examination. What if the plaintiff didn't admit that a lawyer reviewed the lease before he signed it? Had he said it in deposition? He flipped the pages rapidly, rereading the entire transcript. Suddenly it seemed ridiculous. Of course he would admit it. There it was on the last page of the lease: "approved as to form," signed by the attorney.

He rehearsed his response to every possible evidentiary objection and made sure the exhibits were in order in their manila envelopes. By eight-thirty, when Gerry's silver Mercedes paused at the curb, Howard felt gritty and damp. Why hadn't he handed in his resignation before this fucking trial? Naïvely, he had wanted a winner, all the facts on his side. Now, as Gerry maneuvered through the traffic to San Jose, he saw this trial with stark clarity. If he won, it was nothing, shooting fish in a barrel the client would say. If he lost . . .

The traffic was heavy. They were going to be late. He asked question after question, until Gerry seemed slightly impatient. "Use your own judgment on that one.

I don't think we need to worry about that. I think we could go either way. What makes sense to you?"

Candy and Emily were waiting in the corridor with the client. Howard remembered his criminal law professor's story about losing his voice in his first court appearance and emitting a craven squeak. He cleared his throat once, very softly, to reassure himself as they pushed through the dark, heavy, double doors into the courtroom.

Three hours later he was standing in the hall outside the courtroom, desperate to tell his anxious jabbering client to shut up.

The presiding judge had already assigned all courtrooms before their case was called. "Come back in an hour and a half," she said, "I may have a courtroom for you then." Otherwise, they would trail, which meant they had to be ready on whichever morning a courtroom opened up.

At eleven, the judge still had no courtroom, but told them to wait. Howard decided to use the time to clean up his cross-examination of the real estate valuation expert.

Gerry was making calls from the pay phone across the hall. Howard left Candy posted outside the courtroom and took Emily to the courthouse library to make a list of exhibits.

He consulted the big *Webster's* with ragged edges to confirm that "custom" did mean "business." These big dictionaries were great. He remembered Gerry's word triage and found it after trying three spellings. He smiled. So his cases were battle victims and he was the Red Cross.

The Red Cross . . .

Emily was seated at the back table in the library, and looked up from her neat stack of documents as he leaned over her.

"How's it going?" he whispered.

"Fine. What's up?"

"Here's a trivia question for you. Do you know whether Gerry fought in World War II?"

"No. Are you getting weird on me again?"

"No he didn't fight, or no you don't know?"

"No, he didn't fight. He was a medic. Let me guess. Four hours after trial was supposed to start you just figured out you need a ballistics expert. Good luck."

"In a real estate fraud case? No, this is perfect. Maybe Gerry will revive me when the judge overrules my objection. Watch for Candy in case a court opens up, will you? I need to make a quick phone call."

A medic.

His hands were trembling as he fished in his pocket in the closed phone booth.

A medic would know the technique.

He didn't have enough change. He started back to ask Emily, saw her standing with Gerry just outside the library doors, laughing and shaking her head. Was she talking about World War II? He went back to the phone booth.

A man in the corridor with a chalk-stripe suit that was too big for him gave Howard a quarter. He punched in the last number of Sarah's office and looked up to see Gerry's face close to the glass.

Gerry opened the accordion door. "You're up to bat. They found us a courtroom. Judge Willis." He seemed oblivious to everything but the trial. He was no killer. Get a grip. As Howard hung up the receiver he heard a voice say "San Mateo Police—"

It took all afternoon to select the jury. When they got back to the office, Gerry and the client settled into the conference room to prepare the next day's testimony. Howard ducked into his office to call Sarah. She didn't answer. Panic began to rise in him again. He dialed her home. No answer.

They worked until nine-thirty, preparing the client for the directions cross-examination could take. Emily brought food from Burger King. Finally Gerry stood up.

"Howard, we're used to this sort of thing, but Joe needs some sleep." He patted Joe on the shoulder.

"You're in pretty good shape, Joe, you'll look fine on the stand, just fine. I know you probably can't forget about this tonight . . ." He grinned. "But read a dirty book or something, will you? We'll see you tomorrow, eight o'clock, outside courtroom four. I'll walk out with you, unless Howard needs me for something.

"I'll drive again tomorrow, seven-thirty downstairs. You're doing fine." Howard jumped when he felt Gerry's hand on his shoulder. Gerry seemed not to notice. "I think we're on our way to a win, don't you? Good. Get some sleep. See you tomorrow."

Howard listened while their voices drifted pleasantly and grew fainter. They were in Gerry's office. He made himself wait, flipping pages in the deposition transcript. He heard them reemerge into the hallway, heard the cheerful *plunk* of the elevator, and then silence except for the air conditioning. He realized he had been holding his breath, and pushed the air out into the stale room. He closed the door of the conference room and dialed Sarah's number. Still no answer. He slammed the phone into the cradle and stood staring at it.

He was flipping out. Gerry Tweedmore was the soul of the firm. He had no motive.

He was also the last person Candy had seen with Leo.

Suddenly Howard had to get out of the office. He began throwing files and notebooks frantically into his two oversized briefcases. The silence was hallucinogenic as he lugged the briefcases out into the hall.

Standing by the elevators he remembered that Gerry had carried the exhibits out of the conference room. He had to have them. He left the briefcases by the elevators and went to Gerry's office.

The light was on. Gerry's desktop was nearly empty, Howard could tell at a glance that the exhibits weren't on it. Maybe on the credenza by the telephone. Or on one of the bookshelves. He saw some loose papers on the bottom shelf behind Gerry's desk. As he bent over to pull them out he saw *Tweedmore's Corporate Taxation.*

That was funny, he'd moved it. It used to be up by his head, where you always noticed it. He stood up and checked. It was still there. Two copies of the same book, only the one on the bottom shelf still had a dust jacket. Which was mashed along the top. Because it didn't quite fit the book it was covering . . .

The book inside had apparently been red once. Now the gold letters gleamed faintly from the mottled brown cover, *Emergency Cardiac Life Support.* The binding was cracked, several of the brittle pages slid into his hand as he pulled it out of the book jacket. U.S. Army, 1945.

Inside the front cover was an inscription:

> Roma, 11 Agosto, 1944
>
> Carissimo,
>
> My family adores you forever, brave soldier, because you have saved my father's life. And I can never forget my first, best love.
>
> Live with boldness, caro. Live with beauty.
>
> Carla

He thumbed the index until he found "Pericardiocentesis." As he flipped to the right page, a voice behind him said, "Isn't it a little late for research?"

31

Last Tango

Gerry stood calmly in the doorway, his hands in his trouser pockets. For an instant it seemed he was referring to the case, and Howard started to smile. Then he saw that Gerry was staring at the book in Howard's hands.

"I, uh, just saw this and it looked interesting." He put the book down and backed away from it.

Gerry's gaze rested pleasantly on Howard's face. "Does it? Sit down and I'll tell you about it." He gestured to a chair and closed the door.

"I have to say I'm impressed, unpleasantly surprised, I guess, by your ability to keep working at this until you got the answer."

"What do you mean?"

"Oh, come, you do realize you've got the answer, don't you? There isn't any doubt?"

He followed Howard's glance toward the closed door and smiled. "No, I didn't think there was. So you know I killed Leo, but I think maybe you ought to know why. You've given up a lot to pursue this the way you did. You ought to know the whole story."

"Holy Jesus Christ," Howard said softly. Where was the guardian angel?

"You know, I wonder if people haven't been surprised over the years that Leo and I could be such a team, could be any kind of a team. He wasn't . . . polished, I'd guess you'd say. Oh, and I don't mean that I am." He waved his hand deprecatingly and flicked his

Stanford club tie. "And I like to think I'm not so shallow that I put much store in all of this stuff. But I do think he had a few more rough edges than I have.

"Well, I'll tell you, the thing about Leo, and I saw it as soon as I met him, he had ambition, and he had extraordinary business sense. Here we were, two little guys in a sunny, easygoing town in California, but we both knew we didn't belong in a backwater practice and we didn't intend to operate one. We intended to set a new standard for success, to become household words in the boardrooms of America, to be the power that the powerful turned to for advice. All across America industry was failing, whole cities dying, and we were poised and ready for an explosion of technology and wealth the like of which this country had never seen before. I knew it, and Leo knew it. Underneath our difference in manners, in education, we shared a vision of greatness, compared to which differences of style were nothing at all.

"So I hired him, but it was never an employer-employee relationship, even before he got his name on the door. I felt we were partners, brothers, in a way I had never believed possible.

"In many ways I was right. He could work harder and longer than any man I ever met. We had a number of moderate successes, they whetted our appetites for a big one. Then, after four years, our dinky little start-up called CryoTech went public. After that there was no stopping us.

"I did think I'd have a problem with Leo and client relations. Even there I was dead wrong. They loved him, with all his vulgarity and childish crudeness and slavering attempts to impress. And his tinsel showmanship. They bought it completely.

"I've wondered why. I think they relaxed around him, all their own crude impulses were welcome. I think Leo set the boundaries of acceptability so far out that nobody was at risk. So in some ways Leo was even better than I expected.

"That's why I didn't see the danger at first of his little indiscretions. Having sex with secretaries at lunch hour and talking about it. Manufacturing billable hours, a habit that spread like a contagion through the firm. Distasteful as these things were to me, I saw that Leo was building a useful reputation, it was actually part of his charm. By 1987, four of the six biggest names in Silicon Valley refused to make a move without consulting us. We were the only 'little firm' west of the Hudson representing underwriters in major securities transactions.

"That was my fatal mistake. I thought his greed, his lust, were petty diversions to help him relax for little snatches from his real driving ambition for power. I was terribly wrong. They were all there was in the world. His greed was insatiable, and he didn't care what the source of the money was . . ." Gerry's voice was rising, he was talking faster and faster. "To him they were all the same. I first began to realize this in the Trillobyte case. You know about Trillobyte? I said, do you know about Trillobyte?"

"Yes," Howard said quickly. "That Leo defrauded the company by withholding information about the circuit boards."

Gerry smiled. "I thought you knew. I found out from that Hite woman. I went to him then. I tried to reason with him. After many years of bone-grinding effort we had an extraordinary hold on the Silicon Valley legal market. We were . . . very wealthy and had every prospect of becoming wealthier. He didn't *need* this risky dishonest crap, he was putting the whole thing at risk . . ." Gerry's voice was pleading. He stared earnestly at Howard without seeing him.

"I tried to tell him these things, and do you know what he did? He treated me like a client. He started bullshitting me, he started with the 'Gerry. What's happening?' crap. I couldn't get him to take me seriously at all. I began to see that I had made a terrible mistake.

"Then CompuStar," he continued. "You know about that, too."

Howard nodded. "Leo messed up on the letter of repurchase and made Mary Belle take the blame for it."

Gerry's laugh was shrill. "You disappoint me. You've missed the point. CompuStar was no error. That would have been bad enough. Originally that's what I thought it was, too. But the day DeLuth's attorney got our cross-complaint, he called me. He said there was apparently a misunderstanding, he'd like the opportunity to come in and clear it up before we proceeded any further.

"I thought they were coming in to settle. But when Emily showed the lawyer into my office, DeLuth was with him. I knew then that something was wrong.

"DeLuth told me himself. It seemed he and Leo had come to an understanding before DeLuth ever left the company. Leo deliberately prevented CompuStar from repurchasing that stock. He confiscated the letter of re-purchase. DeLuth kept all the stock, lay in the weeds un-til it became valuable, and split the profits with Leo. Do you understand what I'm saying?"

Howard nodded.

"And Mary Belle just got in his way.

"I began to feel desperate. This law firm is my life. My youth is buried in these walls, and two failed mar-riages, and my children . . . Suddenly the whole founda-tion was riddled with termites. I had put myself at Leo's mercy, he was rendering my life meaningless.

"Miraculously, we buried the CompuStar affair by making it look like Mary Belle's mistake. To my great shame, I couldn't tell the insurance carrier the truth. But I knew we could never be that lucky again. Leo had to be stopped.

"I didn't intend to kill him that day. You see," he

said, searching Howard's face, "I didn't want to kill him at all. After all, I'm a deal maker first and foremost. I believe that if you can just find out where everybody's real interest lies, what each party *has* to have and what he can give up, then you can forge a compromise.

"I became obsessed. I couldn't get my other work done. I decided to go and tell Leo I wanted to split the firm. I wanted him out.

"Again he wouldn't listen. He sat looking at me, pretending to be earnest, refusing to acknowledge the magnitude of what he had done. He wouldn't take me seriously at all. 'Hey,' he said, 'Gerry old man, you're losing your perspective. We're partners, remember? Together we made this gold mine, we're not going to mess it up now. You've been working too hard, you need a vacation. Why not fly up to the island for a few days, take the wife. Better yet, leave her home, I'll provide the company. On Monday, I guarantee, my little faux pas will have shrunk to its proper size. Me and you, Gerry, always will be.' Then he turned his back on me and started to dial his telephone. I was sitting there looking at his back.

"I was carrying a bunch of office supplies. It was silly, but I had been so upset I had to walk around. Office supplies seemed like an excuse. While he sat there with his back to me I pulled out the message spindle.

"He was dialing, he didn't hear me come up behind him. I heard a phone ring down the hall, the click of a door closing. I knew I had to pin him against his seatback and stab him in one fluid motion. Just as my arms were spreading to surround him, he tapped his fingernail on the credenza, oblivious. . . .

"After I killed him my thinking seemed unnaturally clear." Gerry's hands were shaking. "I knew it was important for him not to be 'interrupted.' He still had his hand around the receiver, I was pretty sure he hadn't finished dialing. I took my handkerchief out of my pocket and propped him on his credenza so he looked like he was talking. I disčonnected the call and redialed, six digits of his home phone number. I picked up the other receiver with my handkerchief and set it on the floor.

"The thing that almost went wrong was the weapon. I didn't want to pull the spike out; blood is messy, you start leaving prints everywhere. But the base already had fingerprints, it was rammed against his chest, I couldn't be sure of getting them all. So I unscrewed the base and took it with me. I was going to take it to Burger King, eat something, throw it into their trash. But I had to get it out of Leo's office.

"I wasn't wearing my coat. All I had was the office supplies. So I wiped the base as carefully as I could and sandwiched it between two of the yellow pads. I was walking past Candy's station when it slid out from between the pads and I dropped it.

"It hit the floor like a bowling ball. But Candy was wearing her earphones, and nobody else was there. It landed in the doorway of your office.

"I couldn't make myself pick it up. I knew I had to pick it up, but I couldn't. I was desperate to be rid of it. And I was afraid of bending over, being seen . . .

"Suddenly Bill was right behind me. He started telling me something. I was smiling and nodding, I couldn't hear anything he was saying. I was waiting for his eyes to flick down to that base.

"The instant he left I reached out with my toe and kicked it into your office. It hit the leg of your chair. I hoped you would find it instead of the police and not realize its significance. I hoped to God I had gotten all the prints.

"I walked over to Burger King and got rid of the handkerchief. Then I came back and mingled at the party. And from almost that day to this I've been hoping that you and I would never be sitting here."

"You've known about me all along. Why didn't you stop me?"

"How could I? Rumors were knee deep about you helping that detective. You even told me about it yourself. Maybe that's what convinced me she had you staked out like a goat to see who went for you. I had to leave you alone.

"There was another reason, too, a simpler one. I underestimated you. We all did that, didn't we? Except for Inspector Nelson.

"So I didn't follow my first impulse to send you into outer space. New York, more specifically, on the PelSol merger, though I came close. Instead I settled for keeping you here and just slowing you down a little. That serious error in judgment seems to have brought us to our present impasse." He closed his eyes, a long blink, and opened them again. His face was filmed with sweat.

"So you found my book." He reached over and picked up the medical manual. "I couldn't bring myself to part with it. Did you see her note inside?"

Howard nodded as Gerry opened the front cover and read silently. "I suppose those were my finest moments, looking back on them. That's a sad thing to say about a life, isn't it, that you were best at twenty? I've kept this with me for so long, it would have been wrong to destroy it because of . . . No point in sullying the best with the worst." He closed the cover and set the book back on the desk.

"I feel badly about what I did. It was a professional failure as well as a personal one. My job is to work things out. But of course I had no alternative. No deal could be made that would span Leo's interests and mine. I had to kill him. He wouldn't listen to reason." He licked his lips. "You see . . . he wouldn't listen."

He lifted his eyes and looked intently at Howard for a moment. He seemed very tired. "And now it's the same. You aren't going to listen, either." He raised the gun and fired.

Inspector Sarah Nelson thought she had long since thought of all the reasons not to wear makeup. There was one she had overlooked. If she had been wearing mascara that night when she walked into her house and heard her phone ringing, her face would have been smeared with black instead of just splotchy when she arrived at the morgue.

Officer Zatopa met her there. When she was finished, he drove her to the police station and walked with her to the room with the bowling trophy, where a figure sat with his head against the wall. He opened his eyes when the door closed and recognized her.

"Not to sound like a jealous lover, Sarah, but where in the *fuck* have you been all night?" He tried to smile.

"For a half-baked lawyer, you did fine on your own."

"Shit I did fine. I almost got my head blown off, my only head in case you never counted. You owe me for this one, Inspector Nelson. I bagged your murderer for you . . . Well, I guess he bagged himself, but at *great personal risk* to me, while you were probably out chasing birds around."

"I thought you were in trial."

"No excuses. You owe me. You have to be sincere with me from now on."

"Come on. Pick something possible." He heard the tears in her voice, and suddenly his face sagged.

"Sarah, why did he kill himself? With me sitting there. And I thought . . ." He closed his eyes. "God, I thought he was going to . . ."

She crossed the room quickly and put her arm through his—to give support, he would still tease her years later, or just to make him feel special?—and they headed for the door.

Epilogue

Rain in June was no crazier than some other things that had happened in San Mateo, California, in recent weeks. Even rain that started abruptly after a cloudless day, and after most people in this bedroom community were already asleep. Even rain so heavy that it drummed onto the roof of the unmarked police car of Inspector Sarah Nelson.

The car was in the dark lot near the entrance of the pink granite office building at Cabrillo and San Ysidro. There was traffic here at this corner, even at midnight. Every time the rain-blurred traffic light turned from red to green, the *whoosh* of wet tires momentarily overwhelmed the stacatto of rain on her roof.

Her legs were stretched along the front seat, and her head rested on the windowsill, cushioned by a bunched-up flannel shirt. She had a camera on the seat beside her, and on the floor of the passenger side were a tripod and two ripped-open bright yellow Kodak boxes. The seat and floor were sprinkled with brown pine needles.

Her face was relaxed and expressionless, except that her occasional sighs were accompanied by something resembling a smile. Periodically she lifted her head to sip from a steaming Styrofoam cup of Burger King coffee.

With her head propped against the window she could look far down Cabrillo at the misty halos that limned the red taillights and the bright multicolored traffic signals. She could also see the front door of the building, with its lighted foyer and nascent gilt lettering on the

glass double doors: "Law Offices of Forman and Val—."
And if she lifted her head and squinted up through the
top of her windshield she could see the band of light that
illuminated the offices on the sixth floor.

A watchman in a flat-topped cap and poncho
rounded the corner of the building. The stiff wind that
whipped around the sides of the building flapped the
loose edges of the poncho and sent a white paper ball
skittering into the dark lot to be battered by the rain.

She pulled a phone message from her jeans pocket
and twisted to see it by the light from the building:
"Going to be a late one. (After midnight.) Call you tomorrow after (and if) he survives closing argument." She
checked her watch: twelve-twenty.

At twelve twenty-five the elevator doors opened and
two people emerged into the foyer. The woman had
stringy red hair. The man was rumpled, and the lines of
his body sloped down and out. Neither of them was
dressed for the storm. She saw them laugh with surprise
and turn their collars up as she leaned into the rain to call
"Howard!"

About the Author

Susan Wolfe is a lawyer who was born and raised in San Bernardino, California. She has a B.A. from the University of Chicago and a law degree from Stanford University (J.D. 1981). After four years of practicing law full time, she bailed out and began writing. She now lives in Palo Alto, California, with her husband, Ralph DeVoe, and their daughter, Catherine. She practices law part time while she is completing her next novel.